a
Hundred
Lives for
You

By the same author:

Eye of The predator
Edge of the Machete

a
Hundred
Lives for
You

Abhisar Sharma

Srishti
PUBLISHERS & DISTRIBUTORS

SRISHTI PUBLISHERS & DISTRIBUTORS
N-16, C. R. Park
New Delhi 110 019
editorial@srishtipublishers.com

First published by
Srishti Publishers & Distributors in 2014

Dedicated to
Mili and Babush, my angels. It does not matter how
tired or tensed I am, the thought of meeting
you after a tough day, your smile, and
the sound of your laughter fills me with joy.

Acknowledgements:

Every time I see my son playing with my father, I can sense Abhimanyu and his Daddu's bonding between them. When I wrote about an infant Simran, I remembered those moments with my first born, Mili. Moments as these inspired me to write a story that shall remain closest to my heart. Then there were childhood memories that have remained etched in my heart. I thought I should reproduce them in a canvas of fiction. A Hundred Lives for You has been a journey of rediscovering myself. It has been a journey of hope not only for the protagonist, but for the writer too.

I am deeply thankful to my wife Shumana and my father-in-law Ashim Sen, my first draft readers and reviewers. My friend Manu Arya, and Chandrashekhar who read the raw manuscript and offered their valuable advice. Team Srishti for their belief in the manuscript.

New Delhi
1984

As he dragged his motorbike through the bloodied lanes of Tilak Nagar that afternoon, the ground under his feet crumbled. It was deceptive and dangerous: insanity scarred the faces of men running around him, screaming, rejoicing, thumping their chests that the Sardars had been paid back. That the Sardars would think twice before branding the Hindus as cowards now. That they had asked for it. How could they assassinate Indiraji? They were, after all, her bodyguards. The 'peace-loving middle class men' scaled their terraces and gasped in horror as clouds of black swirled across the wretched Delhi skyline.

His feet felt numb, as if frostbitten in the burning city. Enfeebled by the mayhem, he struggled to hold the motorbike, its tyre punctured by shards of glass strewn across the last turn. The shards of the tinted glass of a car. A Sikh family trying to escape. All they needed was to get across to Dhaula Kuan, the cantonment area, to a relatively 'safe zone'. At least the Army would not stand as mute spectators. But the bastards got them at the bend. When he passed the car by, he saw the bloodied and manicured hand of a woman hanging out of the window. He bowed his head, as if apologizing, as if ashamed of the crime of the majority that day.

The six-feet tall man, broken in will by the bloodshed, strained his eyes to see his destination ahead of him. The hospital wasn't too

1

far. He kept mumbling incoherently, praying that the insanity had at least spared the hospital. They must have, he thought, for who could they hurt there! The dead, or the burnt? He wiped the grease off his face with the sleeve of his blue shirt. The stains of red on it brought back the burden of watching so many die, even some of his own. His cheeks shivered and he gasped in pain. He wanted to cry, but nobody could assuage his pain.

He took the next left, and the hospital stood in front of his eyes. They had left it untouched between buildings that were once houses. He reached the doorstep of the two-storey hospital, crashed, rather abandoned the motorbike with disdain, as if unburdening every whiff of guilt and anger on the ugly and broken piece of useless metal junk. He walked past the reception; a line of bodies covered in white shrouds lay across the long and bleak corridor. Except for a distant wail of a woman in some corner of the hospital, it was dead quiet. Most people brought there that day were dead. Unclaimed. And would perhaps stay that way till the city decided to unmask itself of its lunacy.

He cupped his mouth and nose with his right hand as he passed through a wing that had been temporarily changed into a morgue. His stomach recoiled with the stench of blood and burnt flesh. He walked faster, nearly breaking into a sprint towards the east end of the hospital which was cushioned from these scars. He climbed the stairs in a hurry, but the toe of his shoe hit the edge of the stairs and he lost his balance. The kneecap crashed on the cracked edge of the stairs and he winced in agonizing pain. He gathered himself and walked faster, though this time with a slight limp. But the pain brought back the past. He had consigned it to flames and was now wary of the future that would stare at him with questioning eyes. He headed towards the nursery; his heart sank. He pushed the door open and saw a nurse sitting at the extreme end of the corridor. She had dozed off, but the urgency in his steps woke her up.

'We have placed her in the nursery, after feeding her...,' she said with a stoic and tired expression, pointing to her right.

The man turned in the direction of her finger. He walked towards the chamber and stood in front of the glass that separated and sanitized the newly born babies from the polluted outer world. There was a neat pattern with cribs lined parallel to each other. His eyes darted from one end to the other, searching for someone.

'There, Mr Sharma...there she is...' she pointed to one side. He jerked his head to look at the baby.

There she was, her wide eyes calm with sleep, and accentuated by her beautiful eyelashes. Her cheeks, her forehead and her chin, all glowing an angelic pink. Her lips with a blush of crimson and a slight pout. She was bundled in a white cocoon. The man placed his fingers on the glass, and gasped seeing the dirt and blood on them.

If death is the definitive truth of this world, so is life! So pure, so unbiased, and so hopeful. Its zeal, challenging the insanity of the city that had forgotten to love and co exist.

He mumbled, 'Can I hold her?'

'Sorry sir,' the nurse said with a thick Malayali accent, 'You will first need to take a wash, and change your clothes.'

The man turned towards the nurse, almost looking at her apologetically, 'I am sorry. I understand, sister.'

What he saw every minute of his exposure to the madness was a city cursed by the wails and shrieks of men, women and children. How could death, he thought, something so violent and vicious, be the final truth? As he saw her breathe in front of his eyes through the glass that separated them, the pain and turmoil of his heart ebbed away. He knew he would have to erase every bit of it from his heart if he had to make a beginning. For him, and for her, the little angel!

Unlike the belief that a man sees his whole life's journey like a movie on fast-forward in the final moments, each and every frame of his life came back to him as he looked at the child. Just like that. The dramatic moments, the lesser ones, the people who had changed his life, those who loved him, even those who had despised him, and the ones he could not hold on to, however hard he tried. And then... like a bolt, she revealed herself. Again.

The girl by the hut...his swansong that had changed it all. That little tale from his childhood that echoed beyond the three pages he had written in that story writing competition back in 1976, the most dramatic year in his entire life. When bonds were being redefined and relationships retold. The man slowly walked to his left and placed his hand on the horizontal grills of the window overlooking the scarred skyline of Delhi. Eight years ago, he was looking at the same skyline from the window of his class in St Mark's School. He gripped the grill tight, feeling the gnarled shrapnel of disintegrating paint on his palm. Panic coagulated in his stomach like a broth of unpleasant and painful memories that had accumulated over the past two days. He placed his head on the grill and shut his eyes.

1976

The dreamy-eyed boy sitting at the window squinted at the pair of sparrows fighting on the branch of the mango tree next to his classroom. He turned around to face the students. Some seemed bored, others were trying hard to put their thoughts on paper, some looking outside the class, amused at some random happening. He looked at the blank white sheet on his desk. A smile crossed his lips as he pressed the freshly sharpened pencil between his thumb and index finger, and wrote the first word...

Rupali...

Rupali stood at the wooden door of her hut and her eyes searched for someone. The fifteen-year-old girl with her hair tied in a plait scanned the neighbouring huts. Her vision was hazy owing to a thin film of tears across her dark eyes. A rock and pebble-strewn dusty road ran in front of her house. Rupali's heart felt heavy. She knew this would happen someday. It was just a matter of time. But now her mind was wandering towards the dark and bleak immediate future. It was lonely, uncertain and hostile. And then suddenly, the tears crossed the threshold of her eyelashes, accompanied by her muffled sobs. She wiped them with her long, mud-stained fingers, but her sobs were now getting intense. With trembling fingers, she clasped her chest, which was heaving rhythmically with her sobs. 'Ma,' she whimpered.

She peeped inside her hut and then came and stood on the edge of the street. She could hear distant chanting, which was getting louder as the procession gradually approached her. The prabhat pheri, *the procession of freedom fighters in that locality of Chandni Chowk. The year was 1946 and there was hope in the air. Not for Rupali, though. It was all over for her. Like a panic attack, pain engulfed her knees as she sat slowly at the edge of her hut with a painful grunt. The prabhat pheri procession at 4.30 a.m. had woken her up every day for almost fifteen years now. She would rub her sleepy eyes daily and look at the men and women chanting hymns and bhajans with the fervour of desire renting the air. Desire for freedom. As the procession neared her hut, Rupali buried her face in the crook of her arm resting on her thighs. The chanting of Mahatma Gandhi's* 'Vaishnava jana tu tene kahiyeje' *was getting louder and she could feel that they were now passing her hut. Rupali had memorized Bapu's swan song by heart because of the daily prabhat pheris. She would often follow them till the arch of the road ahead, but never beyond.*

The sound was getting gentler in the chilly December morning, and as it gradually faded, Rupali knew that the procession had crossed the arch round the corner. She raised her head and rested her chin on her arm. It was quiet again, except the sound of her toenails scratching the soil and a distant howl of a dog pack. And then from the arch of the road, she saw a tall man walking towards her. The man was walking straight towards her. It was dark, but she could make out that the man was clean shaven and was wearing a mud coloured dhoti kurta. Rupali looked at him confused, tears still caressing her cheeks.

The man spoke with a hint of an apology in his voice, 'I am sorry, but I could not stop myself…I was with the prabhat pheri and I saw you sitting at the edge of your house. I could see that you were sobbing….is everything okay?'

Maybe it was the helplessness of the situation and her own vulnerability that the hint of sympathy in his voice sounded genuine to her. Rupali had been longing for solace since last night. But now that someone was standing in front of her, she did not know what to do. She buried her face in the bend of her left arm again and started sobbing uncontrollably. The man moved ahead and bent down, resting his right knee on the ground.

'What is it, please tell me… It was as if the vibe of your pain drew me to this hut.' Rupali was still sobbing, and the man raised his hand and reluctantly placed it on her head.

'I don't know what your pain is, but I am sure that there is some way out… There is some hope…'

It was at this point that Rupali stopped sobbing and raised her head. The pain vanished and a strange hardness filled her face. She wiped her tears and stood up.

'There is no hope…not for me…'

With a small pause, the man spoke again, 'I don't know what your story is, but this entire country is thriving on hope. Our prabhat pheris are all about hope. We hope that our words bring this sentiment back into the lives of nearly thirty crore individuals of this country. I am sure there is a way ahead.'

'There is no hope for me, for my last hope is lying in my hut…shattered and lifeless,' Rupali turned around to walk back to her hut, but then stopped after taking a few steps, 'and you want to know why....come with me!'

A strange panic filled his heart as he started following the girl. An earthen lamp lit one corner of the room that was very stuffy. His eyes scanned the room, while the girl walk towards a charpoy. His eyes were still trying to adjust to the light in the room and he could not actually figure out if there was something on the bed. The girl sat on the edge of the charpoy and he realized that someone was lying on it with the entire body covered in a black tattered quilt. Rupali gently removed one end of the quilt. From that distance, the man could see the forehead of a woman as the girl started caressing her hair. Tears filled her eyes as Rupali looked at the woman.

'This is my last hope, my mother. Last night, she died....'

She left the last word hanging. The man stepped back in shock, letting out a gasp. Hope had suddenly acquired a different meaning in this small space, this world of hers.

'You talk about hope,' she said faintly, 'My mother died last night and that is what this word means to me.'

'What happened?

'She felt a sudden pain in her chest while cooking and I asked her to rest. I had my back to her when I heard a groan, but I ignored it. I kept cooking and did not look at her till I finished the chores in half an hour. She must have died that very moment.'

The man looked at her in stunned silence. The stuffiness of the room and the shock of what he had just seen and heard were now engulfing his senses. He inhaled the musty air and it made him even more uncomfortable. He wanted to breathe fresh air now.

'She could never recover from my father's death a year ago, when the police rained lathis on his head in a freedom *rally in Red Fort. Ironically, my father was not even a part of the rally. He was just a bystander. My father believed that the freedom struggle was not his fight. His war was against hunger. We are daily wage workers from Uttar Pradesh and had come to Delhi for a better life. This city and your fight for freedom took away my father...and now...,' she pointed at the lifeless body of her mother as her voice broke.*

The man had seen death closely so many times during rallies, but this was not some martyr. This was certainly not death with dignity. And certainly not death with hope at the end of the tunnel.

'My father would come back in the evenings after a hard day's work and sit with us and talk endlessly about his day, the freedom struggle, the men leading the movement – Bapu, Chacha Nehru. He was fascinated by them, but never did he muster the courage to go and participate in these rallies. I would admonish him and ask him if he was afraid and that he could be construed as a coward. But he was never apologetic. He just said that his world was his family and that the condition of his lot would be the same, whether it was the British or our own people. I could never understand his pessimism. He said that our society functions according to a strict feudal norm. He said that he was a worker, a labourer, and that the powers to be would conspire to see that he continues to be at the lowest echelon. He was not resentful though. He said that all of us have come to this earth with a distinct karma and that his karma was to serve.'

Rupali now looked at the man and said, 'Your freedom struggle is yours, not mine. I have no share in your hope. My world stands here...right in front of my eyes, dead and lifeless and hopeless on this wooden charpoy...'

The man realized that every stain of tears on her face, every unruly hair falling across her eyes and every pain-filled frown reminded him of just one thing – uncertainty. Dignity and self respect acquired a new meaning in her world. After all, this was what they were fighting the British for. He would have never understood her father's stand had it been some other time and situation. But here he was, staring at the girl's dead mother. Hope was certainly not meant for her. It was romanticized and overrated here. After half an hour, he asked the girl to wait in the hut, as he hurriedly got some of his friends to arrange for the last rites of her mother.

The funeral was performed in the next two hours as the man's friends bathed and clothed Rupali's mother for her last journey. From a distance, Rupali watched the funeral pyre being lit by the stranger. A stranger whom she had met a few hours ago. As the fires leapt and kissed the chill of the morning, the sun rose at a distance. When the first ray of the winter sun hit Rupali, she felt a strange sense of relief. It was indeed the end of all the trauma that her mother had been enduring for the past one year. She was alone, but her mother was not. Hopefully in a better and a just world, with her father. She looked around and saw many faces, all strangers to her. Then she saw him. The stranger in her life.

The man put his hand on Rupali's shoulder and she looked straight into his eyes. She did not know how to read them, not yet. She was not completely sure what that grip on her shoulder meant. She did not know if she could trust him. She wanted to feel reassured, though.

Trust was still an ambitious word for Rupali. But he was her final hope.

Hope....
Rupali did not know that she would find her share of
hope at the funeral pyre of her mother. But it was certainly
something she was ready to cling on to.

The winter morning sun, the funeral pyre, Rupali and the
stranger slowly melted into the blue ink on the third page, bit by bit.
Mrs Jain turned over the third page and saw the details of the entry
in the short story writing competition of the school.

Abhimanyu Sharma,
9th B,
Roll number 11
Title of the story: The Girl by the Hut

Mrs Jain was the invigilator in the story writing competition,
and kept staring at the name 'Abhimanyu Sharma' for some time.
Something about the story was unnerving. Something that left a
mark of melancholy. This, she thought was the most radical thought
that she had encountered on the freedom struggle of the country
and that too from a thirteen-year-old. The topic for the competition
was 'Stories revolving around the freedom struggle' and she had
a fair idea of what students would write. But this...this was just
incredible. Her eyes searched for Abhimanyu in the class. Most of
the students were still writing, so she called out the name.

'Abhimanyu Sharma?'

Still peering at squabbling sparrows, the boy's trance was broken
by Mrs Jain's authoritative voice. He suddenly got up on his seat.
Mrs Jain saw the gangly, thin boy with pronounced frontal teeth.
His hair dishevelled, strands falling on his eyes. But his eyes were
curious and wide. His mouth, slightly open like a hungry fledgling.

As he stood up, he tightened the belt that held his blue trousers to his waist. Mrs Jain smiled at Abhimanyu as he walked towards her and stood in front of her with his hands tied behind him.

'What is this, Abhimanyu?' asked Mrs Jain.

Abhimanyu glanced into his paper and then looked at Mrs Jain with confusion writ large on his face. He mumbled, 'Something wrong, ma'am?'

'No, I just want to know what went on in your mind when you wrote this story.'

Abhimanyu was still not sure if he was being praised or censured. He gave a rather forced smile, 'I don't know, ma'am. I just wrote what came to my mind.'

Mrs Jain placed her hand on Abhimanyu's shoulder and reassured him, 'This is just brilliant! I am stunned that someone of your age can write something so profound; something so sublimely tragic, and yet so hopeful. The story ends so beautifully, leaving us wondering what happened to the girl and the stranger. You have given a totally different dimension to the freedom struggle. Rupali is so prophetic when she talks about the have-nots of our society. Abhimanyu Sharma... well done!'

Three decades of independence later, the honeymoon with hope had long ended. It was ironical that the Congress and the daughter of the first Prime Minister of independent India had imposed Emergency. It was even more ironical that Satyagraha – which was the most potent weapon of the Congress against the British – had turned out to be its biggest nightmare.

Abhimanyu smiled, with a hint of shyness in his eyes. He bowed down, and chose to look at his dust-smeared black shoes instead. Without looking at Mrs Jain, he raised his head and saw the unsolved trigonometric equations right behind her, scribbled across the blackboard. Mathematics was his worst nightmare, so he looked at Mrs Jain and spoke with a hint of hesitation, 'I read newspapers, ma'am, and I see so much disillusionment. It is not even thirty years since we attained independence. And now this emergency...'

Mrs Jain looked around to check if anyone undesirable was hearing this conversation. She said in a hushed voice, 'Be careful Abhimanyu. You might be in trouble for those views of yours. These are strange times.' She cleared her throat and patted his back, 'Nevertheless, I see conviction in your writing. You can go a long way in life. Early days, I know, but you would certainly have an impact. God bless you son!'

Abhimanyu bowed his head and mumbled thanks under his breath.

'I shall speak to the principal and recommend your name for the inter school story writing competition, Delhi zone. For me, the competition is over. This is brilliant!'

Principal Dr Sanjay Matthew was a Keralite with tremendous contempt for north Indians. He had lived in Delhi for more than ten years and had faced enough stereotyping from the Punjabis to fill him with venom to not miss out on a single opportunity to get back at them. His high was Punjabi parents begging for admissions in his school and even better, begging for not rusticating their wayward children. He was just a 'Madrasi' for all of them. He detested the word and the ones who used it.

Dr Matthew had just finished lunch and was busy digging the cavity of his teeth with a tooth pick, patting his perfect French beard, when Mrs Jain knocked at his cabin door.

She held Abhimanyu's story in her hands, 'Sir, you should see what this boy has written. He is just brilliant. I think we have a prodigy amongst us...'

'Mrs Jain, the children are what we make of them. How many times have I told you? This is a very prestigious competition and Shweta Varma has been winning it for us for the past three years. We needed to replace her only because she has had a loss in the family. This boy that you are talking of... what class does he study in?'

'Ninth standard, sir.'

'Ninth? I hope you know that the other schools will send in students from higher classes. You want to send him?'

'Sir, please at least have a look at what he has written,' she held out the loose sheets.

Matthew smiled and started looking at the papers. After ten minutes, he took a deep breath and kept the papers on his table. He began fiddling with the paperweight, his lips forming a curve arched downwards. He kept nodding and shaking his head as Mrs Jain waited impatiently for his answer.

'Well Mrs Jain, I see glimpses of a radical in his writings...a sort of a Naxal! How can someone question the freedom struggle like that, and that too in the circumstances like we have nowadays?'

'But sir, is he really questioning the freedom struggle? He is just questioning our priorities. The theme given to them was freedom struggle, and look at what this boy has written...and that too coming from a thirteen-year-old!'

'Mrs Jain, I will not question your judgment, but please do think about it. I don't want to antagonize and create trouble for anyone.'

'Sir, please trust me,' Mrs Jain pleaded as she bent forwards on the principal's desk, her left hand clasping the edge of his table. Matthew raised his hands and shrugged his shoulders, all in one movement. Mrs Jain had finally triumphed. With the smile of a winner, she rushed out of the principal's room towards Abhimanyu's class.

'Abhimanyu Sharma, congratulations. You will now represent St. Mark's in the Delhi Zone story writing competition.'

Abhimanyu bit his lower lip with his frontal teeth and folded his fingers into fists as he whispered a triumphant 'Yes'. He had already conquered the world. This was a first for him, representing his school in a competition. The lack of physical prowess was a big hindrance for him to even attempt any form of sports; his awful memory and a gnawing stage fear ensured that he stayed out of elocution or singing competitions too. The only thing that he could do on his own terms was story writing, where there were no rules, where he was the king. He had hidden a huge collection of stories back home. If his father – who was a scientist with the Ministry of Environment – ever figured that he was actually writing stories rather than trying to salvage his average grades, it would be his last day on earth.

'Now listen to me carefully, Abhimanyu. For the past three years, Shweta Varma has been representing us in this competition and getting us the coveted trophy. This time she can't make it as her grandfather, may he rest in peace, just passed away. You have to, and I mean *have to,* prove me right.' Abhimanyu saw something in Mrs Jain's eyes that he had never seen before. Faith! And that meant a lot for him. It wasn't an expression that he was used to.

The story writing competition was exactly one month away, and the venue – Kendriya Vidyalaya, Tagore Garden – was walking distance from Abhimanyu's house. He stayed a couple of blocks away in what was originally a refugee colony, with a straight long row of flats facing another identical long row. People who had migrated from Pakistan after the Partition had landed there, and the government had turned the refugee camp into a permanent residential colony. Abhimanyu's family was tenants of the Salujas from Lahore. Their landlord was fond of Ujjwal, Abhimanyu's father, not just because he taught his chubby twins without fee, but also because he was a patient listener. Mr Saluja often mentioned the great life they had in Lahore and in the same breath abused the 'circumcised bastards'. *Katwe*, as he put it! It must have been a painful experience for him as a child when his elder sister was kidnapped by the local thug in Lahore as they left the city. They found out five years after they reached India that Vimmi Saluja was now Vimmi Akhtar and had already borne three children for Mr Shahid Akhtar. Vimmi had died for them since then.

Abhimanyu's dust-kissed face shone with a smile. He decided to break this news to his parents in the evening when his father returned from office.

His father Ujjwal was a tall, slim man who had come a long way from his education in a village school in Santpur in the Chindhwara district of Madhya Pradesh. His father had been a clerk in the postal office of Chindwara city and was the first in the village to step beyond the district. Ujjwal's younger brother Prakash was a professor in Makhan Lal University in Bhopal, and the youngest of the three, Om, was in the customs department. Financially, both the brothers were doing much better than Ujjwal, and that was cause of trauma for the young Abhimanyu.

The compulsory summer vacation in Santpur was a source of constant torture for him as his younger and more affluent cousins would often show off their belongings. Abhimanyu's father often told him that since Prakash was a professor and much in demand, gifts were common. And Om was a customs officer. Abhimanyu did not understand the logic for the latter till two decades later, when the CBI raided his uncle's residence.

When Abhimanyu's mother Mahima saw him that afternoon, she knew he was up to something. Abhimanyu did not even crib about the lunch that day and was unusually quiet, though happy. As if trying to conceal something.

Abhimanyu smiled, fiddling with the spoon in the yellow dal. His mother looked hard at him as he spilled the dal outside his plate, his fingers dancing with some hidden excitement.

'Okay, enough!' she frowned, though that look did not intimidate Abhimanyu anymore.

'What is it Babu?' she asked calling him by the nickname she had so lovingly given him.

Abhimanyu shook his head and smiled.

'I don't know what's going on in that mind of yours, Babu, but just be careful. Your father does not like surprises and you know that.' Abhimanyu still did not respond and the silly grin on his face just grew wider.

It struck 6.30 on the wall clock and Abhimanyu heard the screech of the chartered bus around the corner of his locality. As the doorbell rang, Abhimanyu rushed to open the door, pushing his mother aside. His father stood there, not too pleased to see Abhimanyu. He knew that look on Abhimanyu's face; it was usually followed by a demand for something. How wrong he was that day! As he entered the house, he smiled at Mahima. That meant only one thing for her: a glass of cold water followed by ginger tea.

'It's been unusually hot today,' he said unbuttoning his sleeves and the top two buttons of his shirt. Abhimanyu was looking for that cue where he could rain that news on the proud parents.

'So have they announced the dates for your finals?' Abhimanyu did not even hear what his father had just said. Instead, he was thinking of ways to break the news. He kept looking at his father with a triumphant grin on his face. On not being answered, Ujjwal glanced at Abhimanyu, 'Wipe that stupid grin off your face and answer when asked. Am I clear, Abhimanyu?' His voice now had an edge to it.

It was at that moment that Mahima entered the room with the cold water in a steel glass and put it on the table in front of Ujjwal. Abhimanyu suddenly sprang up and stood between his parents, holding his mother's hand and asking her to sit down. Ujjwal looked at Abhimanyu, with confusion bordering on irritation.

'I have to tell you something. It's the biggest news of my life, and probably yours too.' Abhimanyu's smile spread wide across his face.

'What is it?' his father exhaled and locked his hands behind his head in anticipation.

'I have been selected to represent the school in the Delhi Zone story writing competition...' Abhimanyu's voice rose as he spread his arms to accentuate the importance of the news. His eyes darted from his mother to his father, waiting for a reaction, but he could see they did not share his enthusiasm. He had wished them to be a little more cheerful.

His father shut his eyes and caressed the bridge of his nose with his forefinger and thumb, and spoke softly but curtly, 'Abhimanyu... you need to understand that this year is like a curtain raiser for what is to follow next year. Next year, you are going have your board examinations where all your papers are going to be checked by teachers you will never meet. These exams will separate the men from the boys. The marks will also determine if you would continue to study in your present school or... you perform so brilliantly that schools like DPS absorb you in their elite sections. In fact, I am not really expecting 90 percent from you; even if you get 80 percent, I can try for a placement there. Prakash has some contacts in DPS R.K. Puram and he has assured me of a placement if you score at least 80 percent.'

There was an uncomfortable silence in the room.

'Your problem is that you just refuse to concentrate your energies in areas that will secure a future for you...'

Abhimanyu was quiet through the dinner and plonked on the sofa where he had been sleeping for a year now. He gazed out of the window, into the starless night. He could hear his parents murmuring in the other room.

'You could have been softer on him today. I don't think he anticipated this reaction...'

Turning towards Mahima, Ujjwal spoke with a hint of irritation in his voice, 'Do you really expect me to encourage him on matters such as these? If he continues getting encouragement from you on such stupid matters, he will continue to falter.'

'He has been selected for something for the first time in his life! Do you realize what that means for our son?'

Ujjwal interrupted rudely, 'So you want your son to be a bloody writer? You want him to work in the godforsaken film industry? Who do you think he is...the next Salim Javed?'

'You know that is not what I meant.'

'Then please enlighten me! If we continue to encourage him in such trivial things, then we can just forget about the placement in DPS next year. And honestly speaking, Mahima, if he messes up next year, I will put him in a government school. I am not going to waste my hard-earned money on a boy who just refuses to recognize what's good for him.'

Mahima retorted with a hint of sarcasm in her voice, 'And you think you know what's good for him?'

'All I know is that he is good for nothing. If he continues like this, he is only going to bring shame to us.'

Ujjwal did not realize that his voice was now loud enough to be heard by Abhimanyu in the other room. Nor did Mahima. But what Ujjwal said next haunted Abhimanyu and determined his relationship with his father for the rest of his life.

'I wish we had the courage to have a second child ten years ago. I am sure the second one would not have been as hopeless as he is.'

Abhimanyu continued staring at the skies as his eyes welled up. A cocktail of various sounds caressed Abhimanyu's ears: someone gargling, a group of young men laughing around the corner, a woman calling out for her son to come back home. He raised his left hand and drew the curtain, turning his back to his parents' room. He grabbed the pillow from under his head and shut his ears to the sounds around him. And then his shoulders started to shake in a rhythm. His muffled sobs did not reach the other room.

With his brown school bag slung on his right shoulder, Abhimanyu was literally dragging himself to school. He would occasionally kick the pebbles strewn on the road with his black school shoes.

'I wish we had the courage to have a second child.'

His mind was so used to everything his father had said about him in the past, that there were no tears this time.

Why don't you ever cut your nails in time?
Why is your hair so unkempt?
Why do you never polish your shoes?
Why are you not studying?

Today, everything he had said in the past had dissolved into just one thing that he had said last night.

'I wish we had the courage to have a second child.'

As he crossed the two-way road that separated Rajouri Garden from Tagore Garden, he was dangerously oblivious to the morning traffic that was zooming with maniacal fervour. Wallowing in self pity was Abhimanyu's favourite sport. He was the zombie on the road: nothing could hit him; nothing could kill him. He thought he was already dead.

'Abe Chutiye! Sadak tere baap ki hai? Marna hai kya?' The man on the wheel roared at Abhimanyu as he stopped his ambassador car just inches away from him. Abhimanyu mumbled a faint sorry under his breath and ran across the road. He just wished that the ambassador had crushed him.

In school, he saw children around him walking in a queue for the morning assembly like a horde of ants. Abhimanyu could afford not to go to the morning assembly, thanks to his class monitoring duty. He was supposed to guard the belongings of other students. It mostly meant having a go at others' lunch boxes. This was also the time for retribution, for monitors could actually mix chalk powder or other undesirable things in the tiffins of those they had an axe to grind against.

Abhimanyu was looking at the morning assembly, ignorant of Jagtar's antics. Jagtar Singh was a Sikh as also Abhimanyu's best friend in the class. He was busy eating some hapless student's tiffin. Jagtar and Abhimanyu were self-proclaimed Jai-Veeru in class, thanks to the *Sholay* wave that had hit the nation a year before. Today, Abhimanyu had found his Gabbar.

'I hate him.'

Abhimanyu's voice interrupted Jagtar, who was gorging the last morsel of Vishal Taneja's *alu ka parantha*. He looked at Abhimanyu and mumbled something with his mouth full.

'I hate my father from the core of my heart.'

Jagtar gave his friend a thumbs-up while continuing to chew the huge morsel, 'Same here, bro! My father is an asshole. But what did yours do *now*?'

'He hates me and wants another child.'

Jagtar choked on the parantha due to the shock and surprise of what he had just heard. But he quickly came over it and said, 'Congratulations, yaar! You will now have a younger sibling. But beware man, these younger ones can be a real pain in the ass. It's painful to see your importance getting eroded once these rats are born.'

Abhimanyu did not respond to Jagtar's lame joke; he was seething with anger.

'It's not that yaar. He can't stand me. Period. I am representing the school in a story writing competition and that means nothing to him. Now he wishes he had another child who could have fulfilled his dreams.'

Jagtar smiled and stood up as he walked across the maze of desks towards Abhimanyu. He said, '*Ye baap hote hee aise hain.* All they can do is impose their will on us. Your father is still a scientist and has some idea about life and all. *Mera baap to kabadi wala hai sala...*a goddamn businessman dealing with metal scrap. Imagine a man who did not even pass his eighth standard asking me to study hard. Giving me sermons on taking my studies seriously.' He chuckled, 'Anyway, what are you going to do about this story writing competition?'

Abhimanyu shrugged and said, 'What am I supposed to do? I will participate and win the first prize. Simple.'

That afternoon during the recess, Abhimanyu quickly finished his lunch and wandered towards the far end of the school. They were constructing a house for the principal there and it was usually deserted at this time of the day. The mulberry tree just twenty yards from the house under construction had always enchanted Abhimanyu. It was one of those days when he wished to be left alone.

As he sat under the mulberry tree, he felt a stinging prick on his buttock. He grimaced in pain as he guided his right hand under his bum to dig the stone out. And while he cursed under his breath, he heard something. Like a muffled sound. At first he decided to ignore it, but then he pushed himself up. He walked towards the under construction house, where the sound was coming from.

He heard someone again. This time something like, 'Please don't!' The same girl's voice.

His heartbeat became faster as a numb fear engulfed him. He continued walking, as if in a trance, his pace now slackened.

He heard again, 'No...please...'

He placed his steps gingerly on the ground, careful not to make any sound over the lumps of mud and stones scattered around. As he walked, the voices from the backyard increased sharply. He stopped. The sound was coming from the supposed backyard of the house, the lawn.

He knew if he entered the backyard, he would see the horror unfolding right in front of his eyes. So he decided to enter the store room instead, a window from which opened towards the lawn. Abhimanyu bent down and started crawling on his fours towards the window.

'Please let me go Ashwini, it hurts...'

He could hear the cries of pain of the faceless victim. Abhimanyu's hands were shaking and tears flooded his eyes. He didn't know what to do. It seemed all the strength in his body had been sucked out and he could not even raise himself to see what was happening.

He heard a painful moan, followed by a grunt of the faceless perpetrator. Abhimanyu rose but only high enough to see the backyard. His eyes scanned the lawn and stopped at the right end.

A girl lay on the ground with her legs raised, spread-eagled, and a boy too huge in comparison to the petite girl was between her legs. The girl was struggling hard to disentangle herself from his enormous body. He had pinned her hands to the muddy slush, even as she tried to break free from his brutal grip. Abhimanyu raised his head further slightly, and then he saw her face emerge. That was the girl from the other section, Shalini. The prettiest girl in class IX-D. She had participated in the group song competition last year. His hands started to shake uncontrollably and his lips quivered as realisation of what was happening set in. The girl was in school uniform, but the guy was wearing a white shirt with black stripes. Had to be an outsider, he thought. Abhimanyu saw his belted black jeans and what seemed like the girl's black underwear heaped up near them.

All he needed to scare the huge boy was to either shout or just raise his voice, but he was stunned. His tongue seemed glued to his mouth. He could hear his own wheezing though, as if trying to rescue his voice from fear. And then the man started jerking. The painful moans now changed to rhythmic gasps and pleading. The girl was wailing as he grunted with his head raised, his hands still pinning down her hands that had lost the will to struggle.

Five minutes later, he lay over her, his back rising and falling, trying to catch his breath as she lay on the ground, stunned and violated, whimpering. And then Abhimanyu saw his face as he stretched his right hand to grab his trousers.

This was her brother, Ashwini! Abhimanyu had seen this guy a couple of times with Shalini in the canteen during school hours. He was allowed entry into the school only because he was Shalini's brother. At least that was what the school knew and the other guys too, including Jagtar.

The tall guy peaking at six feet rose and grabbed his jeans and started putting them on. He mumbled something to the girl to which she retorted by screaming, 'Leave me alone! Don't come near me.'

Abhimanyu cowered down under the window, shutting his eyes and covering his ears. Trying to lock away the reality.

Ashwini said, 'Wear your clothes, someone might come!'

'Leave me, just leave me! I hate you,' she howled like a woman possessed. Abhimanyu could not see her face, but her voice echoed with violation.

'I am sorry, but you know, we...it's been so long, I couldn't control...'

'You...you...' she wailed, 'You couldn't control yourself? I trusted you and this is what you did to me?' The girl now broke into angry but hysterical weeping. It must have scared the man, 'Please don't shout, Shalini, someone will hear us...you know that I love you...'

'Shut up, and leave me alone...just leave me....' Her voice disintegrated into cries that would haunt Abhimanyu for many days to come.

As Abhimanyu cringed under the window, he saw the profile of the man walking out of the house, and waited for his footsteps to fade away. He was now alone with the girl. He was feeling guilty for he had let him violate the girl, and he had let him get away. His cowardice was now seeking shelter in her misery.

Mustering all the courage in his body burdened by shame, he got up and started walking out of the store room, towards the backyard. The girl was lying on the ground, coiled and curled with disgrace, hiding herself. Her imaginary cocoon was no solace from the dishonour and betrayal. Abhimanyu crossed the wooden threshold of the lawn, and his right shoe hit a rock with a thud, startling the girl. Abhimanyu looked at her with guilt, and she looked at him, first in shock, then fear, eventually breaking down. She hid her face and started crying.

He couldn't utter a word; how could someone give solace to a broken spirit. She tried to rise, only to fall down with a loud and painful moan. She clasped her stomach and started crying again; a stinging pain rose from below her stomach and spread across her body through her spine. Abhimanyu saw that her hands were muddied by the slush and the back of her white shirt had gone dark brown. There was no way she could leave this compound like that.

'Please don't cry. I don't know what to say...' He paused and then spoke again, 'I am leaving my shirt here and going out. Please wear it. You can't go out in this condition. Please.'

Abhimanyu stepped out and took off his shirt and then peeped in. She was still lying on the ground and sobbing uncontrollably. He walked in and placed the shirt next to her.

'Please leave your shirt behind. I would need one too.'

Abhimanyu waited for fifteen minutes, the longest in his life, while his mind oscillated between a feeling of guilt and pity for the girl. He heard some sounds, like the sound of a running tap. She was probably washing herself, he thought. He heard sounds of her sobs that would break into hysterical weeping.

In a few minutes she emerged, in his shirt and her skirt, walking with a limp. Her eyes could not meet his.

And then, just for a hundredth of a second, she looked at him, straight into his eyes. In that moment, she poured all her agony, her contempt at his spinelessness into him. He would never know what she was actually thinking at that moment. Without speaking a word, Abhimanyu sprinted towards the lawn. Her shirt lay on the ground, muddied and dirty.

It took him another ten minutes to wash the stains off her shirt under the same tap she had used to rub clean her scarred body. But the scars won't go so easily. Abhimanyu scaled the boundary wall of the school and started walking towards his house, praying that none of his teachers notice his absence from the remaining three periods after recess. He was lucky, no one did.

He never saw Shalini after that. He never heard anything about her too. As if she had just vanished. But the memory of the look on her face and the guilt in his heart stayed with him for a very long time. All he needed to do was raise his voice.

Scarred by that memory, Abhimanyu kept a low profile at home. His parents thought he was sulking because of their reaction to his participation in a story writing competition. Abhimanyu's father did not believe in assuaging a man's hurt pride and his mother thought he would be fine soon. But he started shirking their presence, particularly his father's. He would lock his room on the pretext of studying, or say that he was going to a friend's place to study. He would then go to a park and spend the evening there. Soon, his mother realized that something was not right and that she needed to talk to him.

That day, his father had to come back late, and Abhimanyu was reading Ruskin Bond lying on the sofa. His mother came and sat next to him. He glanced at her, but ignored her presence. This was all the confirmation she needed. Something was wrong with Babu.

'What is it Babu? Why are you sulking like this? I hope you remember what we do to people who sulk...' Abhimanyu turned his head towards his mother and saw her smiling.

'We spank the sulky ones on their bum,' she raised her right hand in a mock gesture. This was her favourite moment with Babu every time he sulked or got angry.

He did not respond. He continued staring at her blankly.

She knew all along that he was upset after whatever his father had said to him that evening. But she did not know that Abhimanyu had heard what his father had so heartlessly said. And she also did not know that he had seen something in school that had scarred him.

If she had known what bothered Abhimanyu, she could have told him that his father had said that out of sheer frustration and that she had protested and admonished him for it. She could also have told him that his father had apologized for his outburst. Had Abhimanyu shared his pain with her, he would not have endured that burden for a better part of his life with disastrous consequences. She could have told Abhimanyu that his father had come to see him later the same night, patting him as he slept, because that was the only way a man terrible at expressing could show his love.

Abhimanyu's mother had a long conversation with him that day. She kept reminding him of the huge expectations they had from him. She kept telling him how they were not his enemies and that they had the best in their heart for him. She talked and he heard.

In the days to come, he would often comfort his guilty conscience by wondering if it was Shalini who had brought that fate for herself. After all, she had lied to the school that Ashwini was her brother. But no amount of wheedling could persuade his heart; he would never forget the moment when her eyes met his. It was as if she had poured those ten minutes of her violation in that single glance. A suffocating feeling was now Abhimanyu's to bear.

Because all he needed to save her was to raise his voice.

There were ten days to go for the story writing competition and Abhimanyu was scarred by the twin memories of the two most gruesome moments of his life. He met Mrs Jain regularly; she informed him that they would get to know the three topics for the competition soon. And then he would have to prepare with her under the watchful eyes of Dr Matthew. Mrs Jain and Abhimanyu were sitting in the canteen, discussing entries that had won the first prize for the school in the past. Mrs Jain was also reading Abhimanyu's stories that he had written over the years. She looked impressed. Abhimanyu was looking at the previous entries that had won the first prize. He looked unimpressed.

'Just a small warning, Abhimanyu. Don't get carried away! These are the entries for the past three years that bagged us the top spot and Shweta Varma the first prize,' Mrs Jain said handing over the papers to Abhimanyu. 'I hope you would like to study them to have a better idea.'

Abhimanyu looked unconvinced and said, 'I have been looking at her papers and I just have one thing to say – if I really have to follow her, then why have me in the first place? In your words, my story writing skills are different. Then why not have something different than what Shweta has been giving them all these years?'

Mrs Jain shook her head and smiled, knowing well how difficult it would be to convince him on this. She just patted his back and turned her head around to face the office peon.

'Madam, principal sir wants to meet you and Abhimanyu.'

Abhimanyu was asked to wait outside as Mrs Jain entered the principal's room. He waited, strolling around, caressing the leaves and flowers of the plants outside his room. His eyes scanned the small placards and notices stuck on the bulletin board next to the door.

'Mrs Kukreja on leave, Mrs Chaddha to replace...honesty is the best...Debating competition on...Flower decoration competitions... PTA to meet on...basket ball team arrives victorious from...'

And then suddenly, the door opened. Abhimanyu had been waiting outside for about fifteen minutes now. An attractive girl, a couple of inches taller than him, emerged from the room. She had her hair tied in a pony behind a round face. She had immensely expressive eyes and a snooty air about her. Through her pristine white shirt, he could see that she was wearing a black bra and his eyes just lingered there for some time till he felt a pleasant tension between his legs. Abhimanyu was suddenly jolted out of his short voyeuristic sojourn by the sound of her husky voice, 'Principal sir wants to meet you.'

Abhimanyu followed her with a smile on his face. As soon as he entered the room, Principal Mathew's Cheshire cat smile greeted him. He saw Mrs Jain too, but she had her back to him. The mysterious girl came and stood next to him. Her polished skin was very close to his and he was tempted to move a bit towards her.

'Well Abhimanyu, how are you?'

Before he could answer, Mrs Jain turned around. She looked sullen as she suddenly got up and walked away. He then saw his story caught under the paper weight on Dr Mathhew's table. The principal gestured the girl to sit down as he clasped his fingers under his chin.

'So?' he said again.

'I am fine, sir,' Abhimanyu said hesitatingly, his mind was now replaying the expression on Mrs Jain's face. The pleasant tension owing to the girl in the room died down.

'Abhimanyu, as you know that the story writing competition is a very prestigious event and we have been winning this for the past three years, thanks to Shweta...' Matthew pointed to the tall girl in the room with his forefinger.

So this is *the* Shweta!

'Unfortunately, Shweta had a tragedy at home and could not come for many days. But she has agreed to come, especially for this competition. The school is really thankful to her for this gesture.'

Abhimanyu suddenly had this sick feeling in his stomach. And then, Matthew's irritable voice struck him.

'I have been reading your paper, and I must say that I see glimpses of radicalism in your writings. I mean, how can you say that Indians were the same under the British and that nothing will change under the rule of their own countrymen?'

Abhimanyu was now losing patience. So, he shut his eyes and bowed his head to keep his surging emotions in check. Even then when the man didn't stop, Abhimanyu spoke, 'But isn't it the truth, sir?'

'What?' Matthew's expressions suddenly changed and there was a hint of hostility on his face.

'If I may say, sir, what really has changed for the poor of this country, for the have-nots, for those who first bore the burden of the British and now of our own people?'

There was a painful silence for a few seconds, broken by Matthew's angry words, 'I think the storyteller should first learn lessons on politeness. Creativity without politeness is an abomination and I can see the proof right in front of my eyes. I called you to inform you that this being Shweta's last year in school, we have decided that she will represent the school this year too. You have three more years with us, so you will get a chance later, provided...you learn how to behave.'

With his mouth slightly open, Abhimanyu just stood there, a lazy drop of saliva stuck unbendingly at the corner of his lip. Shweta was now looking at him, her beautifully manicured fingers clawing his story paper. Abhimanyu dropped his head, his gaze blankly stuck to the floor.

'Say something and don't just stand there like a log!' Matthew spoke with irritation all over his face. Abhimanyu heard a muffled giggle. It was Shweta.

'This is unfair, sir,' Abhimanyu spoke loudly. Matthew's face had a look of bemusement. No student had dared to use that word in front of him. His ears turned red, as if someone had cracked a slap across his face. How dare a bloody north Indian, Hindi speaking kid question him about being fair! Regaining his composure, he looked at Shweta and forced a nervous smile. He then looked at Abhimanyu and his face hardened.

'If you would have been just another kid, I would have thrown you out of this room,' Matthew said coldly. 'But you had been selected to represent the school for a competition and I would like to give you one last chance to rectify your behaviour. You come here after a high recommendation from Mrs Jain! So I will spare you.'

Abhimanyu thought, 'Why don't you say that I have shown you your true face, that you are so ridden by guilt that you won't dare to touch me today, you lousy sonofabitch!'

'Now please leave and get back to your class. I will have a word with Mrs Jain on your behaviour. This impertinence will not be tolerated in my school. And one more thing, it's not a prophecy, but mark my words – *You will get nowhere in life.* You will bring a bad name to your parents, to your school, and everyone you know.'

As Abhimanyu walked back to his class, clasping "The Girl by the Hut" in his hand, his mind swung between two voices.

You will get nowhere in life.

and

I wish we had the courage to have a second child.

In a few moments, he stood in front of IX–B, and the Math teacher gestured him to enter the class. Abhimanyu quietly entered and moved towards the second last bench, half occupied by Jagtar. His friend immediately realized that something was wrong with Abhimanyu. He nudged him and asked, 'What happened?'

Abhimanyu stared at the blackboard, at the sin and cos equations, turned his head and looked at Jagtar, forcing a tired smile as he whispered, 'Nothing'.

Confused, Jagtar nudged him again and asked, 'What?'

This time, his voice was loud enough to be heard by Mrs Chaddha. She had never really liked the two anyway. She had heard from one of her chums in the class that Jagtar and Abhimanyu often said nasty things about her. Every time she would climb the stairs from the teachers' rest room on the ground floor to the classroom on the first, they would shout, '*Chaddi chad rahee hai*'. And every time she would finish a class and head back downstairs, they would yell, '*Chaddi utar rahee hai*'. Jagtar's voice fulfilled her dream of catching them red-handed. She threw the chalk in her hand at him, which unfortunately landed on the hapless boy sitting behind Jagtar.

'Stop talking or I will throw you out of my class,' she roared.

Chaddha's class was the last period of the day. That day Jagtar walked with abhimanyu, instead of taking the usual bus to his house in Tilak Nagar.

They went and sat in a park near the school. Jagtar raised his right hand and put it on Abhimanyu's shoulder, patting, 'It's just a story writing competition yaar! And that Appam Rascal said you will get a chance in the years to come. Shweta will leave the school next year and then the world is yours.' Jagtar's nickname for Matthews didn't have any effect this time.

'You don't get it, do you? It's not about getting a chance next year! I needed it this time. I wanted to prove myself to that father of mine.'

Jagtar retorted, 'Just go back and sleep for a few hours. You will be fine after that. *Sapnon me khoja, goti pakad ke soja!*'

Jagtar laughed out loud and after a bit of reluctance, Abhimanyu shook his head and joined in. They slapped each other's backs and cracked bawdy jokes for the next few minutes, before both took off.

Abhimanyu sat on the dining table to force food down his mouth and his mother stood next to him, gently caressing his hair. Probably it was her touch, what else could have triggered the tears. The mother's touch bares the vulnerability in a man's soul. Without asking anything, she just pulled him to her bosom and wiped off his tears. Abhimanyu spread his arms around her waist and held her tight.

Perhaps she understood what had happened, 'There is always a second time, if you like to believe in it.'

He cried himself to sleep. And that afternoon, he dreamt something really strange: he was hurting Matthew, torturing him actually. He dreamt that he was slapping Shweta. That tickled and amused him. But then a sudden sound woke him up from his blissful existence.

'Abhimanyu...get up! Its six thirty already. Get up!'

Abhimanyu woke up dazed, still trying to make sense of where he was. He looked at the blurred face of his father. Even with that fuzzy vision, he could make out that his father was angry. Abhimanyu rubbed his eyes and his mother handed over a glass of water to him. His father gulped down the cold water, but his gaze on Abhimanyu was colder. His mother also looked worried.

'I got a call from your principal today, that too in the office. He said you misbehaved with him, that you dared to disobey his authority?'

Trying to make some sense of what his father had just said, Abhimanyu yawned and stared at his father blankly.

'Say something! And don't look at me like an owl,' his father roared.

Abhimanyu's mother appealed for him to stay calm and said, 'He has just woken up. Just give him some time.'

'Mahima, just shut up! It's time he woke up and he has had enough time. I never thought I would get a call from his school and be berated like this in front of my colleagues.'

It now started making sense to Abhimanyu. He had hurt Matthew's ego, prompting him to call his father. And his father had felt hurt because Matthew had insulted him in front of his colleagues. It all boiled down to one thing – his father was embarrassed because of him. Abhimanyu saw his mother walking towards the kitchen and with it, his last hope of being defended.

'How dare you misbehave with your principal? Is this what we have taught you?'

Abhimanyu was shocked that his father did not once ask him what had happened. What had been his provocation? He wondered if he had even asked that question to Matthew.

Abhimanyu protested, 'But I did not misbehave with him. I just protested. I was supposed to represent the school in the story writing competition and they just...'

'So what? Does that give you the license to question his authority? How long am I going to tolerate this? And how long will you continue making life hell for us?'

Abhimanyu could not comprehend his father's hostility. He knew that his father would never appreciate his talent, but couldn't he be fair? Couldn't he have come to him and asked what had happened in school before deeming him impertinent and a duffer?

But his father just wanted to know one thing. 'How long will you make life hell for me?' He had half a mind to actually tell him, 'Till you have your second child.' He should have said that. It would have shut his old man. But instead, he said something else.

'I don't know what I am doing to make your life hell, papa. But I know that I shall continue to do what I do. I think the only redemption for you is to disown me. You don't have to tolerate me because I can't give you the mental peace that you so desperately desire.'

Ujjwal watched his son for some time and his face turned crimson with rage. His jaws tightened and his open fingers closed into a grip. He should have waited for another five seconds to calm down but the rush of blood was so sudden that he did not realize when his fist flew and struck Abhimanyu's jaw. The thin frame of his son crumbled under the force of his blow. The impact of the fall was tremendous; his frontal teeth broke at the roots, piercing his gums. Abhimanyu shrieked, and cried in pain as blood gushed out of his gums. Mahima was used to her husband thrashing her son, an occasional slap or a wringing of ears. But this time, her son's moans were painful and scary. She ran from the other room to the drawing room, and saw her husband looking at something on the floor. And then her eyes followed her husband's gaze. Her son lay on the floor, his dull eyes gaping at the ceiling and his thin hand reluctantly touching his bloodied mouth. Mahima ran across and bent down, lifting her son's head and placing it on her lap. With blood oozing from his mouth, he mumbled, his voice soaked in pain, 'Ma, my teeth'. Mahima tilted her head and saw the crushed teeth. Her eyes moistened. She looked up, her eyes shifting from Abhimanyu to her husband. She had an expression of disbelief, 'What did you do?'

'Get up beta, sit straight! Don't worry, we will take you to the doctor. You are going to be fine.'

Abhimanyu's father bent to pick up Abhimanyu, but Mahima pushed him aside. The anguish had turned to rage.

The dental surgeon surveyed Abhimanyu's teeth as his mother stood by. Ujjwal waited outside the clinic, pacing around, restless, with a surge of guilt engulfing his senses.

'The problem is that his frontal teeth have pierced his gums after breaking. We need to remove the remaining teeth and after that perform a root canal operation. Since he is 13 years old, we cannot have a replacement, like a crown. For that we will have to wait till he is 18.'

'So does that mean that he will stay like this...his teeth exposed to the world?' asked a worried Mahima.

'I can give him a temporary cap, but...I may have to operate him, time and again. So putting a crown or capping it may not be advisable for the next six months.'

Mahima stared at her son, his mouth full of bloodied cotton. A drop of tear trickled from the extreme end of his left eye and moistened his stained cheeks. Abhimanyu was groaning feebly as the effect of the anaesthesia was wearing off with every passing moment. His pain rose, so did the loathing. For the first time he gave words to his hatred for his father.

'Bastard!'

Ujjwal strolled outside the clinic and occasionally peeped inside. From his dental chair, Abhimanyu saw his father walking in a lazy swagger, yawning and looking bored. And then suddenly he stopped, as he lifted his right foot, trying to extricate the pebble stuck in the sole of his brown leather sandals. As he saw his father taking out the pebble from his sandal and flinging it away, he knew his place in his father's life. The pebble stuck in his shoe. The irritating bit of dirt in his eye. Self pity was his favourite sport!

About two hours later, Abhimanyu lay on the sofa, pressing a large piece of cotton on his mouth. His father and his mother sat on the dining table with his mother staring blankly into a vacant space.

'Come on, Mahima! It was a mistake. I did not mean to hurt him like that. Listen to me...'

Mahima raised her forefinger, her eyes dug deep into Ujjwal's, 'You will never ever touch him after this day. Ever! I promise I will make you look like an absolute idiot in this locality otherwise. I will create such a drama... Mark my words!'

His blood boiled, but he sat without a word. This time he had crossed the *Lakshman rekha* and even he knew it.

Abhimanyu looked at his parents, arguing on the dining table. The pain was now unbearable as the effect of the anaesthesia had worn off completely. The point of impact was pulsating heavily. The dentist had removed the broken teeth and had applied cotton around it. The pitch of the argument grew and with it Abhimanyu's pain. Garnering all his strength, he removed the swathe of cotton from his mouth and mumbled something. His feeble voice broke the argument, 'I know... that I continue to bring shame to you papa. You... may not say so in front of me.... but I know.... that you consider me.... a...disgrace....'

Ujjwal looked at his son and shook his head. He got up from the dining table and started walking towards the next room. Stopping at the turn, he turned around and looked at Abhimanyu, 'I can see where all this is heading to. You are unapologetically dramatic and seek self pity. Unremorseful about your behaviour. Instead of being so dramatic, you can at least accept your mistake and start taking life seriously. And shockingly Mahima, you support this....'

Ujjwal always wanted to have the last word. As he walked into the bedroom, he thought he did. Abhimanyu turned his body and head away from his mother's view. A drop of tear trickled down his left cheek, not out of the pain from his gums, but that of the heart. Rupali, the girl by the hut, kept flashing before his eyes. Since the day he had written the story, her vulnerability had always haunted him and deep down... he knew that someday he would complete her story. He wasn't sure if it would be a happy ending, though. He saw Rupali coming back to her hut alone, from her mother's funeral. He saw her shutting the wooden door of her hut, not strong enough to shelter her from the world. The world... that was waiting for a chance to pounce on her. He wiped off the lone drop of tear from his eye as Rupali sat on her charpoy staring blankly at the choolha in one corner of her hut. Separated by a thirty years, Abhimanyu stared at Rupali. For her, it was a desperate fight for survival. For him, it was a dream that lay shattered.

Shweta Verma and her batch were being given the customary farewell. She wore a black gown that was held by thin noodle straps to her shoulders. Her stilettos further accentuated her height and even without them, she was one of the tallest in her class. The party was on, but she was not there. She was searching for someone in the playground in the scorching heat of that afternoon. Faint whistles rent the air, but she ignored them. Her eyes lit up as she found him sitting under the mulberry tree, a book in his hands. Shweta stood in front of him; she rounded her lips in an 'O' and exhaled. She was out of breath, having walked the length of the football field. Shweta cleared her throat audibly. That's when Abhimanyu's eyes rose from the pages of the book to her perfectly manicured red toenails and then her calves. There she was...any boy's dream come true. Her presence at that moment, in front of him...at the edge of the football field was unexpected. Abhimanyu stood up, nearly falling off in the process and looked at her blankly, tongue tied.

'I know this sounds and looks really strange...but I have been wanting to speak to you after I won the first prize in the story writing competition.' As she spoke proudly, Abhimanyu noticed that not once did she look at him. Why the hell was she telling him? Was she trying to rub it off on him....further? One hell of a snooty bitch, he thought!

'I was wondering if we could speak for sometime...maybe somewhere quieter!' It was at that moment that she turned her head and looked directly into his eyes. By God, she was magic! She had stolen the most precious opportunity from his life, but right now, he stood mesmerized in front of her.

'I don't know,' mumbled Abhimanyu.

She cut him short, 'It's okay, we could take a walk and maybe talk. Just that I don't want to be disturbed by those rowdies on the football field. I am sure we can have an uninterrupted talk in the senior wing.'

Abhimanyu looked around and absent-mindedly touched his frontal teeth that had been recently carved and cut to their roots.

'You look different,' she said. 'Your teeth....'

Abhimanyu became even more conscious as he lowered his head, covering his mouth with his right hand, his gaze on his unpolished shoes.

Sensing the discomfort in Abhimanyu about the subject she had just broached, she smiled. It was like a kick. Someone else would have apologized or probably changed the topic, but she just smiled.

'So how were your exams?'

Another uncomfortable question. The results were supposed to be out in a couple of days and the past three months had been nothing short of a nightmare for Abhimanyu. He was hoping to clear his exams and probably pass it with bare minimum this time.

'What is that you want to talk to me about?' Abhimanyu's eyes were still fixed on the ground. He could feel the blood rising to his ears.

'Come...' she demanded, 'Let's walk!'

Walking with the hottest chick in the school was no mean achievement. More so, when *she* wanted to. As they walked across the edge of the football field, the play stopped again as the players started looking resentfully at the unimpressive company she had.

They climbed the stairs to the first floor and made their way to Class XII-B; Shweta pushed the door that opened with a creaking sound. As she sat on the teacher's chair, Shweta gestured to Abhimanyu to sit on the front seat of the classroom.

'I read your story...I also had a long chat with Mrs Jain about your story. She told me why you wrote it and what she felt about it. I have known Mrs Jain since I was in the sixth grade and I have always been her favourite student. Never has she praised anyone in front of me, knowing how possessive I am about her....till you came along...'

Shweta glanced outside the window that opened to a view of the other wing and then turned her gaze back at Abhimanyu who lowered his eyes as their eyes met.

'My mother died when I was seven years old and my memories of her are very faint. I have often been affected by her absence in my life, till Mrs Jain came along. I guess even she was drawn to me because I did not have a mother. So when my grandfather died, and I called her up to find out if someone was representing the school in the story writing competition, I came to know about you. I was stunned at the praise that she showered on you and your so-called amazing story. As I told you, I am possessive about her and then... this was my forte. How could anyone be better than me? So, I came back. Just because I could not see anyone taking my place in Mrs Jain's heart.'

Abhimanyu looked at her intensely and noticed a subtle change in her expressions. From the arrogant and snooty air that she carried around her, a strange insecurity and helplessness filled her eyes.

'I was in pain because of my grandfather's death. But when I heard Mrs Jain speaking about you, I promised myself that I will not let you take my place. Not in the final year of my school. I knew if I had gone to Mrs Jain, she would not have allowed me. So I went to Principal Matthew. I saw that there was a bit of resentment in him about your participation in the competition. I just had to cash on it!'

Shweta smiled, 'Mrs Jain has not spoken to me since then. She thinks that I have usurped your chance and she is absolutely right. Though she still does not know why I did it. I guess she will never speak to me again in her life if she found out.'

With a uncomfortable pause she said, 'They call me an arrogant bitch in the school. Not that I care. I don't mill with people and I am happy with the tag of being a loner. I have always been a topper in my life, so the question of losing simply does not arise. You were the first person who actually showed me what staring at defeat means. I had to bring you down... and I did it in style. I saw you in school later with your mouthful of cotton and I realized that incident had some ripple in your life. You looked sullen and even shattered. It was at that moment that I realized that I had crossed the line. For the first time in my life, I thought that I was wrong.'

Shweta looked at Abhimanyu intently and he stared right back at her. A mixed feeling of self-pity and a simmering rage engulfed his senses.

'I have to say...' she spoke as her voice broke, 'that you wrote a beautiful story. So profound....so... it was just....I don't really have the words to describe it. This is in fact the first time I am praising someone. And this is probably the first time I am going to say this ...'

Abhimanyu was listening.

'I am sorry....I really am.' A thin film of tear filled her left eye. 'I am not going to ask for your forgiveness as I am still the arrogant bitch this school thinks I am. And then, you still have three years. But I realize that if you had participated and won this year, it would have changed your life. An Indian publishing giant is publishing ten short stories of students from across the country, including mine. I have also been offered a contract by yet another publishing house to expand my story into a novel.'

Shweta paused and bit her lower lip as Abhimanyu stared at her blankly.

'You don't have anything to say...?'

Abhimanyu shook his head and got up from the seat and started walking towards the door of the class.

'Please, just talk to me once....'

Abhimanyu turned around and said, 'I have nothing to tell you. Nothing whatsoever. This incident has brought on a storm in my life that you cannot even imagine. And frankly speaking, I don't care. I have moved on. You don't have to feel sorry for me and then...you don't even desire my forgiveness, so we are even.'

Abhimanyu turned back to walk, but she stopped him.

Shweta moved ahead and stood right in front of him. Very close. He could hear her breathing and the smell of the perfume that she had put on, teased his senses. She was a couple of inches taller than him and even if he wished to, he could not avoid the view of her cleavage.

Shweta whispered, 'I had always thought that my first kiss would be to the man I love...but I am ready to make the biggest exception of my life.'

Shweta cupped his cheeks in her warm and perfectly manicured fingers and pressed her lips to his.

As she pressed her lips and then tantalizingly inserted her tongue in his mouth, the first reaction was instant numbness. And then gradually, he felt a sweet taste of strawberries engulfing his senses. The moistness of her lips had by now completely drenched his lips that were parched just a moment ago. Shweta shut her eyes and started relishing the moment. Abhimanyu was too shocked to even move a nerve, she but started moving her fingers around his neck. A hard on was not new for a thirteen-year-old. But a sudden hard on is what he learnt for the first time in his life. He was so numb at that moment that he did not know what to do and how to respond to this dream of a damsel. Shweta then held his right hand and guided it to her left breast.

'Aah....,' they moaned together. Abhimanyu was now breathing heavily as he raised his other hand to cup her right breast.

'Gentle...,' she whispered while licking his earlobes and neck. Abhimanyu moved ahead and pressed his hard on between her legs. Not that he was ever tutored on what to do, but he started to press himself between her legs, and started kissing her passionately.

She moaned louder this time as she felt him between her thighs. And then just like that, she pulled out her lips from his. Shweta pushed Abhimanyu away, as if she was pulled out of a deep trance. Abhimanyu fell back on the desk behind him and she wiped her mouth with the pink handkerchief in her hand.

'That's enough,' she raised her right hand trying to catch her breath. The cold look was back on her face, as she turned around and walked out of the class.

That was Abhimanyu's first kiss and what a way to do it. And what a girl! A dream for any boy in St Mark's. They would not have believed him, even if the word got around.

That night was special for another reason; it was a night of another first. He thought about her, absent-mindedly put his hand inside his pyjamas and started touching himself. As if she were doing it. He could now see her, next to him. He could feel the taste of strawberries in his mouth as he licked his lips. Abhimanyu rubbed harder; he gasped and he moaned. And then something incredible happened. Like a burst of light, something just took him by force and he exploded.

His ninth standard results had been a nightmare-come-true for Abhimanyu, causing a lot of heartburn to his father. Though his father couldn't touch him now, his disappointment was reflected in other ways. The annual trip to Santpur was fast approaching, and Ujjwal would have nothing to say to his brothers for his son's broken grades and teeth.

Abhimanyu's cousins were always complaining of the village life in Santpur and how if they had a choice and their parents hadn't forced them every summer, they would never come here. There were no cinema halls, no ice cream parlours, and no restaurants. Just a village built on wood and cow dung with lush green fields and a reserved forest a couple of kilometres away. Abhimanyu's grandfather, the seventy-year-old Prem Lal Sharma lived in one such house. His grandmother had died long ago, so his grandfather lived alone in a sprawling house, one of the biggest in the village. The summers were the only time the house would be teaming with his city-bred grandchildren. If he wanted to, he could have sold the house and the field and moved in with one of his sons, but he did not. He too was a loner just like Abhimanyu, and that's why he liked him the most.

He was the lone reason Abhimanyu looked forward to the summer break at Santpur. Daddu was full of tales and experiences from his youth. In the afternoon, when everyone was asleep or complaining about the torrid heat, Abhimanyu would step out with his grandfather to the fields and climb the *machan* (a shelter built in the branches of a tree to monitor animals entering the field) on the mango tree. The labourers would be ready with a sackful of mangoes and berries for Abhimanyu to devour.

His uncles and his cousins had already arrived when Abhimanyu and his parents reached that morning. Daddu had sent a bullock cart to the main road to fetch them. Abhimanyu was excited to see Daddu and also because he was told that the labourers had plucked fresh mangoes and berries and spread them on the machan.

Without wasting any time, Abhimanyu stepped out with Daddu to be able to relish the fresh fruits. 'Easy and slow Abhimanyu,' Daddu shouted as Abhimanyu sprinted across the pathway of the cattle shed right in front of the house. It was deserted as the cattle was out grazing, but was still slippery with the dung.

Abhimanyu stopped and came back to hold his grandfather's hand, 'Why don't you tell me that you need my support, Daddu. You have now become old,' he chuckled.

'Me and old?' Daddu feigned an angry look. 'I can still stuff your father and his brothers single-handedly in a fist fight!'

'That must be a thousand years ago, Daddu, isnt it? ' Abhimanyu teased his grandfather as he raised his hand to tickle his white upturned moustache.

'Ha...' His Daddu faked a loud laughter that boomed across the shed to the field nearby, indicating to the labourers that the old man and his grandson were on their way.

'Your father looks tense Abhi. Is everything ok? Have you been behaving properly?'

Abhimanyu now turned his head and looked straight into his Daddu's eyes. Suddenly he felt a lump in his throat. It was so easy for him to just let it out, but he turned his head away and swallowed the lump.

'Must be the journey Daddu! And my results haven't been too good...so maybe....'

The old man put his old but burly hand on Abhimanyu's shoulder and gently patted it.

'I know that you will make it big someday. I have absolutely no doubts about it...'

'Don't raise too many hopes with me Daddu. You are going to get hurt...just like papa.'

Daddu swatted the air with his hand and said, 'Forget about studies...tell me something about your writing. Have you been writing anything lately?'

Abhimanyu turned his head away, his moist eyes now scanning the approaching machan, 'No! I haven't. Haven't had the time.'

'Don't stop, Abhimanyu! I have always been interested in writing, and had your grandmother been alive, I would surely have followed this passion to its logical conclusion.'

Abhimanyu suddenly stopped and interrupted him rather curtly, 'Logical conclusion?'

He searched and fumbled for words, 'Err...ah...maybe become an author...a writer.'

'At the cost of raising your family?' Abhimanyu asked again with a straight face.

'No, I know that I could not earn my bread and butter with writing, but maybe strive to strike a balance.'

Abhimanyu shook his head. Something about Abhimanyu's expression unnerved his grandfather. It was downright patronizing. A more careful scrutiny of his expressions revealed much more. He looked frustrated.

'Your times were different, Daddu. Now we are taught that the only world we know are the pages of our textbooks. You talk about me becoming an author? I have to hide my written work from papa... what if he discovers it? He will die of shock.'

'Abhi! What kind of language is that? Is this how you speak about your father?'

Abhimanyu stopped walking. He smiled and turned around to face his Daddu, arching his skinny arms and pressing his waist with fists of his hands. 'So, you are hurt that I abused your son? Are you also going to disown me? Just like your son did?' As he spoke the last word, his voice broke and a tear started rolling down his left cheek. But he was still smiling. Still trying hard to smile, or perhaps trying hard to suppress his tears.

Digging his knees on the dusty earth, Daddu cupped Abhimanyu's cheeks in his hands. He raised his face, but Abhimanyu reluctantly jerked himself away. His grandfather shook his head with pain and slowly wiped off Abhimanyu's tears with his thumb. He embraced him, and as he did so, the surrounding sounds got muffled by his Daddu's heartbeat. Abhimanyu's earliest and the most reassuring memory was the warmth and the sound of his grandfather's heartbeat.

'Abhimanyu, how can you carry so much anguish in your heart? Do you know your father bore the agony of losing his mother when he was ten years old? I have lost many loved ones too. And you are just thirteen! I have no idea what your pain is...and I am going to talk to your parents about it....'

Abhimanyu interrupted, 'No Daddu...please...'

'I will not let my grandson suffer like this. I am sure either your father can change, or you can see some sense in his words....we have to chart out a way. This is a crucial year of your academic life, and I cannot see you so distracted by other things.'

His grandfather's eyes shifted sideways, his mind overflowing with thoughts. And as if he suddenly remembered something, he said, 'And why did you say Ujjwal disowned you? What did he say to you? Tell me!'

'Nothing...' Abhimanyu shook his head with his eyes shut as he wiped off that lazy stream of muck from his nose. His Daddu started walking towards the field with his hand on Abhimanyu's shoulder. Dry leaves from the mulberry and guava trees lay scattered on the ground. A nightingale perched high on a mango tree cooed endlessly.

That afternoon, when he sat with the old man on the machan, Abhimanyu poured his heart out. He wasn't afraid to be judged. He knew that he would be heard. His Daddu heard every word and nodded, sometimes in disapproval... but mostly in acknowledgement. But he never lifted his old hand off Abhimanyu's back. It was then when Abhimanyu drew 'The Girl by the Hut' from the pocket of his trousers. Daddu dug out his reading glasses and started reading it.

'I am sure he must not have meant it. He loves you. Just that he does not know how to express his emotions. He is my son and I know this of him...'

'No! I know what he said. And I know that he meant every word of it.'

'I will speak to him tomorrow...' Abhimanyu was trying to protest again, but was cut short, 'I know if I don't, you will continue to torture yourself like this. And if there is a flaw in the way they are bringing you up, it has to change.'

And then he paused.

'And you....will not stop writing. You don't have to hide it from your father. I am sure there can be a balance between your dreams and his expectations from you.'

And then he lowered his glasses and locked his old eyes with Abhimanyu's dreamy ones, 'This is just beautiful, Abhimanyu. I am proud of you.'

Daddu was lost in thought for a while and then he spoke suddenly, 'Abhi, have you seen that book rack in my room? Someday, I will proudly keep your first book in that rack. And what a moment would that be!'

A warm breeze blew across the fields, and Abhimanyu felt sheltered. A faint smile played on his lips as he held the sleeves of his grandfather's kurta.

'Now go back! I have work here. I have to sort out these rascals in the field. Go and play with your cousins!'

'No Daddu,' Abhimanyu grabbed his hand, 'I want to be with you. They can wait. And I don't think that they are missing me. So if you don't mind, I will be with you till you go back home.'

Daddu patted his head and called out for a worker to help him come down the machan. Abhimanyu saw that even at seventy, his grandfather was a hands on man, directing workers around. He wondered what would happen to all the fertile land and agriculture after his grandfather. It was clear that neither his father, nor his uncles were interested in carrying out his legacy in the village. How he wished he could be here with his grandfather to look after these vast expanses that led up to the edge of the reserved forest.

'Daddu, can we go to the forest?'

'Not now. But I have planned a safari for all of us in a week's time; two nights in the buffer area of the jungle. I am told that there is a very good chance of spotting tigers in this region.'

Abhimanyu was scared at the mention of tigers. 'Don't worry, you restless monkey. I have everything sorted here,' Granpa tapped his temple and laughed lightly.

Abhimanyu held the old man's hand as they walked across the field. He would occasionally turn his head and sniff his Granpa's sleeves that had the mixed aroma of betel nuts and the soil from the fields. That would remain the most comforting fragrance of his life.

Abhimanyu noticed how after every half a minute, Daddu would caress his moustache and tweak it upwards. There was so much pride in his eyes. After all, his sons did make him a proud man.

'Abhimanyu bhaiya, you got just 50 percent marks?' said one.

The other was more dramatic, 'That's shocking...'

'What did *bade* papa say?' the third one butted in.

'But what were you doing the entire year?' came another.

He was now surrounded by four of his meritorious cousins, the ones he loved to hate. The un-identical twins Sharmila and Rajesh were as old as him and alike only in their top grades. What else with a professor father! His customs officer chacha had two high-scoring children too – eleven-year-old Mala and ten-year-old Jeetendra. All named after film stars of that decade.

Abhimanyu sat there surrounded by his cousins in this 'once a year' conversation with the same topic this year too. He was dreading the evening dinner when his entire family would have the grand congregation in the veranda under the open starlit sky. Daddu was an early sleeper and an extremely early riser.

That day too he finished his dinner by 7 p.m. and was in bed in an hour. The dinner for the others had just started. A huge table was laid outside with all sumptuous vegetarian delicacies and the servants were bringing warm chapatis as the Sharmas sat and ate. The veranda and the dining table were lit by lamps and a lone bulb at a corner.

'I think you have to think of some desperate measures bhaiya.... barely getting a second division is unpardonable! And this year is tenth class boards,' Prakash lit the fire.

Om uncle sitting next to Abhimanyu patted his head and said, 'What have you been doing the whole year, Abhimanyu? You need to pull your socks up, young man.'

'Are you sure Abhimanyu is not in bad company, bhaiya?' Prakash bit on a piece of cucumber.

Abhimanyu's father looked at Abhimanyu and said, 'He is usually with that good for nothing Sardar...'

Abhimanyu was till that moment eating with his head down. He suddenly raised his head and said, 'He is my best friend, and I would appreciate if you did not speak like that about him.'

'Shut up! I will not tolerate this insolence. You obviously aren't doing things properly...and the results are there for everyone to see...'

Prakash intervened, 'But bhaiya, coming back to the main point, what are you planning to do about him? If he does not get at least sixty percent this year, he won't get admission in the science stream. His future will be doomed!'

Abhimanyu retorted, 'You mean to say that everyone who is not in the science stream or is not an engineer is doomed in this country?'

'Abhimanyu!' His father's voice rose alarmingly even as his uncle raised his hand appealing his brother to stay calm.

'Let me handle this bhaiya.' He shifted his gaze to Abhimanyu and said, 'Beta, ours has been traditionally a family of academics and government servants. The problem with our generation was that we did not have anyone to guide us. But you have far better exposure and options that we did not have. So you have to take the next step... you have to think seriously about cracking the entrance exams to IIT in the next three years.'

'But I am not interested in IIT,' Abhimanyu mumbled.

Ujjwal banged his fist on the dining table and said, 'So what are you interested in, you idiot? What do you wish to do with your life? Join the movies? Become an author?'

It was at this moment that everyone on the table turned their heads towards Abhimanyu. Their eyes said it all. He was the outcaste, an anathema in their perfect lives.

He should have kept quiet, but he still spoke, 'Why not? What's wrong in being an author? I am not even interested in the science stream. I would prefer social sciences or language to science any day.'

Ujjwal pointed his forefinger at Abhimanyu menacingly and then shifted his glance to his wife, 'Just ask him to behave himself. I will not hesitate in breaking the rest of his teeth.'

Abhimnayu retorted calmly, 'And what makes you think that I am going to take it lying down this time?'

There was a sudden hush in the room, spare the sound of the clanking of a spoon or someone munching. Even that stopped. No one had retorted like that to Ujjwal in the family. Not even his brothers, or Daddu. He commanded the kind of respect and adulation that was unparalleled. Mahima thought Ujjwal would throw a fork or knife at Abhimnayu owing to the pent up rage. But he did not. Probably realizing that his father was sleeping in the other room, he just slumped back on his chair and smiled.

'See, this is what I have been dealing with. You guys are so lucky to have children like these.' He pointed at the four, who looked stunned.

'All I have is this!' Ujjwal stopped at that. His face was bloodshot as he stared at his plate. Meanwhile, a sense of déjà vu struck Abhimanyu. *I wish we had the courage to have a second child.* It was pin drop silence in the room.

The matter could have ended there itself, but then Om uncle spoke, 'No use crying over spilt milk, bhaiya. You have to think in terms of options. If he is not interested in science, maybe aim for commerce. He could become a chartered accountant.'

Ujjwal muttered under his breath, 'I guess we will have to set up a grocery store for him somewhere in Tagore Garden. But he will mess that up too.'

Ujjwal did not actually mean it, but Om latched on to it and said, 'You don't have to worry about that bhaiya. I will finance it.'

Abhimanyu raised his head and turned towards his uncle, 'And what makes you think that I would be interested in starting any venture with your ill-gotten wealth?'

'Abhimanyu!' Ujjwal roared as a serving spoon flew from the other end of the table, missing Abhimanyu by a whisker. Abhimanyu had now braced himself for another thrashing. Ujjwal got up and started walking towards Abhimanyu menacingly. Mahima rose from her chair to calm her husband down. It was then that a voice stunned everyone in the room.

'You dare not touch Abhimanyu.'

Everyone turned their heads towards the entrance of the house. It was the patriarch of the family. Daddu stood at the entrance with his trademark walking stick in his hand.

'Get back to your chair, Ujjwal!'

'But Pitaji...'

'I don't want any arguments on this. Just get back to your chair!' He looked at Om and said, 'Are you out of your mind? That boy has just reached tenth class and you people are thinking of setting a grocery store for him and you....you are talking about financing it. I am shocked!'

'But Pitaji, he is...'

'I know what he is Ujjwal! And a dining table is not exactly the place where you discipline your children. We will talk about this in the morning. This is no way to raise a child, however wayward he is. And mark my words, Abhimanyu…is a bright boy. The best!' Abhimanyu looked at his old man, his saviour, and his eyes welled up. He wanted to get up and hug him, but seemed glued to the spot.

'We will all sit after breakfast and sort this out. And I am sure we will.'

As Daddu turned and started walking back, he looked at Abhimanyu. The old man looked agitated but his eyes said it all: We will sort this out and sort this out your way! He smiled and then slowly walked back to his room.

That night Abhimanyu slept with his mother inside the house while all others slept in the veranda. A gentle breeze blew, rattling the windows of Abhimanyu's room. He wondered what the fields would look like if it rained. Also thought what would Daddu do if it rained. Daddu was a man of plans and he made the best out of every situation. He was the Jinn to his Alladin. In the little time that he slept, he dreamt of his Daddu. They were staying in a cottage in the dense forest. The one that bordered their fields. He kept drifting from one dream to the other. But his Daddu was always with him. And then in the dream, he heard a voice…

'Abhimanyu…Abhi! Get up…Abhi!'

At first he could not open his eyes to the sharp morning light He saw the blurred image of his father, 'Get up Abhimanyu,' Ujjwal said softly. His voice was too soft for it to be real.

Abhimanyu turned his back to Ujjwal and mumbled, 'I want to sleep.'

But Ujjwal still insisted.

As Abhimanyu rubbed his eyes, the sounds in the house started permeating his ears. He was not sure, but he thought that he heard muffled cries. He was groggy, but still could not understand why his father was holding him so tenderly. Had Daddu's reprimand worked last night? Even grown-ups needed scolding once in a while. With these thoughts, he exited the room.

And then he saw it.

The white shroud extended up to the neck. And the muffled cries were of his mother and his aunts.

But why was Daddu lying on the floor? Abhimanyu walked towards his Daddu and his eyes met his uncles' faces soaked in tears. Abhimanyu looked back at his father who looked stunned. Why was Daddu wrapped in the white shroud? Ujjwal walked towards Abhimanyu and whispered as his voice broke, 'Your Daddu passed away in his sleep, Abhi! Just touch his feet...'

Abhimanyu looked back in anger, clearly enraged by what he thought was some sick joke by his father.

'What do you mean passed away?'

He was now standing in front of his Daddu's body. His face looked immensely calm. Abhimanyu collapsed to the ground as his knees gave in beneath him. The ground beneath him suddenly started crumbling, the reverberations of which rose across to his heart.

He turned back to his father and said, 'Are you saying he is dead?'

A trickle of tears started flowing from his father's eyes.

'But how can he die? He can't!' Abhimanyu bent down further, his face close to his grandfather's. And then suddenly, he started rocking back and forth as if hit by a fit. Abhimanyu clenched his fists and his teeth as a strange wheezing sound started rising from his mouth. Like an animal in pain, he started whimpering. With all his strength, he banged his head on the ground. Ujjwal rushed forward; Abhimanyu's eyes started turning over and blood started flowing from his clenched teeth. He had bitten his tongue. Mahima rushed to her son as Ujjwal clasped Abhimanyu to his chest. Pushing his father away, he spread his arms around his grandfather and embraced him. That was the first time in so many years that he could not find the old man's heartbeat. For some strange reason, he still tried to find it. Maybe. Maybe he would still rise. He kept pressing his ear to his chest...maybe...maybe he would finally find the heartbeat. Daddu could not die like that! He could not die on him!

Abhimanyu's grandfather had died in his sleep. It was a heart attack. Ujjwal discovered that his father, who would normally be up by five, was still asleep at seven. One look and he had known. But he still called the doctor. It was only around an hour later that they woke Daddu's favourite child. Abhimanyu was shifted to the city hospital, some thirteen kilometres away from Santpur, and was put on a drip. He had collapsed. It was only in the evening when Abhimanyu returned that they consigned his grandfather to flames. Bit by bit, he saw his Daddu melt away in the evening sky. His Jinn had finally been released.

Abhimanyu did not leave the funeral pyre till it was reduced to smouldering ashes. It was then, a rare moment, when his father embraced him and started crying uncontrollably. But Abhimanyu, his eyes filled with tears just stared into the emptiness that lay ahead of him. Once again, Rupali flashed in front of his eyes. The funeral pyre of her mother, the uncertainty, the helplessness and the scary vacuum that lay ahead. Rupali's tale had got stuck in three pages, refusing to move ahead. It was screaming to be told. Dying to move ahead. But Abhimanyu would not understand that. His own predicament was somehow linked with Rupali's misery. But he could not see that.

Abhimanyu would spend the days dazed and the nights sobbing quietly. Sometimes his mother would wake up and clasp him tight to her chest, but mostly he endured his pain alone. They had to take him to the hospital a couple of times as he kept collapsing at regular intervals. He had become weak and dehydrated and whatever he ate came out in a vomit. For the first time since his birth, Abhimanyu became the centre of all attention. For the wrong reason this time. He was, after all, the old man's favourite child.

Fifteen days later, they decided to leave the village and move to Bhopal to Prakash' house. Two bullock carts would drop them to the highway. Then, a bus would take them to Chhindwara and from there to Bhopal. As everyone else waited in the veranda, Abhimanyu sat in his Daddu's room staring at his garlanded photo kept on a pedestal. He looked into the serene and proud eyes of his grandfather and saw his own reflection in the glass of the photo. And then his grandfather's voice started haunting him. Like echoes from the past, like waves on a rebound, it started coming back to him.

And you....will not stop writing.

I will seek a solution, so that you don't have to hide it from your father.

I am sure you will shine someday.

...there can be a balance between your dreams and his expectations.

Abhimanyu...I am proud of you.

Abhimanyu inserted his hand in his shirt pocket and drew out the papers. The story of Rupali. He looked at it and a faint smile played on his lips.

*Abhi....have you seen that book rack in my room? Someday,
I will proudly keep your first book in that rack with my own
hands. And what a moment that would be...*

Abhimanyu stood up and walked towards the rack. Abhimanyu
looked at the papers in his hand and drew out Daddu's favourite
book. Charles Dicken's *Great Expectations*. And incidentally his
favourite too. He turned around to look at his grandfather's photo
and said, 'I am sorry Daddu...for this is as far as I could get!' He
felt that he would choke with the surge of emotions engulfing
him at that moment, but he did not cry. Instead, he calmly put
the papers in the book and shut it. A hint of dust rose from the
impact. Abhimanyu then walked back to his grandfather's photo
and kissed the frame.

'You died because of me, Daddu. And I shall never forgive
myself for that. I have now buried my dream. Forever. But I shall
certainly fulfil your son's dream. But he will discover someday that it
will come with a cost...'

Abhimanyu shut the door of his grandfather's room and locked
it. He saw his parents and uncles waiting for him. The bullock carts
were there to take them to the main road. Abhimanyu handed over
the keys to one of the caretakers of the house and then walked
straight to the bullock cart and sat next to his mother. Mahima
caressed her son's hair. Abhimanyu looked at his mother blankly
and then turned his head away. Something had died inside him.

And then, the bullock carts started to move. Every year, year
after year, his grandfather would stand there and wave his hand
as the bullock carts left. Abhimanyu would cry while leaving his
grandfather's house. As dust rose from the wheels of the bullock
cart, everyone covered their mouths with hankerchiefs and towels.
Abhimanyu saw Daddu's house disappearing as they took the next

turn. Village children perched on the top of their boundary walls, watching the bullock carts wobble and jump on the rocky tracks of the village.

The Sarpanch of the village had bought all the agricultural land and cattle from the Sharmas but for some emotional reason, they decided to keep the house and did not sell it. A caretaker was appointed who would maintain the house and clean it daily. The patriarch was dead and everyone in Santpur knew that things would never be the same again.

'I thought he was invincible! I thought he could never die,' Abhimanyu said wiping off the single tear on his left cheek. Jagtar placed his hand on his shoulder and patted it.

'I should not have told him Jagtar. I shouldn't have...'

'No, it's not like that. Why are you blaming yourself for his death?'

'You don't get it, do you?' Abhimanyu turned and looked at Jagtar with anguish in his eyes. 'He had a perfect life. He had no tensions in his life, till I riddled him with mine. I still remember that look on his face, when he moved back to his room. The night he admonished papa...just those last few moments before he shut the door. Those last few seconds...when I saw him alive. I can never forget the look on his face. So much anguish, yet so comforting. What I realize now is that I had never seen so much worry in his eyes. I never expected that he would take it so seriously...'

'Now will you let me speak for a moment, Abhi?' Jagtar clasped his shoulder, 'I have seen my grandfather die...And he had a miserable life in those last few days. He was eighty. Now just imagine something like that happening to your grandfather. He deserved a peaceful death, and he got it.'

Abhimanyu suddenly got up brushing off Jagtar's hand off his shoulder, 'What kind of logic is that? Are you justifying his death, just because he had to die peacefully?'

Jagtar tried calming him down, 'No! But Abhi, he loved you. And would be really hurt if he came to know that you blame yourself for his death.'

'But this was no time for him to leave me, Jagtar.' Abhimanyu spoke loudly even as his voice crumbled. Tears started rolling down his cheeks and he crashed on his knees on the pebble strewn ground.

Jagtar bent down and patted his back. 'Come on Abhi! I know it's hard, but it shall pass.'

Even in that state, Abhimanyu realized something. Jagtar was unusually calm and mature. Jagtar was growing up, so was Abhimanyu. But at a cost. Something indeed had died inside him during this summer of discontent.

That evening when he went back home, he received a call on the landlord's telephone.

'Hi, it's me.'

'Who me?'

'No guesses? I wish you could smell me on the phone...'

'Shweta!' Abhimanyu's heartbeat went out of control, 'How did you get this number?'

'Does that really matter? Aren't you happy we are talking?'

Abhimanyu was stunned. He hadn't imagined this even in the wildest of his dreams.

'I am leaving India Abhi...tomorrow.' There was a painful silence. 'I know I should have informed earlier, but I was wondering if it really mattered to you.'

Abhimanyu just listened to each and every word, preserving Shweta's husky and velvety voice. He did not know how to react to what she was saying. He had not defined his feelings for her till now. And this sudden sting on hearing the news was a bit surprising for him too.

'Are you even listening to me, Abhi?'

'Every word of it,' he responded. 'When are you leaving?'

'I have a flight at 8 a.m. and our check in time is 5 a.m.'

'You could have told me earlier.'

'I wasn't sure if you'd care. But I could not leave this country without telling you. My dad is going to be settled in London now with his English girlfriend.'

'Do you really have to go?'

'I *want* to go. I love London and wouldn't miss it for the world. But for some reason, I thought I should tell you.'

'Thanks,' Abhimanyu breathed out on the phone as he felt slight discomfort in his chest.

'Was that a sigh of relief, Abhi?' Shweta giggled.

There was a brief and uncomfortable pause again. 'Can I see you one last time?' he pleaded.

'But how? It's impossible! You can't come—'

Abhimanyu interrupted, 'I can see you tomorrow morning at the airport. I will be there at 4.30 a.m.!'

'What?' Shweta was pleasantly surprised and flattered by Abhimanyu's determination.

'Don't ask how, but I will be there!'

Abhimanyu's next call was to his crisis manager, Jagtar.

'What do you mean you want me to take dad's scooter at 4 a.m.?' Jagtar whispered into the phone and turned his head around simultaneously to see if someone was listening to this conversation.

When Abhimanyu told him, Jagtar refused point blank. 'No way, Abhi. I cannot take you to the airport at four in the morning.'

They were zooming to the airport on Jagtar's Lambretta scooter at four, and the only sound barring the scooter's was Jagtar's cussing. Abhimanyu could not hide the wide grin. The butterflies in his stomach and the excitement was alien to him. And he was loving every bit of it. At ten minutes to five, they stood in front of the departure gate.

It was around five that an ambassador car came and stood in front of the same gate. Shweta alighted from the car wearing blue jeans, white top and her signature ponytail. Her father was fiddling with the baggage. Abhimanyu got restless as he stood at a distance with Jagtar who looked confused as hell. Shweta turned her head around as her eyes met Abhimanyu's. She looked at him and coldly turned her head away. Shweta's father dumped the two huge suitcases on the trolley and dragged it towards the entrance.

'What? Is that all?' Jagtar sounded pissed as he said that. 'Dude, she saw us and did not even respond. Are you sure you spoke to her? Have you been hallucinating? I mean, we came all the way to this bloody airport to do what? To be...'

Abhimanyu put his hand on Jagtar's shoulder who now had his back to the entrance gate of the airport. 'Look!' he pointed to the entrance again.

She walked elegantly out of the entrance gate. Her eyes met Abhimanyu's again, and this time, she smiled. Jagtar stood there stunned, his eyes darting from Abhimanyu to Shweta.

'I had to let dad enter the airport before I met you. I told him I saw some friends standing outside.'

'It's ok, I understand. I am glad that I could see you one last time.'

Shweta turned around to see if her dad was watching them and moved a step towards Abhimanyu. She raised her right hand and placed it on Abhimanyu's cheek, 'You have grown taller since the last time I saw you.'

She had surprised him the last time and she was no different this time too. She moved further ahead and pressed her lips to his. Jagtar felt ignored between the two, and even he hadn't expected this. She withdrew her lips from Abhimanyu's, but her eyes were still shut. Numb, he opened his mouth and gently licked his lips, savouring the moment. But before he could open his eyes, she had turned around and was running towards the entrance gate. Abhimanyu felt a sudden jab in his heart. He raised his hand to call out her name, but did not. He wanted her to turn back again, maybe just look at him once before she entered the airport. She did not. But then, just as she vanished from his view forever, he saw something. She wiped her eyes with her crimson handkerchief.

Driving back slowly to Rajouri Garden, the scene at the airport played over and over in Abhimanyu's mind. They reached their favourite park in Tagore Garden and walked towards their pet haunt after parking the scooter in the no-parking zone.

'I always thought you were lying to me about Shweta. But boy oh boy, when I saw her walking towards us...I was stunned. And then she kissed you, dude. Wow!'

Abhimanyu was lost in the joggers and walkers in the park. Jagtar nudged him, 'So did you do the naughty stuff with her?'

Abhimanyu started coughing as he turned his head towards Jagtar in absolute bemusement. 'What?'

'You know what I mean. Don't give me that "cookie in the jar" expression.'

'Shut up, Jaggu. Nothing of that sort happened.'

Jagtar nudged him, 'You don't have to hide it. I am your best friend, after all.'

'One, nothing like that happened. And two, if it does happen someday, I am not going to share it with you.'

'Not fair! What are friends for?' Jagtar tried being overdramatic in order to dish out some juicy details.

'To shut the hell up!'

'Come on Abhi, did I not tell you when the tenant in our house let me feel her up?'

'That's so gracious on your part Jaggu but everyone is not as selfless as you are. Some have a mean streak like I do.'

'You know, I have always had the hots for Shweta. I am so jealous of you.'

'You can have her. What are friends for!' Abhimanyu sniggered.

'Very funny. By the way, would you have dropped me for her?'

'At the very first opportunity! Don't you know I am the devil?'

Jagtar rose dramatically and made a mock expression that would put a B grade Bollywood actor to shame. Abhimanyu shook his head, while Jagtar started to hum *Dost dost na raha*.

Abhimanyu became more of a recluse in the year of the board examinations. Abhimanyu didn't go out to play, spent more time at home. His father became even more actively involved in his studies. Abhimanyu scored seventy percent marks in the half yearlies, which was a surprise and a relief for his father. But he also knew his son was unpredictable. So while he waited with baited breath for the board results, sweltering May had already set in. And then, one day as he had just come out of a meeting, he received a call from home.

'What? Are you sure?' Ujjwal said. Mahima was on the line, barely able to control her emotions.

'Yes, it's true! He has scored 86 percent marks! Imagine getting 94 in Mathematics. He stands fifth in the class...' Tears started flowing from Mahima's eyes, 'Didn't I always tell you my son will make us really proud someday. I always knew...' Mahima's voice broke.

On the other end of the phone, Ujjwal stood stupefied, a lone drop of tear rolling down his left eye. 'Is he around, Mahima...Is my son around?'

Mahima went quiet, 'This is the first time you have used the expression "my son". Here, talk to him!' Mahima turned around and handed over the phone to Abhimanyu. He moved ahead slowly and pressed the phone to his ears as his mother started caressing his hair.

'Hello...'

'Hey Abhi,' Ujjwal bit his lower lip, trying to steady his broken voice.

'Yes papa,' Abhimanyu responded coldly.

'You did it champ! You did it!'

Abhimanyu smiled with a hint of sarcasm on his face and said, 'Yeah, kind of. It was all your hard work that paid off finally. And thanks for never losing faith in me.'

'You are *my* son; Ujjwal Sharma's son! It was just a matter of time...This is just the beginning Abhi...I promise you, now that you have proven yourself, you can do whatever you want! Let's plan a vacation, son. Any place of your liking.'

'It's ok, papa! We need to save that money for my studies. You know I am not into holidays and visiting places.'

'My son is a big event player,' Ujjwal laughed exaggeratedly. 'I always knew...now no one can patronize my son! No one can dare to...'

Abhimanyu smiled again as echoes from the past started striking him again.

I wish we had the courage to have another child.
We may have to set a grocery shop for him.

Abhimanyu said, 'If I underperformed, it was not because of anyone. If I excelled today, I don't owe it to them. So why should we even talk about them papa?'

Ujjwal moved back on his chair and smiled, 'Hmm, I see my champ has suddenly become so mature that he can teach his old man a thing or two. I wish your Daddu was around...'

Ujjwal left the last word hanging and then suddenly like a panic attack, Abhimanyu's heart started sinking. That same wretched feeling when his Daddu had died. The realization that he wasn't there anymore. And without saying anything, he just kept the phone on the cradle and started walking away.

Mahima was standing by his side and asked, 'What did your father say?'

'I have made him a proud father today. I am sure Daddu must have felt the same. I am going out for sometime Ma, will be back before papa comes back.'

Abhimanyu walked in the sweltering May sun. The road from the school to the park was filled with children from various schools. The results were out and the summer break had begun. The vacations did not matter to Abhimanyu anymore. His was already over. Exactly a year ago in Santpur.

The park looked desolate, except for a distant chatter of some retired old men playing cards and talking loudly. Three years ago, Daddu had come to visit them during winters. That was his last memory of Daddu in this park. They would often come during the day and sit there and talk endlessly.

Abhimanyu murmured under his breath, 'I miss you Daddu... always will.' He was angry with his grandfather; he felt betrayed. He looked at the old men exiting the park with contempt and cursed them. They had no right to live while his young-at-heart Daddu had died! As a collage of disturbing thoughts pounded him, Abhimanyu shut his eyes and ears and wandered off to neverland.

Six hours later, Ujjwal and Mahima discovered him sleeping in the park as they searched frantically for him all around. Unlike his usual anger, Ujjwal gently woke his son and embraced him warmly. As they walked back home, Abhimanyu looked around dazed. He felt the old man's presence around him. The feeling was so powerful that he started looking around, searching for his Daddu.

One life-changing incident and not more than one year later, Abhimanyu had changed dramatically. He grew tall and the dental operation got rid of his buck tooth. He was now a handsome boy. His parents noticed the physical changes in him like everyone else, but ironically missed out on the changes in his person. His decent run in science stream continued to bring joy to his father who was also happy that Jagtar had landed in the commerce section, leaving his son alone. The teachers loved him because he was a hassle-free student who would never create a ruckus in the class. But something else had died inside him.

Mrs Jain would never forget that look in Abhimanyu's eyes when she met and spoke to him about the story writing competition. She saw an emotion in his eyes that was disconcerting. After the long chat with him, she knew that the Abhimanyu she had known was gone. Never to come back. They had murdered his innocence. And his dreams.

In his last year at school, he was back to the mulberry tree near the now-complete building of the principal's house. Alok Bhatnagar paced under the tree and others, including Abhimanyu, sat on the pile of bricks. And when Alok Bhatnagar spoke, others listened in rapt attention. He was the tallest, darkest and the most intelligent lad in the XII class.

'There is no way we are taking NO for an answer! Appam Rascal can't do this to us...' Alok mumbled.

'So what are you going to do? Rebel?' Sharad pushed his thick spectacles up the bridge of his nose as he squinted, his eyes never leaving the sight of Alok who was still staring at something on the ground. Alok bent down with a feeble groan and picked up a sharp rock.

'Well, this country has shown time and again that rebellion is the way out...so why not here? In our school!'

Sharad shook his head and started to look around to the other three, 'You can't be serious, can you?'

The others stared blankly at Sharad. With the look of shock on his face, Sharad spoke again, 'We can't be serious. Abhi...what do you think?'

Abhimanyu exhaled softly, 'We need to have a plan. Or we wait for an opportunity. A rebellion works only when we have an alternative in place. The management will never support us and even if we convince the students to join us in whatever that you guys have in mind, they can arm twist us by pure blackmail. Don't forget, they still decide how many marks we get in the science practical. And if they do the unthinkable – by failing us in the practical examinations, which I know Appam Rascal is capable of – we get screwed for life!'

Vishal's hair were dripping with coconut oil, which seemed to be the source of his intelligence. 'Why even bother man? You know we don't rely on Chaddha for studies.'

Mrs Chaddha had delivered awful results for class IX students, so Matthews had appointed her to teach class XII instead. Pandering or politics, whatever it was, it wasn't going very well for the students. Alok turned to Vishal and spoke with an edge to his voice, 'It's not about dependence on Chaddhi, it's about principles. How can she get away with this? Imagine, she actually screws up on basic trigonometric equations.'

'Dude, she could be nervous teaching us,' Vishal sprang to her defence.

'What's your problem, Vishal? Why are you being an asshole?'

Before Vishal could say anything, Abhimnayu spoke calmly but firmly, 'I might not be totally dismissive of what Vishal said. We do make her nervous! But then, if you can't handle the heat, she better get out rather than play with our careers.'

'Exactly!' said Alok. 'And if she does not on her own, we will help her!'

They knew that something had to be done. The best way was to make Chaddha's life a living hell. Maybe they could scare her away.

That day as she entered the class, the look on the faces of the students meant only one thing. She was up for a rude shock. As she carefully entered the class, there was a muffled guffaw, the sound of which originated from the back benchers. Mrs Chaddha looked hard at the students sitting at the back bench and carefully took the chair. The murmurs and giggling continued and Mrs Chaddha admonished, 'This is the most undisciplined class I have come across.'

The giggling now changed into a loud laughter as the other students also joined in.

'Shut up! Don't you dare forget that your science teachers are very good friends of mine and if you continue harassing me, I will see to it that none of you gets good marks in the practical exams.'

It was at this moment that Alok stood up and said, 'Is that a threat?'

Stunned at the retort, she fumbled for words, 'Behave yourself! I am not finished as yet.'

'But you seem to be threatening us,' Alok clenched his right fist and it scared Mrs Chaddha. She raised her shaking right index finger and said, 'Enough! Sit down now or you may never get a chance to sit in this class.' It was at this moment that she opened the compartment below her desk to keep her purse. As she looked at the open compartment, she thought she had seen something that should not be there.

She moved her eyes to the class, then back to the compartment before she saw "it". It sat there looking straight into Mrs Chaddha's eyes with its tail raised and pointing upwards. The mud smeared chameleon jumped and grabbed at Mrs Chaddha's mangalsutra.

It was the loudest shriek that the school must have heard in its history. Mrs Chaddha tumbled back and the chair that she was sitting on went crashing down. Luckily for her, the chair landed on its back and so did Mrs Chaddha. The frightened chameleon slithered across the classroom and then headed straight for the exit. It was not a very pleasant sight. Mrs Chaddha sprawled on her fours, her hands spread across and her feet spread across wide, a posture that was till that moment only known to Mr Chaddha, her husband. A hush descended in the class, but Mrs Chaddha now had tears in her eyes as she struggled to get up. And when she finally did, she walked out of the class, without even looking at the students, her purse firmly clasped in her right hand.

The girls stood by the window of the class and saw the guys sweating it out on an unusually hot October day in the football ground. This was probably the first time a science section was given punishment on such a massive scale. Principal Matthew stood next to the sports teacher Khatri as he scanned the faces on the students. His eyes stopped at Abhimanyu.

'Abhimanyu Sharma! Why am I not surprised to see you?'

Abhimanyu continued looking straight into Matthew's eyes, his face blank and devoid of any emotion as a drop of sweat trickled down his sideburns.

'Is that chameleon straight out of your tales, Abhimanyu?'

Abhimanyu turned his face away. Khatri, the sports instructor moved ahead menacingly and growled, 'Principal sir is asking you something. Speak out!'

'No sir. I didn't do it.'

Matthew rounded his mouth and blew out as he simultaneously shook his head and smiled, 'You know Mr Khatri, this entire class is going to the dogs. They have this misplaced sense of hurt and pride which will only take them to a very dark end.'

Matthew shifted his eyes back to the students, 'I need names... and I need them fast! I want to know who placed the chameleon in the drawer. I know that your final examination results are not in my control, but your practicals still are! Do I need to say more?'

Matthew walked back to his room after that. He knew he had instilled doubts in many minds and sown seeds for rebellion within the ranks of the rebels. He just needed to wait for a day or two and the name would be out in no time. But Alok Bhatnagar was not the one to be messed with. After the Principal left, Alok ran his gaze through the faces of the students. He did not have to say anything, but the look said it all.

Abhimanyu, Sharad and Alok walked towards their houses after the last bell rang. The plan to intimidate Mrs Chaddha wasn't working the way they had planned it. In fact, she continued to teach the class, minus the boys! The best of both worlds for her basically.

A hoard of children dressed in blues and whites walked across the dusty road. Skirts bounced as girls walked and chatted energetically. The sounds of rickshaw pullers shouting at students blocking their way and the high pitched call of the sugarcane cube seller rent the air. Children gathered around the candy floss, ice cream and churan sellers, holding the five paisa coins. Amidst all this chaos, Abhimanyu thought someone was calling out his name from a distance. He saw Jagtar and his gang waving and shouting wildly at them.

'Congratulations guys, you have broken all previous records! You now have the dubious distinction of the first science section being punished in the open.' Jagtar roared as he high-fived a weary Abhimanyu.

Alok stuck his middle finger out and waived it at Jagtar.

Jagtar laughed and slapped Abhimanyu's back. 'So now what? I mean, it's just a matter of time when someone speaks out and...'

Alok butted in, 'No one would dare to. The principal will have to give up.

Another guy spoke, 'Listen, Diwali is around the corner. Do we expect some fireworks from you guys...or do we have to do the dirty work?'

Alok was lost in thought, but his suddenly brightened face meant he had a plan.

After all the murmuring in the group, Sharad looked the most disconcerted. 'Are you serious about this?'

Alok patted his back and said, 'Gotchya! We aren't that crazy Sharad. Relax! It was a joke.'

Abhimanyu wasn't sure if it was.

The boys continued to be punished for the next two days. It was only a day before Diwali that Principal Matthew allowed them inside the class. And ironically, the first period was their favourite teacher's.

Mrs Chaddha entered the class, and without sparing any student a glance, slowed down as she approached her desk. She carefully opened the drawer and closed it. This was followed by muffled sounds of laughter across the class.

'Enough!' Mrs Chaddha shouted at the top of her voice.

Meanwhile, Sharad had been late for school and was running like a maniac towards the class. His eyes were fixed on the broken desk that was kept outside his class for the past few days and no one had bothered to dispose it off. Sharad thought like he did every other day, "Someone is going to get hurt because of this..."

Sharad was rarely late for classes. Perhaps it wasn't his day.

The synchronization of the events that followed was just seamless. Sharad appeared at the door, Mrs Chaddha turned her head towards him, Abhimanyu raised his eyes from his book on trigonometry to the door, Sharad asked for permission to enter the class. And then, just then, the agarbatti timed Gola cracker hidden in the wreckage of the desk came alive.

Boom!

As a reflexive action, Sharad cupped his ears and bent down. He saw Mrs Chaddha crashing to her right with a look of sheer terror in her eyes. Sharad rushed towards her to lift her up. But the reaction from Mrs Chaddha was not what he had expected. As he stretched and offered his hand to help her get up, her hand stung his left cheek. Sharad's glasses flew across the floor of the class. A collective gasp from the entire class reverberated across the corridor.

Sharad picked up his glasses and turned to look at Alok, 'This time you have crossed all the limits.' Sharad said nothing after that and took his seat. They were now waiting for Matthew to walk in any moment. Their classroom was situated just above his room and they could hear sounds of a hysterical Mrs Chaddha. The entire wing was out to witness the drama. The biggest soap opera St Mark's had witnessed. Till now.

That day Matthew realized that Mrs Chaddha not only looked like a man because of that thin line of hair above her upper lip, but also sounded like one. Particularly when she was shouting incoherently. All that he could understand was – XII-B, cracker, harass, can't take it, and Sharad.

Matthew walked inside with clenched jaws and gestured Sharad with his index finger all in one go. His shrill voice cut through the school corridors as teachers in the adjacent classes stopped teaching, ears cocked and trying to listen in. Dumfounded, Sharad stumbled through his desk and walked slowly towards the principal. He looked back at Alok, who could not understand that look. It was a hurt look, with a hint of betrayal.

'Sir, I...'

Matthew slapped him hard, this time on the right cheek. Sharad mumbled something again, but Matthew pushed him, making him crash on his buttocks on the floor.

'This boy sir,' Mrs Chaddha choked on her flowing eyes and nose, 'This is the guy who blew the cracker in my class sir.'

'Don't worry, Mrs Chaddha, I will see to it that he isn't in a position to do anything whatsoever after this...' roared Matthew.

Abhimanyu sprang up on his feet and banged his fist on the desk, 'I saw Sharad entering the class sir, and he was just as shocked as Mrs Chaddha. He did not do it. You are being unfair.'

'Shut up!' Matthew pointed at Abhimanyu to come out. 'I think this is all your brainchild, Mr rebel. Come out! You are nothing but a bunch of spoilt brats whose parents haven't taught them anything.'

Abhimanyu pushed aside his desk and stood tall and intimidating with his fists clenched. Matthew saw him and felt a sudden surge of panic engulfing his chest. He knew using force with Abhimanyu could lead to dramatically different consequences.

Matthew stood there muttering something under his breath and then swung around, turning his back to Abhimanyu. He walked a few steps, then stopped and turned around, his eyes meeting Abhimanyu's, 'I hereby announce the suspension of this entire class. And you, Sharad...you are expelled!'

Sharad had never been slapped by his teachers in his entire life, and today he got two. And then the unthinkable. Rustication! Matthew's last word rang in his ears. Sharad grabbed Abhimanyu's sleeve but crashed on the ground. He grabbed his throat and started choking before he threw up. His eyes rolled over as if hit by a fit. The sight of a sixteen year old crying is always a disturbing one. Abhimanyu clasped Sharad tightly to his chest

'Do you realize what you have done, Alok?'

'I am never afraid of owning up. But I did not do it.'

'Give me a break! You think anyone else has the guts to do this?'

'You can screw your assumptions, Abhimanyu. I did not do it, and that's about it! Now don't test my patience.'

Abhimanyu walked back to his home across the dusty by-lanes of Rajouri garden. Sharad had left early with his father who had been summoned by Principal Matthew. Sharad had looked crestfallen. His father's face was red. Without even hazarding a guess, he could imagine how Principal Matthew must have berated Sharad and his father. And knowing Sharad and his father, they would have just put their heads down and listened without even protesting. Matthew may have expelled him, but they thought that Sharad still had a chance of rejoining the school, and it was for that chance that they were not even contesting Matthew's accusation. Sharad's father was convinced of his son's innocence, but he thought that this would pass and that Matthew would ultimately reverse the decision of rusticating Sharad.

That night Abhimanyu went to Sharad's home. Not just because he felt guilty at not being able to save Sharad, but also because his father along with the fathers of other boys in the class had received calls from the Principal's office to be present at a meeting that was convened a day later. His father would have questions and he was in no mood to answer any.

Sharad and Abhimanyu sat in the veranda of his sixth floor house in Ramesh Nagar. With his chin on the iron railing of his balcony, Sharad stared blankly at the children playing cricket. His face bore testimony to the deathly chill that had engulfed his life after the incident in the class. His confidence bordering on arrogance had always stood him apart in the band of boys in the class. But now, his vulnerability was so frightening. Sharad had planned his life ahead. He had already finished his course for entry into AIIMS and was on his way to complete the two correspondence tutorial courses that he had subscribed to. But it was scary and unnerving to even look at his new avatar that evening.

'It is all over,' he mumbled.

'Don't be daft! This is just a phase...'

Sharad turned his head towards Abhimanyu, his watery eyes now simmering with rage, 'They have expelled me! Do you realize what that means?'

'I know what that means...but don't you see that the school needs you too. You are the pride of the school.'

'Still,' he whispered. 'I just don't have it in me to face anything now.'

Sharad's voice suddenly rose, 'At times when I realize that I have shattered my parents' dreams,' his voice broke, 'I just feel like ending my life.'

A sudden chill engulfed Abhimanyu and he felt as if the chirping evening birds, the children playing in the park and the chattering women had been silenced by Sharad's shocking confession. He knew this feeling. Death was not just a dramatic word for Abhimanyu. It was something that he had endured. It was something that he felt responsible for.

He had come there to counsel his friend, to make him see the light at the end of all the doom that he saw around himself. But now he felt stark naked in front of him. He felt vulnerable. He mumbled a quick 'goodnight' to Sharad and left.

When Abhimanyu reached home, his father was waiting for him in the drawing room. 'Where have you been? And what have you done in school?'

Abhimanyu did not even slow down and went straight into the bedroom. He was lying on the bed with the bend of his left arm covering his eyes. As his father entered the bedroom, Abhimanyu sighed and turned around on the bed. It was clear that he did not want to talk. Ujjwal stood by the side of his bed and then slowly sat at the edge. He could see that Abhimanyu was restless.

'Take your own time Abhi. I am not here to cross question you, I promise I won't. I just need to know what happened. That's it!'

How could he cross question him, thought Abhimanyu. How could he do anything that could disturb the fragile balance of his mind in the most important academic year of his life? Abhimanyu was enjoying this pampering by his father. There was a pause before Abhimanyu started speaking.

'It was not his fault...'

The next day, Principal Matthew sat in front of the fathers of nearly two dozen boys. His Cheshire cat smile today had an edge to it. It was such an amazing high for him to see those bloody north Indians sitting in front of him, at his mercy. They sat in front of him in half circles. Ujjwal sat in the second row.

'For the St Mark's administration, there is nothing more important than discipline. Sharad was the brightest student of the class, but when found flouting discipline, he was expelled. I am sorry to say that there is sense of "I can do whatever I wish to" in the boys of this class, and I am afraid to say that you as parents have been miserable failures. But as a school, we shall not shirk from our duties. I will not tolerate such behaviour.' There was silence in the room as Matthew paused, his eyes scanning the faces of the petrified fathers.

'The decision of suspension and rustication is irreversible. I have called you gentlemen to inform you that if any of your children repeat this condemnable action, a similar fate awaits them.' Matthew's eyes then started to search for someone, 'Who is Abhimanyu's father here?' Ujjwal raised his hand.

'Aah, Mr Sharma! Your son was lucky to escape expulsion. Defending a culprit is also a crime.'

'I am sorry Mr Matthew.'

Matthew aggressively leaned forward and said, 'I am not finished, Mr Sharma...please do not interrupt me!'

Ujjwal mumbled a sorry again to which Matthew responded with a wide grin. 'Thank you! I have seen streaks of rebellion in your son, and that is harmful for him in the long run. I am told that he is performing very good in his studies, but that, as you know Mr Sharma, is hardly a license for rebellion. I shall keep a close watch on him in the days to come...a very close watch. I hope you will cooperate.'

The rest of the meeting was addressed to Abhimanyu's father and Principal Matthew did it with a vengeance. Ujjwal had never felt so miserable in his entire life. Based on what Abhimanyu had told him, he indeed had many questions for Principal Matthew, but speaking at that moment would have been disastrous. He wanted to defend his son but he kept quiet. Rather, he apologized for his "behaviour". And promised that it would never happen again.

Abhimanyu saw his father walking out of the school from a distance. He did not take time to guess that Matthew had meted special treatment. Even from that distance, he looked like a man whose pride had been trampled. And he felt good about it.

Two days later, Sharad walked into the school and headed straight for Principal Matthew's room. He wanted to accept that it was his fault and apologize. He knew that there was no other way to get back into school.

'I am not shocked at what you did. You have shown that intelligence and laurels in academics mean nothing unless you have family values. And in your case, I can clearly see that you have none.' Matthew smiled at Sharad, tapping his fingers rhythmically on the table.

Sharad had been driven to the edge already, and trying hard to control his tears, he said, 'I am already apologizing sir. And honestly speaking, I never burst that cracker...but I am still sorry.'

Matthew interrupted rudely, 'Shut up! You are still in denial. Now how do I convince myself that you really mean it! I don't know what to say...' Matthew raised his hands, 'I think you should go back. I don't feel the need of reviewing my decision.'

'I am sorry, sir. Please think about my career and my future.' Sharad's voice was cracking.

Unperturbed, Matthew said, 'You should have thought about this before messing with me, son.'

Wiping the tears off his eyes, Sharad hardened his voice, 'Can I ask you something sir?'

Matthew nodded.

'The cracker was timed with an agarbatti, which means that it must have been lying there for some time. Why do you think I would come back just at the time of the blast? It wasn't as if I lighted it and lobbed it. No one saw me doing that. Even Mrs Chaddha did not. In fact, Abhimanyu saw me entering the class and then ducking when the blast happened.'

'Don't!' Matthew raised his forefinger pointing it at Sharad. 'I don't want to be told by lumpen elements like you on what justice and fair play is. Don't defend your actions in cock and bull stories like these. And since you're not even apologetic, I think I am wasting my precious time talking to you!'

The school needed Sharad; his academic laurels were a must for the school's reputation. But he underestimated himself and couldn't fathom that Matthew was just playing hard with him. He would have reversed the decision in a week. But as he walked out of the room, he thought it was all over for him.

In the recess, Jagtar and Abhimanyu were walking in the huge playground teaming with children playing football and cricket. There was a distant guffaw and catcalls as students of a particular class rose their hands in high fives for something. Children from the junior wing ran around randomly as others sat at the edge of the playground eating their tiffins.

Abhimanyu said, 'Let's go and sit somewhere. I don't feel like walking today.'

Suddenly Jagtar nudged Abhinmanyu, 'Hey look! Someone is standing on the roof.'

Abhimanyu's gaze followed Jagtar's finger and he saw a student standing at the edge of the railing on the fourth floor. The boy suddenly slumped on the railing, as if he had collapsed or lost consciousness. Jagtar ran towards the building shouting and frantically waving his hand at the boy, 'No...no!'

Abhimanyu ran towards the door of the building to try and make it to the balcony. Even while running, his eyes were fixed on the student at the edge of the railing. His foot tripped on a rock and he fell chest down. Mud and blood trickled from cuts on his palms as a result of the impact. He looked at the roof wondering about the sudden silence.

The boy slipped and there was a collective gasp in the ground. Abhimanyu saw the boy falling from the roof and hurtling towards the ground. As he came crashing down, the boy first landed on his feet and then his buttocks. His entire body jerked violently with the impact, and his back twisted and turned to the sound of a crack.

Sharad lay there on the ground, his legs twisted like a coil and his eyes half open. Abhimanyu ran towards him, jostling with students who had assembled around him. Jagtar had just raised Sharad's head and placed it on his lap, gently patting his cheek, his own eyes reflecting the horror of what had just happened.

Abhimanyu bent down and saw that Sharad's legs had broken into two, bone sticking out from the flesh of his calves. His cheeks were dark with stains of tears and sweat.

Sharad was rushed to the nearby hospital and doctors tried hard to revive him. Shattered and aghast, his mother stared blankly at the sea of students around her as she swung between sobbing suddenly and then going quiet for some time. His father looked bewildered and shocked at what had happened to their only son. The news did appear in the next day's newspapers as an incident of a student slipping from the balcony of the school. They did not even bother investigating it and instead printed what the school administration had fed them. Matthew convened a meeting of the students of class XII–B and warned them against leaking anything to anyone. Sharad's expulsion was also revoked.

Sharad made it, but not completely. He would never be able to walk normally, the doctors had said, and his back would take a painfully long time to heal.

Two weeks later, Abhimanyu sat next to him in the hospital.

'What are you thinking?' asked Abhimanyu.

'Nothing...just angry with myself. Why did I act so foolishly? I mean, Matthew would have taken me, sooner or later. I don't know why I went to the terrace that day.'

'Were you out of your mind, trying to kill yourself?'

'I am not a coward, Abhi. I just wanted to be alone for a while, and the ground was teeming with students. I went to the terrace for that. I had been crying, and the dehydration must have caused me to faint.'

Abhimanyu looked at Sharad, his eyes now unwavering of him. He wondered how it would feel to not want to die and still end up almost there.

'I have a plan,' Abhimanyu murmured.

'What...what do you have in your mind? I am not in a shape to take another risk,' Sharad managed a faint smile.

'Can you write down a suicide note?'

'What?'

'A suicide note!'

Sharad jerked as he tried to get up but realized he could not. 'Why? What is that you want to do?'

'We need to get back at Appam Rascal. You write a suicide note. I take it to a newspaper. The newspapers will be filled with what is your suicide note. Imagine, once a newspaper prints a story that it was because of the pressure by the principal that made the student take this extreme step...they're gonna screw his happiness!'

Sharad was listening to him intently. He whispered, 'Then what?'

'Then, with all the muck flying around, they will have to remove him.'

'Is that so simple? And what if it screws me instead of Appam Rascal.'

'No, it won't! Because I am going to be the face of this story. I will take this letter to the newspapers and tell them I discovered this at your place, and that I was dying to get even with Principal Matthew for the blatant injustice he had been handing out to the students.'

Sharad was shocked at the cold manner in which Abhimanyu was going about it, like a shrewd strategist. He seemed so sure of what he wanted. But Sharad wasn't! He wanted to nail the bastard but the plan was fraught with tremendous risk and any mistake would only lead to collateral damage.

'But Abhi, ultimately this is a lie. We are concocting a story. A false one.'

Abhimanyu smirked, 'That's my speciality, isn't it? Making stories. And trust me, it will be the perfect plan to eliminate Matthew. And even if something goes wrong, my future would be at stake. And how is this a lie? You may not have committed suicide, but Mathew certainly drove you to it!'

Sharad seemed unsure. So, Abhimanyu asked him, 'Do you want that rascal to go scot free? Tell me!'

'I don't know what I want Abhi... but I would love to see him suffer.'

Subodh Jha blew the smoke out of the window as his eyes turned towards the traffic dragging itself lazily on a Sunday afternoon. He was the head of the city bureau at *The Times of India*. He was a man with a lean frame and a five o 'clock shadow.

'Come on! Don't just stand there. Speak out!' Subodh mumbled with a hint of irritation to the peon who had been lurking around for a while.

'Saab, there is a boy to see you!'

Subodh pressed his dark-rimmed glasses further up on his nose and bent his head towards the door. There he was. Abhimanyu Sharma.

'Let him in.' Subodh now looked curious. He rolled the right sleeve of his khadi brown kurta up as he peered under his desk to find his brown sandals. As he slid his feet into the sandals, he leaned back on his chair only to find Abhimanyu standing in front of him.

'My name is Abhimanyu. I study in the twelfth standard of St Mark's School.'

'Is that the same school —'

'Yes, sir! The same school where a boy tried to commit suicide.'

'Suicide?' Subodh's eyes grew wide with curiosity. 'I thought he fell down accidentally. That's what we have been told by '

'The school administration. I saw the trash you published.'

Subodh looked hard at Abhimanyu and then a gentle smile played on his lips as he pulled the drawer of his desk and took out a file that had some newspaper cuttings. As he flipped through the pages, he glanced at Abhimanyu who stood there nonchalantly.

'Why do you say that it was an attempted suicide?'

'Will you print the story?'

'That's none of your business. Answer my question!' Subodh's voice had an edge to it now.

Abhimanyu coldly drew out a letter and a notebook from a jute bag he was carrying.

'This is Sharad's suicide note and this is his class notebook. This note states...'

'I can read,' said Subodh as he started reading the letter. 'What is this?' Subodh held the notebook up in his right hand.

'This is his English notebook. I know you would want to ensure the letter is in his handwriting.'

Subodh smiled again he mumbled 'smart' under his breath. As he read the A4 size paper and its contents, his eyes turned pensive. He read it again and again. And again.

'How did you get this?'

'I went to meet him. He is in a mess. That is when he confided in me and told me about the suicide note. His life is over. I don't think he will ever be able to walk normally. He and I, we think there is only one man responsible for this. Principal Matthew. We want justice. Sharad was the brightest in our class. Circumstantial evidence pointed out to the fact that he could not have burst that cracker. But Matthew just followed his whim. They screwed him. For life! I know that the media is not aware of the fact that there was a cracker incident in the school and that is what triggered this incident. You did not even bother to talk to anyone of us and find out the truth.'

'That's because your school administration had requested us not to and did not want negative publicity for an accident and we believed their word.'

Abhimanyu shook his head and said, 'How naive!'

Subodh drew out another cigarette and then realizing that he was in front of a XII standard student, kept it back. He opened his drawer and took out some gum and offered one to Abhimanyu who accepted it without any hesitation.

'So if I correctly understand this...You guys burst a cracker outside your class—'

'No, we did not!'

'Ok, whatever. So this cracker burst, and then the school punished a boy who has been a topper throughout his life, with no history whatsoever of any indiscipline. The boy goes into depression. As this letter states, he even met the principal who refused to take him in, rather he insulted him! So he jumps from the terrace of the school.'

'Yes.'

'But why are you into this? What do you want here?'

'I want justice and I am ready to testify about this.'

'On record?'

'Means?'

'On record is when you give me an interview and I publish it attributing it to you. Are you ready for that?'

'If that's what gets us justice, I am ready to come on record. I am ready to testify the highhandedness of Principal Matthew. I am ready to speak on behalf of the students, but no one else would come on record on this matter. No one.'

'Are you aware of the consequences? The school will expel you and no school will touch you after that?'

'I don't care,' said Abhimanyu. Subodh was shocked at what he saw on Abhimanyu's face. He saw a boy who was so sure about what he wanted and he was so cold about it. There were no emotions on his face. Just absolute brazenness. This seemed like a boy possessed. With the zeal of a revolutionary.

'Have you told your parents about this?'

Abhimanyu smiled again, 'You think they would have let me come here had I told them about this? No way. I am on my own.'

Subodh was stunned. It usually took at least two cups of strong coffee to spring him into action on a lazy Sunday. But now, he was wide awake. He wanted to question his motives. His real intentions. But how could he? Here was a boy ready to put his life at stake for a cause that clearly wasn't his. Or maybe it was. The boy sitting in front of his eyes did not look like a fool. He seemed so sure of what he wanted. It was the coldness with which he went about it that fascinated Subodh. The angry young man.

'Ok...what happens if the school does not remove Matthew even after our story is published?'

'We make a spectacle out of them till they meet our demands. We all go on a strike! But I don't think they have the guts to go against the newspapers. These are missionary schools. They don't want to be in the news for the wrong reasons. I have realized that they have conservative values and they like to keep a low profile. That is one publicity they can afford living without.'

'You have answers to all questions, don't you, Abhimanyu? Well, I would need contact details of your classmates, even Sharad. I need to speak to them and only then shall I tell you if I am interested in this story or not!'

'But my classmates are not aware of Sharad's suicide attempt...'

'Leave that to me. You just get me the numbers and I will take care of the rest.'

Abhimanyu gave him contacts of around five boys and three girls from his class. All of them corroborated Abhimanyu's version that Sharad was indeed innocent and that he was crucified just because of the whim of an individual. Subodh was careful not to reveal anything about the suicide note, but he got enough dope on how depressed Sharad was after being rusticated from school.

So a suicide attempt would not have come as surprise to anyone. As he spoke to the students and made a few enquiries on his own, including speaking informally to some teachers in the school, one thing was clear – Matthew was an unpopular choice for a principal. Subodh could not afford to be too intrusive and probing. He could not have let Matthew know through anyone that he was attempting a story on a boy's suicide attempt. But before getting his version, he had to be sure that he had a water tight story against Matthew.

Even then, there was something that was bothering him throughout. What if it went wrong? What if Abhimanyu had to pay the price for this story? There was no way that the school would let a student who was making a spectacle of it on the front page of a newspaper stay in the school. So he took a call. If this was to make its way to the newspaper as a story, then Abhimanyu had to be an unnamed and faceless source. He was the deep throat of Schoolgate.

Subodh went to see Sharad along with Abhimanyu during the day. Sharad's mother was told that Subodh was Abhimanyu's cousin. Abhimanyu had ensured with Subodh that it would be an 'off the record' interaction; he had briefed Sharad about handling it – to keep mum and look sullen on questions that he was uncomfortable with or had to lie about. For the rest, have short answers and avoid details.

Abhimanyu had won half his battle when Subodh entered Sharad's room and saw him in that condition. His legs plastered, bandages all over his bare chest. The shrivelled boy was just wearing an underwear. His fingers were swollen, and nails uncut and laced with dirt. As Subodh came and sat next to him, Sharad's mother moved out of the room. After a two minute uncomfortable silence in the room, Abhimanyu spoke in a whisper, careful that they might not be heard by someone.

'Sharad, I told you about Mr Subodh Jha, remember?'

Subodh pushed his chair towards Sharad's bed as his eyes scanned Sharad's frail and bandaged body. 'I am not here to remind you of that unfortunate incident. I am just here to ask you some questions which you may chose not to answer. And don't mind, it's my job to confirm a few things.'

Sharad looked blankly at Subodh and a strain of melancholy caressed his eyes. His eyes then shifted at his bed pan that he had used in the morning. A lump moved up his throat as his eyes lined up with tears.

'I just want to know Sharad, if you had written this letter?'

Sharad looked at Abhimanyu and the film of tear in his left eye crossed the threshold of his eye lashes, spilling over his cheek. Sharad bowed his head and nodded while wiping his tears with his bandaged right arm.

'Are you sure that you wish to go public with this suicide note? Are you aware of the consequences?'

Sharad now looked at Abhimanyu and said, 'I am not sure if I really wish to go ahead with this....'

Abhimanyu thought their lie was about to be exposed. If Sharad was not in such a mess, Subodh would have grilled him into spitting the truth out.

'Mr Jha, Sharad is very disturbed. He was reluctant about going public with this suicide note initially and I think he—'

Sharad butt in, 'I am not scared. I just don't know what to do. My future is destroyed and there is only one man who is responsible for this!'

After a ten second pause, Subodh said, 'I totally empathize with your condition Sharad, but you see, we can take the story ahead only if you cooperate. I am aware of your condition, but I just need a few answers and then I will be off. I need to investigate and get to the bottom of things. You need to understand that it isn't as if Matthew had pushed you from that building...'

'Did he not?' Abhimanyu interrupted.

'Well figuratively, yes! But—'

'And driving someone to suicide is also a crime, isn't it?'

'Sharad is still alive. Are you even ready to go public with accusing Matthew for driving you to commit suicide? Are you ready for the consequences? I am not sure how the school will take it or how the education fraternity would view it.'

After another pause Subodh spoke again. 'I have been thinking about this since last night. As a human being, I realize that if this story goes into print, it will have consequences.'

'So what are you going to do?'

'This is more than a story for me!'

He did not say it, but it was a mission for him now. The meeting went on for another ten minutes till Sharad's mother entered the room. Despair written all over her face, she looked utterly helpless. That was another picture that got imprinted on Subodh's mind.

When they came out of Sharad's room, Abhimanyu said, 'So when are you printing the story?'

Subodh suddenly stopped and turned to face Abhimanyu, 'It will take its time. It is a decision that I will take. I need to speak to your Principal, and then I shall discuss it with my boss. Just stop badgering me; it's really getting onto my nerves now!'

'It's just irritating for you. For someone, it's his life!'

Subodh bowed his head and put his hand on Abhimanyu's shoulder, 'I am sorry but it's complicated, and it will require a lot of thinking before we actually go to print. You have to be patient.'

'My friend Sharad is one...for life.' Abhimanyu smiled wryly.

Subodh sought an appointment with Principal Matthew but was refused. But he did have a chat with him over phone and that gave him an idea of what he was all about.

Subodh asked him, 'Did your student Sharad try to commit suicide?'

Matthew was enraged, his voice venomous, 'What rubbish? What kind of silly journalist are you? Get your facts correct or else I will bang the phone.'

Subodh was persistent, 'Isn't it true that you expelled Sharad from school, in spite of students testifying in his favour. You just refused to take their version.'

'I am the principal of this school and I decide what goes around,' Matthew spat. 'I decide whose testimony to be taken and whose to be thrashed? Who has been speaking to you? The students?

Subodh had feared this, 'No, Mr Matthew. But hasn't Sharad been one of the brightest students of your school? He had no reason to burst that cracker. Isn't it true that you just took the whim of a teacher as a proof and your own hunch?'

Matthew replied, 'Yes, I took the statement of the teacher as my primary proof. So what? You think I am going to trust those vagabonds in the class? If I had my way, I would have chucked everyone from that class out of this school. Anti- social elements... all of them! Listen Mr Jha, or whatever your name is, I run this school and I do it on my own terms. I don't want some journalist to tell me what to do. Most certainly not those students who have a bleak future ahead of them. If that student attempted suicide because of me...so be it!'

Subodh was shocked, 'What?'

'I don't need such sissies in my school. This is a school that will build the future leaders of the country. Not some freak on the verge of suicide. I am not going to miss such students in the school,' Matthew barked into the phone.

'Well, Mr Matthew,' Subodh almost gave away the tinkle in his voice, 'I did not imagine that the interview would be over so soon. I have you voice on tape now and I got the quote I was looking for. I am sorry, I should have informed you. But then, how does it matter to you? You are not a sissy! You are a strong man and I am sure you can handle the storm, The one that's going to hit you so hard that you won't know what happened.'

Subodh had disconnected the call before Matthew could respond to his bare threat.

In Editor Pranay Sengupta's room, Subodh wasn't sure if he really wanted to do the story. Pranay was a balding, middle-aged man, who was a naxalite at heart and causing real dilemma for Subodh. 'I have no doubts in my mind that if we publish this story using this boy's name, they would make his life hell. I am not sure what would happen to that other boy...what's his name...Sharad.'

'What do you suggest?' Subodh looked at him intensely as he sipped his coffee.

'Are you really sure you want to do this as a story? I would rather suggest that you meet the school administration and speak to them off the record. Tell them that you are thinking of doing this story and that you have damning evidence against the principal.'

'Blackmail?'

'I won't use that word. Call it a noble cause. Treat it beyond just a story. You have done bigger and better stories. Maybe you could step back and treat it as a mission.'

Subodh smiled as Pranay Sengupta used the word he had in his mind. 'Just explore the waters and see. If they are evasive, then we screw their happiness. Big time! But I doubt they are going to stand behind this Matthew chap at the cost of the reputation of the school.'

The appointment with the media friendly Dean of management Father Peter Alva came by easily. He had no clue why Subodh Jha wanted to meet him. As the sixty-year-old, clean shaven Father Alva sat in his flowing white robes in front of Subodh Jha, he was grace personified. But it soon started dissipating as Subodh Jha started narrating the 'tale in his backyard'. In precisely ten minutes, Alva reached for the glass of water. He gulped down the water and a line of sweat dragged itself along the edge of his jaw and paused at the tip of the chin. As Subodh narrated Alva's tale of agony, he noticed the nearly comical singular drop of sweat shining at the tip of the Dean's chin. Alva was breathing in and out rounding his lips into an O, as he patiently listened to the journalist. The rhythmic heaving of his chest was increasing every moment. And then Subodh drew out the suicide note. He also drew out his Philips compact cassette recorder that had recorded his infamous conversation with Principal Matthew. After Alva finished reading the letter, and heard Principal Matthew's voice, he felt a sudden jab on his chest. His ears were now crimson. The man was clearly scared. Father knew once the news was out in one newspaper, the others would drag it too. The press loved news about scandals in schools.

That was not the attention he wanted. He was also out of favour of the new Education Minister at the centre. Father Alva had pro-actively supported the Congress government during the emergency and he knew that the Janata Party regime will not leave any stone unturned in embarrassing the school. In embarrassing *him*. Subodh was with Father Alva for another thirty minutes. He made his intentions clear. He told him what he wanted. Father Alva could not look him in the eye because he knew that the journalist sitting in front of him was different from the rest. This man just wanted justice for the students. He wanted Matthew's neck. It was a small price to be paid for the prestige of the institute.

Seething with anger, Matthew barged into XII–B like a raging bull. His sudden entry in the class frightened the English teacher who gasped in shock. He stood in the middle of the class, his clenched fists on his waist and his eyes red.

'You rascals dared to go to the press against me? Don't you have any desire to have a future? I want the culprit to step out right now!' Matthew's voice echoed across the corridor and teachers in the other classes moved towards the doors to hear what was happening in the most controversial class of the school *now*. Matthew's infamous temper was a terror across the school.

A peon in khakis walked towards the class, clutching an envelope. He looked petrified as he had to deliver it to Matthew himself.

'Come on! Who dared to challenge me? Who?' Matthew's eyes scanned the class till they stopped at Abhimanyu. 'Come out, right now! I know it's you...it has to be you.'

Abhimanyu clenched his fists and calmly walked towards Matthew. As Abhimanyu stood a few inches taller in front of him, Matthew raised his forefinger and said, 'I will ask you just once, did you go to the press?'

Abhimanyu mumbled, 'No.'

Matthew's right hand flew with immense force aiming for Abhimanyu's cheek, but Abhimanyu was clearly prepared for this. He moved a few steps back and defended himself with his raised left hand. Matthew's right hand crashed on Abhimanyu's and the former winced in pain. He spat, 'You dare raising your hand on me! I will finish you...'

Matthew could not even finish his words as the peon entered the class and said, 'Sir!'

'Not now! Don't you see I am busy, you illiterate rascal?'

The peon pleaded, 'But sir...'

Matthew moved towards the peon menacingly and what he did next stunned everyone in the classroom. The sound of the slap reverberated across the corridor.

The peon stood there stunned, clasping his cheek. With one hand on his cheek, he raised the other to hand over the envelope to Matthew.

'The Dean wants to meet you right away. He has asked me to bring you along.'

With the look of bemusement on his face, Matthew grabbed the envelope and tore it open: *Mr Matthew, please meet me as soon as you read this letter.*

Abhimanyu smiled. He knew what this was about. He now stretched out his chest and stood there, his hands on his waist. Matthew was shocked at this posture of defiance, but his eyes were shifting between Abhimanyu and the letter by the Dean. Something was not right, he thought. The tone of the Dean's letter had a sense of urgency and maybe even intimidation. Or was his mind playing tricks on him? Matthew rushed out of the class and Abhimanyu mumbled loud enough for Matthew to hear: 'All the best, sir!'

Meanwhile, the peon muttered something under his breath that did not have flattering references of Matthew's mother and sister, and walked rebelliously towards the Dean's cabin.

He caressed the hurt cheek by touching it to the door of the Dean's room, Matthew's predicament his balm. The dean was loud enough to be heard outside.

'The press is going to rub this on my face as well. That reporter has been speaking to parents and students, and apparently some teachers too. I hope I don't need to tell you what reports or impression you carry.'

Alva paused and then said, 'This is serious, Mr Matthew. It could have a direct impact on our funding. Blame me if I am paranoid, but this is not the kind of attention I want. Not from my financiers and or trustees, least of all the press.'

It was at this point that Father Alva and Matthew both heard some commotion outside the room. This was followed by sloganeering and chants. It was the peons and the clerks. They were up in arms and were shouting:

'Matthew down down! Matthew go to hell! We will not tolerate injustice on any peon of this school. Peon Unity Zindabad!'

The sullen face of Father Alva was now turning a shade of red with shock. He looked like a man who could get a heart attack now.

'Now what is this Matthew?'

Principal Matthew held his head with both his hands and buried it on the Dean's table. He cursed himself. It was all over, he knew at that moment.

The next day, Matthew's slap and the strike found a mention in every newspaper of the city. Subodh was tempted to club this story with his own and make that big splash; but instead, he waited. He did not have to wait for too long, though.

Matthew always had grand designs about his day of retirement. He often dreamt how he would stand like a king in the assembly and declare with moist eyes that he is leaving the school and with it, a legacy of brilliance and perfection. But one sixteen-year-old had brutally snatched his moment from him. His tearful farewell where everyone in the school would be crying copious amounts of tears for the most historical principal independent India had seen.

He dreamt how he would be honoured by the President's award, the most prestigious award a teacher could get. But it was all over. Matthew wiped his tears with his fingers and wondered when he had cried the last time. Maybe after a thrashing when he was in school. In exactly two weeks, he left Delhi with his family, never to come back.

May 1980

Jagtar and Abhimanyu sat on their favourite bench in the park; Abhimanyu slanted and rested his head on the bench, his hands spread across the length of the bar. Eyes half open, half a smile playing on his lips, he was deliberately trying to have a blurred view of the light falling on them through the golden leaves of the eucalyptus tree. Jagtar turned his head towards Abhimanyu and said, 'Weirdo!'

Abhimanyu raised his head from the bar of the bench, his eyes still half open, the mysterious smile still playing on his lips, and slapped Jagtar on his neck.

'O benchod, sambal ke! Meri pagg.' Jagtar readjusted his turban with mock irritation on his face, and mumbled something under his breath. Perhaps cursing his father, Abhimanyu guessed. Jagtar had been issued a strict directive to wear a full turban instead of just a *patka*, a cloth tied around the head. It was really cumbersome for Jagtar to actually tie a turban every morning. His father was getting increasingly religious and his interactions with the Khalistani separatist ideology was on the rise. Jagtar was not aware of this, neither did he espouse the cause, but he was the victim of the new code at home.

'Why are you smiling, fucker?' said Jagtar still adjusting his cumbersome turban.

'You called *me* a weirdo, that's why!'

Abhimanyu and Jagtar were catching up after long. The board exams had been taken care of, so were Abhimanyu's entrance exams for engineering colleges. What remained were the results, anytime now in the sweltering May heat.

Finally the day Ujjwal Sharma was waiting for arrived. Abhimanyu delivered a cracker of a result. Standing third in the class, he scored 91 percent in PCM (Physics, Chemistry and Maths). No college in Delhi would refuse him. For Ujjwal, it was like the world was at his feet. He would not stop making calls and the calls just wouldn't stop coming in. He was now on the verge of irritating the Salujas who were tired of calling him and informing him of a phone call. It was celebration time at the Sharmas. Sweets in the kilos were ordered and were distributed across the block. By his standards, it was a lavish display and he seemed to have forgotten that there were many in the block with bad results too. The eldest of the Bhushans had in fact flunked, but still was the first to grab a handful of sweets from the jubilant Ujjwal.

It was the biggest party of Ujjwal's life. But there was more to come, a little while later.

Admissions to Delhi University had started soon after results. Abhimanyu was seeking admission to the honours course in Physics which he was sure to bag easily in the first cut off list. Ujjwal was just hoping that there would be better news in the results of the engineering entrance exams.

'Is he mad? How can he even think like that?' Ujjwal was fuming, frothing and boiling with anger. He would lunge towards Abhimanyu intimidatingly every time he spoke.

'You heard me, papa. I am not joining IIT! This is not what I want to do for the rest of my life,' Abhimanyu responded calmly.

'So what is it that you want to do, you idiot? No one thinks of not joining the IIT after getting selected. Does he even realize what he is talking about?' Ujjwal now turned his head towards Mahima who was the silent witness to this dramatic exchange.

Abhimanyu shook his head and said, 'It's my life, papa, and it's me who decides how I live it.'

Ujjwal got up from his chair and moved closer to Abhimanyu, 'When I was in class XII, there was no one to guide me. Someone asked me to study chemistry, and I did. You have all the guidance you want, and even a goddamn option. Now that you have cleared IIT, you don't want to join it just because you think this is not what you want to do?'

'Precisely! You finally got it.'

It was at this moment that Ujjwal could not stop himself and slapped Abhimanyu. He could not fathom why his son was hell bent on ruining his own life and career. Abhimanyu fell sideways and his head crashed against the edge of the dining table. It was his worst memory repeating itself, all over again. Abhimanyu touched his forehead and saw his fingers; thick and dark red blood stained his fingers. He looked at his father and smiled. The blood gradually soaked his entire face, but Abhimanyu kept smiling like a man in a drunken stupor.

Abhimanyu had struck gold with the 112th rank in a list of 2000 students who got selected for IIT. Ujjwal came to know of it through an evening newspaper. He immediately called home to inform Mahima of the big news. A jubilant mother then rushed to Abhimanyu to inform him of the news. But instead of jumping with joy, he coldly put a bookmark on the fiftieth page of *The Hobbit* by JRR Tolkein and said the unthinkable.

He was not interested.

After her initial disbelief, Mahima realized that Abhimanyu really meant it. The news was finally broken to Ujjwal when he entered the house with stacks of sweets and three tickets for a midnight show of Amitabh Bachchan's *Don*.

Abhimanyu really meant it. Hell had to break lose.

Now, after the dramatic episode, Abhimanyu lay on the bed, his head bandaged. Jagtar had come to congratulate Abhimanyu, but had ended up rushing him to the doctor on his scooter with Ujjwal. The defeated father now stood alone on the terrace, his mind oscillating between a hurt ego and deep guilt. He mustered courage after a long rumination; hesitating a bit, he came and sat next to Abhimanyu's bed. Mahima turned her head away from him and wondered why everything between the father and son boiled down to this.

Clearing his throat, Ujjwal said, 'I am sorry, Abhi. I should have controlled myself—'

'Don't be sorry... I am not the weak, lanky, pushover whose teeth you broke three years ago. So, please don't waste your efforts; you can't change my mind. You just can't! IIT is a closed chapter for me.'

Tears welling up in her eyes, and torn between her love for both these men, Mahima said, 'This is absolutely no way to speak to your father, Abhi.'

'I wish you had defended me like that, Mom! I wish you did. Things would not have come to this!'

Jagtar stood at one corner, uncomfortable at witnessing this exchange till he decided to walk out. Ujjwal gestured to Jagtar to stay. He slowly got up with the expression of a man who had lost his final hope. He slowly walked out of the house, his shoulders drooping and a blank expression on his face.

Abhimanyu murmured under his breath, *'Now we are even!'*

Ujjwal's IIT dream was finally over as Abhimanyu enrolled himself in St. Stephen's College for the honours course in Physics. Abhimanyu also knew he could not stay under the same roof as his father now, so he rented a room in the North Campus, close to his college. They could not have disowned him, so they kept sending him money every month. Soon, Abhimanyu walked beyond that obligation too. As he walked out of his class at the end of the very first day, someone was waiting for him at the main gate of his college.

'I just could not stop myself. I wanted to do a story on this. But instead of sending one of my rookie reporters, I thought of coming and seeing you.' It was Subodh Jha from *The Times of India*.

Abhimanyu was surprised. 'So you are indeed weirder than I thought. Joined Stephen's instead of IIT?' Subodh teased him.

Abhimanyu gave a wry smile, 'Can we talk of something else please? I have had enough of this topic at home and outside. I have been giving cock and bull stories to my professors here in the college about why I did not join IIT.'

Subodh stood in front of him and placed his hand on his shoulder and said, 'Let's take a walk, shall we? Or better, let me treat you to lunch.'

Subodh Jha was familiar with the campus. He had landed from Patna and completed his graduation from the Hindu College, so he knew every nook and corner of the campus. As they sat in a dhaba and ordered food, Abhimanyu started opening up. He told Subodh that he was now at a point of no return when it came to his relations with his father. He had taken up Physics honours because he thought physics was the most dynamic subject known to man. But that was not enough to give him a direction in life. He still did not know what he would be doing three years from now when he passed out of Stephen's. But that was hardly an issue. Subodh heard him out. He knew that there was something more to this young man with a bizarre streak. There were too many ghosts to be exorcised and a dark secret that he would not let go of.

After hearing Abhimanyu out, Subodh proposed that Abhimanyu contribute to his newspaper by reporting on issues that he saw around him. Issues that would interest a metropolitan reader. The young reader. He told him that he would pay him for each article that he contributed. He also wanted him to be his eyes and ears about what was happening in the campus and its politics. Subodh realized that there could be instances when Abhimanyu could be at direct conflict of interest with his college, so he would write with an alias. A nom de plume. And it was simple. He called himself Babu.

Little did Subodh realize that Abhimanyu would be such a prolific contributor. Abhimanyu would travel across the city in the DTC bus with his camera and draw interesting and exotic colours in his story board. By the middle of his first year, he was already contributing half a dozen articles per month. That also sorted his finances. He was earning an amount that would be the envy of even a staffer in *The Times of India*. Subodh was his passport to the inner circles of the newspaper.

By the second year of his graduation, his contribution to the newspaper doubled to a dozen and by the end, he was hitting nearly twenty per month. The accounts section went into panic mode and suggested that hiring him instead of paying him per article would be a better deal. So by the end of his second year, and by the beginning of his third year, he was already a staffer of the reputed daily. They had hired him as a reporter. Meanwhile, Abhimanyu continued to perform reasonably well in his academics. He was not outstanding, but he managed a distinction. He informed his parents only after two months of his joining the Times. Mahima was happy, for journalism was still a respectable profession. But Ujjwal's reaction bordered on cynical to indifferent. He had already given up on him.

During these three years, some of Abhimanyu's stories had even hit the front page of the newspaper. These included the rise of extremist student leaders in the Khalsa, thanks to his unsuspecting source in the form of Jagtar who was pursuing a degree in Commerce. His alias Babu struck big with the story of sexual harassment of one of the students by an English professor in the college. The college knew that the story was an insider's job, but they could never find who.

Another big one highlighted the plight of students from the northeast. It was while researching for this one that he met Dipali Das. The hot chick from Uzan Bazar in Guwahati, who Abhimanyu lost his virginity to. The short story of lust lasted only for six months till Dipali moved on to a Imran Siddique and Abhimanyu to Sugandha Verma, a student of Botany honours in Miranda House. Abhimanyu thought that he had a future with her, but then he realized that he enjoyed sex more than listening to her when she spoke. It took eight months for her to realize that. Abhimanyu thought that sex was highly overrated and he could not demean himself by further getting involved with someone just for the fuck. So here he was: sex was over rated and love, nowhere in sight. But deep down, he knew he missed that special someone.

1983

'Mr Sharma!' the nurse tapped on Abhimanyu's shoulder. 'You can wear these clothes.' It was a medical gown drawn from the store. 'And if you wish to hold the baby, you will also need to take a bath.' She pointed to the other end of the corridor.

The gush of cold water crashed on his hair and followed his back to his buttocks and then to the unevenly cemented floor. It felt therapeutic. His mind was still stained by the events of the darkest afternoon of his life. How he wished to unclutter his mind. How he wished he could erase his mind of those memories. He wanted to hold on to something powerful to release the demons. Something from the past, something powerful. And then out of nowhere, it came back to him.

It was a humid day in June in India but in London, Kapil's devils were about to make India proud. Mohinder Amarnath ran lazily to the bowler's end in his typical run up, and Mahima entered with a plate of hot samosas. Amarnath released the ball, Michael Holding swung hard, missed and was caught plum in front of the wicket. Ujjwal rose from his chair and lifted his hands as if *he* had just claimed Holding in that historical ball in the finals at Lords. Mahima kept the plate on the dining table and rushed towards the television. Abhimanyu rose from his chair and started clapping. But Ujjwal was uncontrollable. He jumped around the house like a little boy. With one hand he grabbed Abhimanyu and hugged him tight, with the other he dragged Mahima towards him. They started jumping in the air as they held each other tightly. For a moment, Ujjwal had forgotten the past and held his son tight. It seemed that all the bitterness that he had in his heart, melted away in that moment of frenzy.

Abhimanyu was elated at India winning the 1983 Cricket World Cup, but his gaze came to rest on his father's face. Never had he seen him so happy. Or maybe he had! When Abhimanyu had cleared the IIT exams. Ujjwal ran downstairs to the Salujas with the plate of samosas to treat the already ballistic landlords. The entire block had turned alive. Everyone was outside, shouting their lungs out. The Singhs had even taken out crackers left from the previous Diwali and started bursting them. Abhimanyu calmly stood in the balcony and looked around. The entire country was celebrating. His father was offering samosas to whoever he met. The Singh twins had started laying the long line of crackers on the streets tied by a string.

The night sky was filled with fireworks as Delhi came alive. Shouts of 'Bharat Mata ki jai' and 'India...India...India' rent the air. The Bhatias staying at the end of the block had even called a Dhol player, and men, women and children danced with fervour to that moment of glory. That moment that bound India and its teeming millions that night and a few more to follow.

Abhimanyu looked around and his eyes suddenly stopped at someone standing in front of the Singhs' house. She stood there, her hands on her ears, eyes half shut and calling out to her first cousin, one of the twins, to be careful while bursting the crackers – "Bunty, *dhyan naal.*"

Is that Jaspreet? How could it be? Jaspreet was the skinny ugly duckling with teeth that could put him to shame when he was bucktoothed. The only image that he had of Jaspreet was this girl wearing thick spectacles, mouth filled with metal to hold her teeth and a long plait moving sideways as she walked with books in her hands. But now, the thick braces were gone. So were the spectacles. The long plait was still there alright, but then she was a *sardarni.* For the first time, he could see her blue eyes. While she covered her ears with her hands, fearing the loud sonds from the crackers bursting, he saw the outline of her breasts hugging her kurta. What a beautiful Sikhni, thought Abhimanyu. He could not control himself and rushed downstairs, only to stand at the gate of his house. Bang in front of Jaspreet.

He felt a sudden surge of energy in his chest that turned into restlessness as he stood there, watching her. He tried breathing out, but he could not get rid of that uneasiness in his chest. *This was so weird.* Abhimanyu walked a few steps towards her and felt better. *Was he drawn towards her?*

Abhimanyu looked at her, but she still had her eyes on her kid brother. He desperately wanted her to look at him. Just that one look. But then she would not recognize him. She would dismiss him as some freak staring at her. Suddenly there was a huge burst of fireworks in the sky. Abhimanyu looked up and saw an amazing display of light in the sky.

His eyes moved back to where she stood; he was totally unprepared for what he saw. She was looking straight into his eyes, even smiling at him. And then, she slowly raised her hand and waved at him gently. Abhimanyu kept looking at her fingers as they moved sideways. Long tapering fingers with a golden ring in her little finger. She was so fair, with a touch of crimson that made her skin glow. She bit her lower lip as she smiled at him. Abhimanyu could not understand what to do except respond with a pitiful nervous smile to Jaspreet's graceful aura.

She walked up to him, while he stood there, frozen. 'Abhimanyu, right?'

'Yeah,' he fumbled for words, 'And you are Jas...preet?'

'Bang on, weirdo!' she giggled.

'Wh-at...weird-o...why?' he smiled nervously.

'A boy who clears IIT and joins Stephen's instead has to be a nutcase.'

Before Abhimanyu could say anything, she said again, 'But I mean respect when I say weirdo.' Her smile was enchanting.

'Really?'

'Yeah, you must be absolutely brilliant, like a genius, to do something as crazy as this!' Jaspreet started laughing throwing her head back and cupping her mouth with her right hand.

She moved a step closer, her hand stretched out, 'Congratulations, India won the world cup.' Just as he took her hand in his, a cracker exploded right behind them with a roar. And as a reflex, Jaspreet let out a muffled shriek and buried her face in Abhimanyu's chest. His senses numb, everything around him went quiet. In those strange few seconds, she wanted to prolong every frame between them too. A numbing sense of comfort engulfed her. Abhimanyu's right hand, as if acting on its own, found its way to her back. She was breathing heavily now, the rim of her breasts gently teasing his chest. Realising that they were now nearly locked in a passionate embrace, Jaspreet rocked herself back from the hug and stood there embarrassed for a few seconds. She raised her eyes, to meet his. Abhimanyu stood there bemused, his mouth slightly open.

'I am sorry.'

'Don't be, it's my pleasure,' he said absent-mindedly.

'What?' She started laughing.

'I-I-I mean, it's okay,' his face was now crimson and the sparkling display of pyrotechnics and crackers did not help him to hide his embarrassment.

'So, are you going to say something or just ogle at me like that?' she rounded her lips in a playful manner.

'I would like to meet you again...if that's ok with you,' he said nervously.

'Why?'

'I don't have a reason, but I want to. And I know that you won't mind.

'But doesn't your job keep you busy?'

'How do you know about my job? I don't have any idea about you. Well, I am a Reporter...so I am on my own usually. I am not bound by office hours. I am out most of the times, so I can be where you want me to be!'

'Well, you know girls don't respect guys who have a lot of time. But I am a student of Master's in history at Miranda House,' she laughed again. 'I am going to be free by 2 p.m. tomorrow. I will wait for you.'

She turned around and walked back, turning around every now and then. When she finally disappeared into the Singhs' house, Abhimanyu was still standing at the gate, a warm smile dancing on his lips. *How did it happen so fast? Why do I feel so enamoured by her? Why do I feel so drawn towards her? Why?*

Once home, he stood in front of the mirror and saw a happy Abhimanyu looking back at him. It was like the memory of his grandfather walking with him through the fields of Santpur. As he lay on his bed that night, he kept reminiscing the moment over and over again. The way she walked back to her house and then gently shut the door. His eyes did not budge from her face till the last frame of the moment when the doors shut. He remembered how at that last frame, the smile on her face grew so intimate, so personal. As if, she sensed his desire. As if she knew that he wished to be loved by her, at that very moment. Abhimanyu started tossing and turning. He was restless, not because of that moment, but because he wanted the night to pass. He wanted to fast forward to that moment in front of Miranda House, watching her come out of her college. He could see himself waiting at the other end of the road, across her college. But for some reason, he could still not see himself cross the road. Just like the previous night. He could still see her walking across the road, looking sideways, carefully looking for traffic, with that smile on her face.

Abhimanyu's first memory of Jaspreet was that of a talkative and plump seven-year-old, who in a fit to flaunt her new pink skirt brought to her by some uncle in Canada, had walked into their house on the very day they had shifted there. So much so that she had gone far away from her uncle's house and landed up in the police station as a lost child. Abhimanyu smiled at the memory of her. He could not imagine how he had never noticed her growing into such a beautiful girl. It was only around five in the morning that he finally dozed off, his eyes fixed at the gate of Jaspreet's house.

The next day, he still could not muster the courage to walk across the road to meet her. Instead, he waited for her to come to him. A tired smile graced her face. It must have been a hard day at college, he thought. She kept looking at his face, and he lowered his eyes, a little embarrassed.

And then she spoke, 'Are you blushing?'

'Who? Me?' He smiled nervously.

'Oh my god, Abhi!'

Abhimanyu raised his eyes to meet hers. "Abhi" had never sounded so musical, so beautiful in his life. He kept looking at her, his mouth slightly open. He could feel a slight restlessness in his chest. He breathed in, but that only aggravated the sudden breathlessness he felt. Raising her eyes, she said, 'Are we just going to stand here, or are we going somewhere?'

Within the next ten minutes, they were on a bus to India Gate. The most beautiful ride of his life. And hers too.

They took the rear end seat of the University special and after the awkward few early moments, started chatting. They spoke of everything under the sun. It was Jaspreet who did most of the talking and Abhimanyu looked at her. They got off the bus at Kasturba Gandhi Marg and took a walk under the sweltering sun to India gate. It just did not matter to them that day. It was a matter of a few minutes that Abhimanyu realized he was smitten by her. The proof: he had never spoken to anyone like that. No one had interested him as she did. He wanted to see her talk continuously, he loved her chatter. And he wanted to talk too. For the first time, he wanted to speak to someone about himself. He wanted to brag. He was so desperate to impress her. This had never happened before. The best thing was that Jaspreet realized that he was striving hard to impress her, and for some reason, she found it very cute. Here was a boy who was so engrossed in her eyes, in every vowel, every word she spoke. She would get a little conscious when she saw him looking at her lips as she spoke, and then shifting his gaze to her eyes. He was soaking up every moment with her. It was a tremendous high for her too.

They walked the lawns of India Gate, without a worry for the sweltering heat at 43 degree Celsius. They stopped and sat under some shade for a few minutes, and had pani-puri before proceeding towards Raisina Hills. Realising that it'd been almost three hours that they had been out in the sun and that Jaspreet was now getting dehydrated, they took an auto back to the bus stop, where they boarded a bus to Rajouri Garden.

After de-boarding at Rajouri Garden, they walked towards Americano. She would occasionally brush her shoulder against his or just get too close to him, touching his hand slightly. He would raise a finger or two, just to touch her. But every time he did that, she would move away – not deliberately, but just his luck.

They sat on a table facing Vishal cinema hall that was showing an Amitabh movie. After ordering two chicken burgers and cold coffee to go along, they sat there in silence.

'I have often observed you from a distance and have found you to be most intriguing. You have always been different from the rest of the lot, Abhi...you are not like the other boys in our locality. I know you are a little weird, and that stunt of yours of not joining IIT only earned you ridicule, but I could see beyond that. I knew there had to be something more. I was really curious. I even spoke to your Mom, but she was very vague. I was so tempted all these years to speak to you about this.'

Abhimanyu smiled, 'Well it's a secret, and for someone to know the biggest kept secret of my life, he or she has to be part of it.'

'So what do I need to do to be part of that secret circle of trust?'

Abhimanyu shrugged and smiled, but Jaspreet felt a little uncomfortable with that look in his eyes.

'I have to say something to you, Jaspreet.'

Jaspreet knew what he would say. The way he had spoken her name said it all.

'But before that, I have to say something to you, Abhi,' her face hardened suddenly. 'I don't know how to say this to you, but I guess I have to.'

'Don't scare me, please, just say it!' Abhimanyu smiled nervously.

'Abhi, I am getting married.' She left the last word hanging.

Abhimanyu could not hear anything for the first few minutes after she had spoken. It was like this strange buzzing sound in his ear, the same that he had felt after being slapped by his father. His eyes were fixed on her, unwavering.

'My father fixed this marriage a couple of months ago. The boy deals in air conditioners. My father thinks he is the best choice for me and I don't see a reason to doubt his word. We are getting married on the 1st of September. I hope you will be there. Will you?' she probed.

Abhimanyu was just staring at her, hanging on to each and every word of hers. He did not realize that Jaspreet had just asked him a question.

'Abhi, are you with me?'

'Yes-yes. Right here. I will be there...for sure! This is great news Jaspreet. I am so happy for you—'

'No, you are not!'

'What? Why wouldn't I be?'

'I know why you wanted to meet me Abhi. I could have said no to you, but I wanted to meet you too. I wanted this moment with you. We have been together for just four hours, but I have never been this happy in the whole of my life. I feel good being with you.' Suddenly a tear appeared out of nowhere, glossing her eyes and hugging her beautiful eyelashes. She wiped it immediately and turned her face away from Abhimanyu's gaze.

'Will you stop staring at me?'

'What? I am not staring. I am just happy that you are happy.'

'Is that all you have to say, Abhi?'

'Yes, what else am I supposed to say now?'

She suddenly seemed angry, 'Okay, I guess, I should leave now.'

'No, wait! I just wanted to say that—'

'Say what, Abhi? Say what?'

'I am genuinely happy for you. And I hope we find happiness in our decisions.'

Jaspreet suddenly got up and walked out of the restaurant. Abhimanyu did not know whether to follow her or ask for the bill and then follow her. Instead, he sat there for the next one hour. Numb and stunned. His eyes vaguely scanned the posters of the latest Amitabh blockbuster and the men standing in long queues to enter the cinema hall.

Abhimanyu had a tough time getting back into his usual grind. He did not speak to Jaspreet after that day; what could he have said! Even when she came to greet his mother while he was walking back home with her, he restrained their conversation to formal pleasantries alone. And about three months later, in September, Abhimanyu and his mother stood in front of the huge *pandal* that was erected near the local gurudwara in Tagore Garden. A huge white Thermocol board read *"Jaspreet weds Harvinder"*. What sort of a name is that! Abhimanyu would have been so much better, he thought. There were no Bollywood songs, just gentle hymns of the *shabad kirtan* filling the air, thanks to Jaspreet's purist father. Just when Abhimanyu was about to enter, it struck him that he was not meant to be here. He clasped his mother's hand as they slowly moved towards the sitting area. Ujjwal was away on a tour, and anyway avoided going to places where he would be seen with his son.

Abhimanyu and his mother sat at a corner of the huge sprawling pandal. Mahima turned her back to the barbeque where different types of meats, chicken, mutton and fish were being roasted. But she could not avoid the aroma, so she pressed her nose with the pallu of her sari. Mahima was a strict vegetarian for religious reasons. Abhimanyu loved to torture his mother during such moments, by deliberately bringing a plate full of succulent and roasted meats and dangling it in front of her. But today, he was sombre. He kept wondering if Jaspreet had expected him to say something that day, the last time they had met. It wasn't as if she was dying to get married to this air-conditioner repairing guy. He remembered her last few words: *Is that all you have to say Abhi?*"

Perhaps she had wanted him to say that evening, something that could have changed things forever. But he could not have. What was there to say? They had just met. Though it was weird how she impacted him, how his senses reacted to Jaspreet! Is that what they say soul mates are? He brushed away the thought as it came, and smiled to himself. But he could not get rid of the sting in his heart that day. The thought of seeing her in bridal wear was making it even worse. He stretched his neck upwards and bent it sideways. That's when he saw a little girl dressed in a pink salwar-kameez, a striking resemblance to Jaspreet, walking towards him. She came, stood in front of him and said, 'The bride wants to meet you!' She gestured towards a room in the banquet hall.

Abhimanyu's mother looked a little confused, to say the least. 'I'll be right back mom!' Abhimanyu walked holding the girl's hand, without another word.

As he climbed the stairs to the first floor, women and young girls dressed in colourful Punjabi attire and flashy dresses zoomed past him, brushing their shoulders with him. A cacophony of sounds rent the air, a cocktail of shrill laughter and conversations in Punjabi. He could hear Jaspreet's father shout from a distance, abusing the caterer in the choicest of expletives. A man carrying a bagful of mogra flowers nearly lost his balance after colliding with a young girl squinting past him. Abhimanyu held him as he was about to fall face down. He thanked Abhimanyu and muttered a curse, all in one breath, as he continued his walk downstairs. Before he could realize, he was standing right in front of a room, its entrance decorated with flowers. Abhimanyu stood there for some time, and with immense hesitation, pushed the door open.

There she was, sitting on the edge of a lavishly decorated bed. She wore a bright red, heavily-embroidered salwar-kameez with a crimson dupatta to cover her head. Her hands and feet were dyed with henna. Her tapering fingernails were painted red. Her neck, nose and her hands were covered with heavy wedding jewellery. As Abhimanyu entered the room, she raised her kohl-lined eyes. The make-up and jewellery made her look older, but she looked every inch a beautiful and elegant Sikhni. He entered the room but stood at a distance from her. He felt awkward and the burden of breaking the ice was wearing him down. He lowered his eyes and looked everywhere, but at her.

'I know it's useless to expect you to say anything. So I thought *I* should do that before I get married. I wanted to speak to you after we met at Americanos, but couldn't really do it. Did you ever wonder what was it that I wanted you to say that day Abhi?'

'How does it matter Jaspreet—'

'It does. It really does! That night when India won the World Cup, it felt so beautiful just standing next to you. It was a beautiful, loving moment for me, and I thought...for you too.'

Abhimanyu nodded in the affirmative, his head still bowed.

'That night and the day after was the most beautiful time of my life. I never felt so connected with anyone. And all that while, I was well aware that I was getting married to someone else in a couple of months.'

Abhimanyu raised his eyes and said, 'Do you believe in soul mates?'

Jaspreet raised her hands and said, 'So finally he speaks...on the day of my marriage!'

'Don't interrupt me Jas, don't!' Abhimanyu said curtly. 'You don't have to burden yourself with that thought, because I felt exactly the way you do. I never felt so happy with anyone.'

'So why did you not say it that day?'

'After you broke the news of your marriage to me, you expected me to say, "Hey, look, here I am! Your soulmate." It does not work like that.'

'I just wanted you to show the same courage that you showed in the face of your IIT admission. I wanted you to have the courage to say that, even in the face of the knowledge that I was getting married!' Her voice was now rising and Abhimanyu looked back at the door just to check if someone was listening.

He turned around and said, 'So what would you have done, Jaspreet? Called your marriage off?'

'I would have stalled it, at least. I would have given us a chance, Abhi. I wanted to hear from you if you felt the same way that I did.'

'The news of your marriage was too sudden and I couldn't react,' Abhimanyu lowered his voice which was now barely a whisper.

Jaspreet moved a few steps and then stopped. She wanted to hug him, one last time. She knew that he would not make any move. Not now. Not today.

Teary-eyed, she said, 'I am happy that we felt the same...on the soul mate bit.' She bit her lip, staining her teeth with the red lipstick in the process. 'Find me next time, Abhi, please! If there is a next time, speak your heart out.' Her voice was now breaking.

'I will. If there is indeed a next time, I certainly will,' he said, smiling at her through teary eyes.

He moved ahead and placed his hand on her head, 'I will always pray for you, your happiness and your future. I wish you...'

Before he could complete his sentence, she moved ahead and pressed her lips to his. Abhimanyu stood there, his lips pressed to hers and his right hand behind her back, a millimetre away from touching her. The door was still not locked and they were at peril of being discovered like this. Suddenly, Abhimanyu thought he heard someone running up the stairs. He pushed her away. She would have fallen on her back with a crash had she not held on to the chair next to her.

'I am sorry. I am really sorry, Jas,' Abhimanyu moved ahead trying to hold her, almost apologetically.

Regaining her senses she said, 'I will be really happy with you.'

'I know that, Jas,' Abhimanyu could see pain on her face.

'Marry me!'

'What?'

'Yes, marry me!'

The shabad kirtan, the chattering women and the cacophony of children and young girls – all sounds died down as both of them stood there gaping at each other.

Abhimanyu smiled and asked, 'Do you mean it?'

'Every word of it,' she smiled back, her tears now staining her cheeks.

The next day, the family bid farewell to the bride after breakfast. Jaspreet hugged her sisters and mother and cried her heart out, her eyes still searching for Abhimanyu. She could not see him anywhere, but knew that he'd be around. Watching her. He sure was. From the corner of the gurudwara wall, his eyes red with tears and the sleepless previous night. She got into the car and sat next to her father's choice, her husband, Harvinder.

She looked back at the place where she had grown up. And then she saw him. When his eyes met hers, she cursed herself for not having taken the right step at the right time. In Americano a couple of months ago, she should just have begged him to marry her. Now she knew, clearer than ever before: she loved him and wanted to be with him for the rest of her life. She felt a hand on her back. Harvinder was trying to comfort her. All that remained of Abhimanyu was a hazy figure disappearing in the morning dust. Abhimanyu was history; Harvinder, her present.

Abhimanyu's visits to his parents' house became rare and fleeting after that. There would be long spells of virtually no contact. His excuse was standard: outstation trips, which was true to some extent. This was the time that Abhimanyu covered a lot of border assignments as Sikh extremism grew alarmingly. He interacted with many extremist leaders and had his share of drama too. But those were the war zones and dramatic scenarios were rather normal.

Strange was when he had his share in Delhi too: the most dramatic was a shootout in Chitranjan Park.

He was fucking his colleague Ipshita Roy in his house that afternoon. They lay on the bed and just when Ipshita lit a fag, Abhimanyu received a call from his source in Delhi Police. Abhimanyu rushed Ipshita to her home on his motorbike, only to discover her father's bullet riddled body. Ipshita grieved her father and Abhimanyu ran around, admitting her mother to the hospital, who kept losing consciousness after every few minutes. He also doubled up as a journalist covering the assignment. Ipshita returned to Kolkata soon after and Abhimanyu was left to himself.

He spoke to Sharad, but their conversations were few and far apart. Sharad had appeared for the XII exams the year after Abhimanyu and the artificial limb to support him while walking enabled him to be self-dependent. Not only had he scored more than 90 percent marks, he had also cleared the entrance exam to the prestigious All India Institute of Medical Sciences. Busy with their respective work, they hardly got enough time to meet or talk.

With time, distance between him and Jagtar also grew. Jagtar got busy with his father's business of spare parts and Abhimanyu was a journalist running around. They discovered gradually that they neither had anything to talk about now, nor any time to be spent together. It was tragic to see the erosion of the innocence that bonded them as friends. They could no longer laugh aloud on inane issues; they could no longer crack lewd jokes and just forget about the difficult times. Abhimanyu stopped visiting Jagtar's house as he could feel a sense of hostility from his father who was becoming radicalized to the core. Jagtar was still untouched by all of this, simply because he was exposed to Abhimanyu and his world and he knew that it was impossible to segregate men on the basis of faith and ideology. He knew that men could be separated only on one ground. Abhimanyu, and the rest. His best friend, and the rest. He would often have long arguments with his father who was troubled that Jagtar did not mingle with other Sikh boys and also did not take seriously issues like Khalistan, the cherished separate homeland for the Sikhs. The conversation would either end by Jagtar rushing out of his house or getting slapped by his father. Khalistan was a dream that was not too far for his father. And he wanted his son to share his dream. Jagtar was pragmatic enough to see where this was leading to. He knew Abhimanyu would stand up for him, come what may. He could see that there was no bitterness in Abhimanyu even as scores of Hindus kept getting massacred by Sikh extremists. Abhimanyu was watching it happen in front of his eyes, but he was not raised on a diet of hate. It went to the credit of his parents that they did not bring him up on clichés that surrounded communities and faiths. But what Jagtar did not know about Abhimanyu was that something was dying inside him gradually. Abhimanyu was going around covering massacre to massacre, story to story in the most clinical fashion. And Jaspreet was the last straw.

Meanwhile, Jagtar was being brainwashed every moment. By his own father. He was trying hard to shut himself to it as hard as he could. He could see the futility of it all. He would see his mother, his younger siblings and wonder what future had in store for them. In a gathering of family and relatives, he would be the minority voice, defending that the work of a few could not be construed as the sin of the nation. Operation Blue Star and the grandeur of a Khalistan had filled his father with immense hatred. Moreover, as his father was a bit too vocal about his beliefs, he had not just lost a lot of clients and ruined his business, but also created many enemies amongst the Hindu majority locality that they were staying in.

Ujjwal had to serve a one-year deputation with a science firm in Cardiff in the United Kingdom starting June 1984. And Mahima was elated that she could join her husband, albeit only after six months. Following that, Abhimanyu had to come and stay those six odd months with his mother.

Mahima went to the airport to see Ujjwal off, and Abhimanyu sat on the balcony after having his lunch. A white Maruti entered the block and stopped right in front of Jaspreet's house. A young Sikh emerged from the driver's seat and rushed to the door on the other side. He opened it carefully and extended his arm to someone who needed help. Abhimanyu cocked his head to have a clearer look. He looked impatiently at the person about to emerge from the car. It was a woman. As she stood out, he could see a bulky lady, clearly pregnant. Flinging her dupatta on her shoulder, she started walking, still holding the guy's hand. And then she stopped, lifting her head to look at Abhimanyu's balcony.

Jaspreet.

Abhimanyu looked at her and so did she! God, he thought. What had the Sardars done to her? She was thrice the size of what she used to be. She looked up at him and smiled. She looked tired, but the pregnancy had not taken away the glory from her face. Abhimanyu absent-mindedly waved at her, and then realized that she was still standing. He rushed downstairs, nearly colliding with someone climbing the stairs.

Abhimanyu stood in front of her, panting and breathless. She was standing alone now. He looked at her and then the bulge of her stomach. Jaspreet bowed her head with a hint of a blush on her face, but then raised her eyes to meet his.

'So?' he said.

She smiled again.

'You look happy.'

'Don't be cruel,' she said.

'Happily pregnant?' he said.

She said nothing.

'But I can see that your in-laws are really taking care of you,' he could not help smiling and she knew what he meant.

'You know, now I understand how Sikh women change after marriage. Since I got pregnant, they have been bathing me in ghee. It has also been a difficult pregnancy. I have been advised complete bed rest. In fact, I got pregnant the month after I got married, but I had a miscarriage.'

'Oh, I am sorry. It must have been painful.'

'No, it's ok!'

'So when is it due?'

'First week of November. At least that's what my gynaecologist says.'

'I am so happy for you Jaspreet.'

'Are you?' she asked.

'Why wouldn't I be? Of course I am happy for you.'

'I wasn't asking about me. I meant your life. Are you happy with life?'

'I have been too busy with work to worry about life.' It was a matter of fact response. 'Hey, I think you should now go in and take rest. Can't keep a pregnant woman standing in the middle of the road like that.'

She mumbled in a whisper, 'Quite a coincidence, isn't it? Most of the things between us happen in the middle of the road.'

Abhimanyu said, 'That moment will always be cherished and will always be one of the most beautiful moments of my life.'

Jaspreet walked into the house and Abhimanyu wondered at his luck. Staying with his mother till she left for London was not exactly a pleasant option for Abhimanyu as it would stifle his independence. And now, it was Jaspreet too. A pregnant Jaspreet. He wondered if he would have to see her day in and day out. He wondered if that would be a pleasant sight for him. But he knew that he had to live with it. After all, it was hardly the drama that he had seen in his life. It wasn't dramatic enough than what the country was about to see a few months later.

To his luck, Abhimanyu's mother did not have to wait for long to join her husband in London. Instead of waiting for six months, she could now join him earlier. It was on the 30th of October that she sobbed her way to the ticket counter looking back at her; he watched her disappear in the sea of people at the airport. He turned around but felt a stinging pain in his spine. He stretched his back and then raised his right arm. He could feel a sudden surge of numbness in his knees too. He wondered if he was going to fall sick. He dragged himself to the parking lot to the official car from his father's office that had come to drop him and his mother.

As he crashed in the seat behind the driver, he shut his eyes only to be woken by the driver when he reached home. He was feeling worse as he tried to get out of the vehicle. He raised his hand to touch his forehead. Boiling hot!

After the effort of climbing up the stairs to his first floor house, he lay on his bed, jolts of excruciating pain ripping through his vertebrae. He smiled, wondering how pain could be such a rush! And then he dozed off.

In his subconscious, he could hear the phone ringing, but his body refused to act. He tried opening his eyes, but all he could see was a blur of a place that looked strange and unknown. Was he in his own house, he wondered in his semi-conscious state of mind. He forced his eyes open. The phone was still ringing.

'Mummy, get the phone!'

His mind was still numb. He was confused why he was lying on the sofa with his shoes still on. He was sweating profusely, wondering all the time why his mother wasn't picking up the phone. The blades of the still fan looked back at him menacingly like the claws of an ancient monster. He stretched his right hand out to grab the screaming phone, but he was some distance away. He stretched further and lost his balance, falling flat on his chest, his chin hitting the floor with a crash. Abhimanyu winced in pain as he held his chin and got up immediately. The pain had woken him out of his comatose existence. He grabbed the phone with trembling hands and pressed it to his ears.

'Where the hell are you? I have been calling you for the past ten minutes! You won't believe what I saw!' It was Sharad on the other end. He was currently interning at the Rajendra Prasad eye centre at AIIMS.

'What?'

I just saw Indira Gandhi taken in a stretcher to the OT. She was bloodied, man! I even saw her daughter-in-law...what's her name... Sonia!'

'What the hell are you saying? Are you sure?'

'I am bloody sure. I was chatting with our chief surgeon, Mr Dhawan when his name was announced for an emergency.'

Abhimanyu pressed the phone harder to his ears. Sharad continued, 'We thought it is some terrorist attack. But soon after, the outpatient ward was emptied by the security people. They even pushed all of us out, except Dr Dhawan and the nurses. I walked towards the OT from another side and Bingo! There she was. I was shit scared man!'

'So what's happening now? Is she fine? What—'

'I have a bad feeling. Dr Dhawan is out. He looks crestfallen. I think she is gone...'

'Gone? What the hell do you mean by gone, Sharad?'

'I think she is dead. I can see this BBC journalist walking around. Don't know his name but I can see him talking to Dr Dhawan. They say she has been shot at by her Sikh bodyguards.'

'Shit! This city is going to burn,' he mumbled.

And then suddenly, Sharad asked Abhimanyu to stay on the line while he spoke to someone. Abhimanyu could hear muffled conversations between Sharad and someone. But his mind was fast racing towards two people who mattered to him – Jaspreet and Jagtar.

'Abhi,' Sharad had an added urgency to his voice, 'She is dead. Declared dead. It's all over.'

Sharad hung up, and Abhimanyu began dialling his office. He disconnected midway and dialled Jagtar's number instead. He drew the curtains of the room aside and glanced out of his window. People were huddled in groups on the street in front of him. He could not see Jaspreet, but her father stood there talking to someone pensively. The voice on the phone was Jagtar's overtly excited father's.

'Uncle, can I speak to Jag—'

'Oye Abhimanyoo! Is that you son? I guess you must be knowing. We heard Indira Gandhi has been shot. Any news on that?'

'Well uncle, that's why I had called. She is dead.'

'*Oye Balley! Chak de phatte*!' roared his father as he broke into an impromptu Bhangra over the phone itself. He started shouting, 'the bitch is dead, the bitch is dead...' Abhimanyu moved the phone away from his ear as his roar got deafening.

And then his father paused and asked again, '*Oye pakka na*? You sure?'

Abhimanyu kept silent for a while and then mumbled, 'Yes.'

Jagtar took the phone from his father and asked him to lower his volume. Abhimanyu said, 'Jagtar, you have to control your father. He can't be heard saying such stuff. I have a really bad feeling about this bro.'

Irritated at his father, Jagtar said, 'What do I do? You have opened the Pandora's box by giving him this news!' He paused, 'Oh God! He is planning to go to the sweet shop.'

'Stop him, Jagtar! You *have* to stop him. If someone sees him celebrating, things are going to get really bad. You stop him...' Abhimanyu's mind was working in different directions and then as if some thought had struck him suddenly, he said, 'You better get your entire family to my place. Fast! I don't want you guys to stay there.'

'Why?'

'Don't ask why! This city is going to burn, and you need to be somewhere safe. Your house is not safe at all.'

Just as Abhimanyu hung up, Jagtar ran downstairs, in time to stop his father from driving off on his Lambretta to buy sweets.

'Papaji, dont go! Let's not attract undue attention. We don't need this.'

Visibly irritated, his father swat his hand in the air and said, '*Oye khote!* Have some balls. Today is the day of victory for us. The whore is dead. And this will be the first step towards the establishment of a separate homeland for us.'

Jagtar now held his hand and said, 'Nothing of that sort is going to happen. You have a family. If you are seen doing this in times like these, we will be in trouble. All of us.'

'What trouble?' He roared. 'You think these impotent Hindus have the balls to do anything?

'You have lost it Papaji. You have totally lost it!'

Jagtar's father was too happy to endure the discouragement of his son. The slap landed on Jagtar's cheek with a mighty roar, bringing his mother to the veranda.

'See, the kind of eunuch you have borne!' he taunted his mother who stood quietly. 'I am ashamed of him. Again! I wish you were never born!'

Jagtar's father sped away, leaving Jagtar and his mother watching him vanish at the turn of the block. His father's words echoed in his ears. Abhimanyu's father had said the same thing, and the turn of events had not been very good. He wondered what he would do now.

Not wasting another moment, Jagtar took his mother, fifteen-year-old sister and fourteen-year-old younger brother to Abhimanyu's house. Meanwhile, the news of an attack on a Sikh family by a mob in West Delhi spread like wildfire. They were targeting anyone who wore a turban and any woman who was a Sikh. Abhimanyu was waiting for Jagtar and his family to arrive so that he could then move out to cover the big story that was developing in the capital. No sooner had Jagtar and his family reached Abhimanyu's home that he dropped a bombshell. Something that was unthinkable.

'You will hate me for saying this, but I am afraid we don't have an option...'

They gaped at Abhimanyu with baited breath.

'I am afraid Jagtar and Joginder will have to cut their hair, so that they can't be recognized as Sikhs.'

Jagtar's mother looked horrified. She moved ahead menacingly but stopped short of Abhimanyu, 'Are you out of your mind? Don't you know what our *kesh* mean to us?' she was fuming and her breath started getting out of control.

'Aunty, no one is asking you to betray your faith! But what you are facing is a mob that is illogical with lunacy riding its head. Preneet can get away as they cannot make out if she is a Sikh or not. But I am sorry, it's not the case with your sons. They will stand out in a crowd and will be targeted. I have news from my office that this will go out of control soon. I have a bad feeling that these mobs will start searching houses and targeting Sikhs. Don't forget, the government is theirs. They will have no problems in identifying Sikh houses. They just have to access electoral rolls and that's it!' Abhimanyu turned towards Jagtar and said, 'Come on, Jagtar! Tell her I am justified. Or am I not making sense?'

'My father will kill me, Abhi.'

'So be it! It's better to be killed by your father than a mob who will violate you and then everyone related to you.'

Jagtar clasped his face and sunk in the chair next to him.

Abhimanyu placed his hand on Jagtar's shoulder, patting him gently. Jagtar raised his head, his eyes filled with tears and said, 'The thought of something bad happening to my family is just...'

Abhimanyu turned towards Jagtar's mother, 'Aunty, we will have to cut their hair. It's going to be a huge risk otherwise. But all said and done, I assure you that the mob will have to cross me to inflict any harm on them. You all are like my family.'

'You don't have to say that son,' mumbled Jagtar's mother under her breath. She grabbed her forehead and started walking around, her mind still on her husband. She suddenly sat on the sofa and burying her head in the bend of her right arm, started sobbing. Through her sobs she kept saying, 'We should have got your father... we should have...'

'I just hope he is safe,' Jagtar's voice broke but he stopped short of crying as he saw his sister and brother breaking into uncontrollable sobs.

'Jagtar, I am going to call a trusted barber who will cut your hair and Joginder's. He belongs to my father's village and will not breathe a word about it to anyone. He will be here in half-an-hour. You all stay here, I will go to your place and get uncle. I assure you Jagga, I will do my best...and nothing will happen to him. I have a feeling, nothing will!'

Abhimanyu was now thinking about Jaspreet and her family, but his landlords, the Salujas had already offered shelter to the Randhawas. Jaspreet's cousins and her mother had shifted to the Salujas'. Jaspreet's father and her husband were still at the shop, oblivious to how volatile the situation was turning into. Every passing minute, every moment gone was like an opportunity lost. The lost opportunity to live. Jaspreet was continuously on phone, pleading her father and her husband to come back home. They were still thinking that the police would come into action and control things soon. They thought that it would subside soon. In all the moments that had passed, the government controlled TV channel and radio had still not broadcast the news of her assassination. The confirmation came from the BBC. It was only after Indira Gandhi's son and successor Rajiv Gandhi took oath in the evening did they announce her death formally. But the mobs were already out. Targeting anyone who was turbaned, anyone who was a Sikh. And amidst all this, Jaspreet's father was hoping that this might be controlled soon. No one thought that the police would let such a thing happen right in front of their eyes, that the police would be passive spectators as mobs went out to murder, rape and plunder in broad daylight. No one had expected that it would snowball into one of the worst genocides of independent India.

The barber finally arrived at Abhimanyu's house and got to his job. Abhimanyu checked his motorbike for petrol and drove towards Jagtar's house in Tilak Nagar. He realized how the mobs had changed the landscape in a matter of hours. Burning cars, tyres and gut down shops lay across the road. Smoke bellowed from houses that were inhabited by Sikhs. Abhimanyu was carrying a camera and would stop to take dramatic pictures as he came cross some. But he was clearly not prepared for what he was about to see in just a few minutes.

From a distance, it looked like a circus. Like a rabid dog circled by boys who were giving it a harrowing time. They had probably ripped his shirt off as they pummelled him. His turban too had been torn to bits and his long hair bounced on his back. Jagtar's father managed to escape somehow and entered his house, only to emerge at the terrace swaying his twenty-inch sword in the air, trying to intimidate his attackers. He had a country made pistol in the other hand and that was keeping the mob at bay. He had not fired a shot till now. He could have easily escaped from the backdoor. But he wanted to teach the "fucking Hindus" a lesson. So he climbed the stairs that led to his terrace and stood at the edge brandishing his sword and gun. That only provoked the hundred odd people who had surrounded his house. They were throwing stones and bricks at him and at the same time, ducking every time he would threaten him with his pistol. Abhimanyu was horrified at seeing a few people from the mob carrying canisters of petrol towards the house. His eyes darted from the canisters to Jagtar's father. The roar of the mob was deafening. Chants of "Death to the Sikhs" rent the air. Abhimanyu looked at Jagtar's father again. His face was scarred red as blood dripped from his forehead to his shoulders. His hairy chest was smeared with thick red. His blood-stained belly wobbled as he moved sideways. Three men with their faces covered with white cloths started pouring petrol at his doorstep, keeping an eye on the armed "Sardar". For the mob that was gathered there, it was like a game. Even the bystanders and his neighbours stood at their windows and doors betting how soon the Sikh will fall. Suddenly an old man appeared from nowhere and started scolding the men who were pouring petrol on the house.

'Are you mad? You will burn the entire block,' he gestured with his hands raised at the men, 'Leave him! You have already punished him for a crime he hasn't committed. Let him go!'

Someone saw sense in what the old man was saying about not burning the house down. But not about leaving him. Jagtar's father saw this conversation, only saw. He did not hear what the old man was saying. From the distance and in the mood that he was, all looked the same. He aimed and shot. It did not find a target, but the bullet ricocheted the wall and hit the old man in his chest. He clasped his chest and fell down. The old man's wife was watching all this. She howled and started running towards her husband who was now on all his fours, clasping his chest and moaning in pain. The crowd got even more enraged; someone threw a bottle that hit Jagtar's father on his shoulder. He trained his gun blindly on the crowd and fired again. And again. And again. And all the three times, nothing came out of his pistol. He just had one bullet loaded. Four men from the mob now rushed inside his veranda and started breaking open the door. They wanted to get in. To the terrace and get the "lunatic".

In a matter of five minutes, the mob started streaming inside his house and started rushing towards the terrace. Jagtar's father now turned around to face his attackers. He threw the pistol away and held the sword with both his hands. There was barely any strength left in his hands. His eyes were blinking as blood oozed from his wounds and dripped over his eyelids. The door of the terrace burst open and people rushed in, only to see the man swaying his sword even more violently. But they waited, for they knew they won't have to wait for long. Watching from a distance, with tears flowing from his eyes, even Abhimanyu knew that it was just a matter of time. He had forgotten that he had a camera. In fact, he had forgotten who he was. And why he was there. Was he a journalist? Or the saviour of Jagtar's father? He knew that he had failed on both fronts as he stood there horrified, watching them tear his father as the mob finally snatched the sword from his hand. Abhimanyu stood petrified and watched the killers of his best friend's father disperse slowly after the kill.

There was absolute silence in the block. Everyone stood where they were. Except for the distant howl of a dog pack and a rioting mob at a faraway place, nothing could be heard. Abhimanyu could not see from that distance, but the corpse lay sprawled on the terrace. All he could see was the blood stained *kada* clad left hand of Jagtar's father hanging lifelessly from the railing of the terrace. His cowardice was dragging him down. He could not dare to save his best friend's father. He did not even give a fight. The thought that there was no way they would have listened to him and would have probably turned their ire against him was secondary at that moment. He had failed to save Jagtar's father.

As he dragged himself to Jagtar's terrace, others followed. In an hour, his mangled corpse was given some bit of dignity by covering it in a shroud. Abhimanyu stood next to the body, clasping his hair and sobbing. He could not dare to pick up the phone and call Jagtar. He could never have.

He drove back, noticing how the roads had further changed in the past one hour. Every nook and corner of West Delhi was haunted by shrieks of the dead. But he had his own monster to face. He had promised Jagtar that he would defend them, his family, with his life. They would have to cross him before they get to his family, he remembered. But he had chosen to save his own life and lost his pride.

An hour later, as he entered his house, he could barely recognize Jagtar and his brother. The barber had done a good job. But he did not have the time to react to this new look. Everyone was looking at him with expectant eyes. Teary-eyed, Abhimanyu hung his head; and Jagtar's mother was the first to start wailing. A stream of tear trickled down Jagtar's left eye. He rose and walked towards his mother and younger siblings who had now gone hysterical. But he kept looking at Abhimanyu, as if reminding him of his promise. Jagtar's mother was now bashing her head on the wall and his sister started crying in a high pitch, clasping her chest. Abhimanyu could not move from where he stood, and tears started rolling from his eyes again. He wanted to go and hug them, but he felt like a criminal. He felt like one from the mob that had violated and scarred Jagtar's family forever. It was only when Jagtar's mother fainted clasping her chest that Abhimanyu moved and rushed to the neighbours, the Bhushans, asking for their Fiat car. She had to be taken to the nearby hospital. It was a fatal heart attack.

While Abhimanyu rushed her to the hospital in a futile effort to save her, Jagtar rode his bike to Tilak Nagar to see his father. He had heard that the mobs did not strike twice at the same place. But Jaggu had lost the fear of death now. The man whose mangled corpse lay in Tilak Nagar was after all his father. He was still oblivious to the shock that he would get in the evening. The death of his mother. The trauma of being an orphan. Abhimanyu's walk in hell was not going to get over any soon too.

Jagtar's parents' cremation was jointly performed the next morning amidst chants of "Waheguru". And it wasn't them alone, but two dozen other funeral pyres, amidst relatives in a state of fear. Verses from the *Guru Granth Sahib* floated in the melancholy of a thousand sobs that morning.

In life and in death, peace resides with those who attain their Guru.
My light merges with the Supreme light, and my labours are over.
The sunbeam blends with sunlight and the water drop is absorbed into water becoming saturated.
Like droplets of water are in an ocean wave and the ripples of a stream, I am immersed in the Lord.

The ritual of reading the *Guru Granth Sahib* was conducted at Abhimanyu's place even as the fires of devastation and lunacy raged all around them. After the ritual ended, Jagtar insisted that he would like to take his brother and sister back to his house in Tilak Nagar. Abhimanyu was wary of such a plan, but nothing could stop Jagtar. It did not matter to him what the mobs could do to him or his siblings. He wanted to visit his parents' home, just this one last time. He had already decided to leave the country and shift with his uncle staying abroad. So much so, that an official sponsorship had been requested and the passports of his siblings already had an English visa stamped. He had to send his brother and sister out of this country as soon as he could, and he would follow soon enough. Jagtar's father had always wanted him to leave India to settle down in London and he had opposed it till his father was alive. He wished he had listened to him then.

After dropping Jagtar and his siblings to their house in Tilak Nagar, Abhimanyu drove back to his house. The Bhushans had been generous enough to let them use the car during these times. It was not just the Bhushans, but many people who with their small but countless acts of selflessness had saved many lives during that time, without really bothering about their own.

When he drove towards his block, he felt his heart sinking. Something was terribly wrong. The sight of burning cars and houses and the smoke besmirching the skies was making it even more unbearable. Every nook and corner of the city was haunted by madness, but his Hindu-dominated block had been spared. What he saw next shocked him so much that he nearly collided with a car parked at the corner of the street. The Gurudwara where Jaspreet's marriage was solemnized was burning. Rioters and goons could be seen running out of the burning structure. They had their hands full of loot, as if they had grabbed everything and anything they could. Loudspeakers, transistors, ration, bed sheets...every damn thing!

Although tempted to get out of his car, he decided instead to race to his block which wasn't too far. A cocktail of slogans and shrill shrieks of women got louder. The air was thick with the stench of burning leather and wood. He stopped his car at the end of the block and rushed out immediately. All he could see was a sea of rioters, their hands raised, their mouths chanting slogans of "eternity to the martyred Prime Minister". He saw that the concentration was heavier in front of his house, the crowd more animated. He raised his head, only to see some men hitting someone sprawled on the ground with sticks and iron rods. And then he raised his head towards his own balcony. It was Jaspreet, pleading with both hands to spare the man who was being battered. It was her shrill cry that was the most definitive sound in that opera of insanity. Mrs Saluja was holding Jaspreet, so that she would not jump off the balcony. She had spread her right hand out, begging and then holding her womb with her left hand which was now a full bump.

Abhimanyu ran towards the epicentre of madness, pushing and shoving the supporters violently. As he approached the centre, his eyes turned towards the gutter to his right. The rioters were throwing the lifeless half naked body of an elderly Sikh. As the body slipped into the gutter, he had one last glimpse of the bloodied face. It was Jaspreet's father. He turned his head back to the centre. He pulled and punched the men who were beating someone. Before he could look at the man on the ground, he raised his eyes back to where Jaspreet was standing. Someone pulled her back and he saw her frame vanishing. He trained his eyes back at the victim. It took him a few seconds, but then he realized it was him. Harvinder, Jaspreet's husband. His last memory of the handsome Sikh was of a man dressed in a traditional Sikh dress. And here he was, his face coloured with red, his right eye gouged out. His hair, cut to half by the rioters. He was as good as dead. All he could see was his lips that were moving feebly in one last struggle to live.

It was at that one moment that someone struck an iron rod at Abhimanyu's back. Winching in pain for a moment, he turned back and swung his right hand in a semi horizontal arc. It came crashing on the man's jaw. The man fell back, immediately vanishing in the sea of madmen. Gathering all his strength, Abhimanyu shouted, 'Leave him, you fucking cowards. He is already dead. Leave him, motherfuckers, leave him!' But the chanting got louder.

Someone started screaming, 'Kill the traitor...kill the goddamn traitor!'

Abhimanyu grabbed the iron rod on the ground and started swaying it violently, hitting a few as it swung aimlessly. From the corner of his eye, he saw someone drawing out metal from his pocket. But he kept hitting the men around him till they had left Harvinder, who now looked like a crumpled lump of flesh. His eyes caught a glance of the gate of the Salujas and Jaspreet emerging out of it, closely followed by Mrs Saluja who was trying hard to stop her. She looked like a woman violated by a hundred devils. She ran towards her husband, pushing the rioters aside. As she neared the blob of flesh that looked vaguely like what her husband used to be, she spread her hands around him, pleading the rioters to spare him. Abhimanyu was still gesticulating like a man possessed with the iron rod in his hand. He knew that pleading would not help. He knew that pleading would only provoke the bastards.

'Please spare them. How much more madness do you want to see? You have already killed the old man,' he gestured towards the gutter.

'Now leave them beta, please go back to your homes. Have mercy on them, please have...' Mrs Saluja was shouting too.

Before she could complete his sentence, the man whom Abhimanyu had noticed earlier, raised his hand and aimed his country made pistol at Harvinder. There was complete silence before and immediately after the shot was fired. The shot echoed in the entire block and beyond.

Someone else had also seen the man raising his gun. Jaspreet. She knew who it was meant for and took a hundredth of a second to spread herself over her battered husband. The bullet found its target. A painful moan and a lazy stream of saliva oozed from her mouth followed by a flush of red, as she stared blankly at her husband's bloodied face. A stream of red trickled from the back of her white Kurta. Jaspreet slowly raised her shaking right hand and caressed her husband's face. She turned around and her eyes met Abhimanyu's. Horror written all over his face, he looked back at her.

It was an expression alien to him. It wasn't a smile; it wasn't even pain. There were traces of grief and an appeal to save her husband's life. He thought that she smiled. He thought she did. And then she slumped over Harvinder.

Abhimanyu bent down clenching his fists, ran his hand over Jaspreet's back and paused at her wound. The wheezing sound from his throat was like a cry wanting to break free. And then he broke loose. It was a cry that echoed till eternity. It was a cry that would haunt him for the rest of his life because he would never cry like that again. He tried lifting her up, but a pregnant Jaspreet was too heavy for him. He wanted to take her to the hospital. He did not want to abandon hope. One last chance, he thought. He looked around, his mouth still open and tears streaming down his eyes. His eyes stopped at Mr Saluja, and he begged him to help him. Mr Saluja rushed forward and they lifted Jaspreet. A few more boys gathered the courage and came rushing towards Harvinder. Abhimanyu and Mr Saluja waded through the crowds to the Fiat that Abhimanyu had parked at the end of the block. The faceless, shameless mob started dispersing.

Jaspreet's mother had lost consciousness as the mob took her husband. She knew what they were going to do with him. Jaspreet's younger cousins were dressed as girls; hence they escaped the mob's ire. The cousins and their parents hid in the basement and were saved. The Randhawas had sent an SOS to a friend in the Indian Army. The help from this friend reached much later. All over for Jaspreet's immediate family, but the military vehicle did take Jaspreet's relatives to the safety of the cantonment area near Dhaula Kuan.

Abhimanyu and Mr Saluja took both Jaspreet and her husband in the same car to the nearest hospital. Harvinder was brought dead on arrival. Jaspreet was still breathing, but there was a problem. It was also the time of her delivery. It was a cruel coincidence that the delivery of the baby was supposed to happen the same day. The gunshot wound on her back had aggravated her condition, and she had already lost a lot of blood. The baby had to be taken out, but that also meant losing blood. The doctors knew that the mother would sink as soon as the baby was born. But she was lucky. She indeed was.

An hour later, the baby lay next to Jaspreet who now had an oxygen mask on her face. She tried looking at the baby from the corner of her half shut eyes. Abhimanyu stood next to the pink little bundle of joy wrapped in white. Jaspreet looked at Abhimanyu, trying to raise her hand, but managing to barely lift a finger. She wanted to say something to him, he thought. He moved closer to her and whispered, 'It's going to be fine. Don't struggle, you are weak.' With anguish written all over her face, she smiled. She raised her finger again. Abhimanyu saw that she had pressed her forefinger to her thumb. It seemed she wanted to write something. Abhimanyu looked around and picked up the doctor's papers from the bedside, digging out his pen. Abhimanyu placed the pen between her forefinger and thumb and the paper underneath.

The doctor walked in and asked him to let Jaspreet rest, but she shook her head. Abhimanyu needed a miracle that day; he wanted Him to save her. He promised himself that he would heal all the scars that the incident would leave. He had promised God that he would. But he needed His help. It was a miracle that the baby was saved, and also that she could write legible words in that condition.

"PLEASE TAKE CARE OF MY CHILD. BE THE FATHER."

Her last words.
Jaspreet's entire family was on the run, and he did not know

anyone in Harvinder's. The unfortunate ones had been wiped out mercilessly. That evening, Jaspreet, her husband and her father were consigned to flames from the same place where Jagtar's parents' last rites were carried out. None of her relatives turned up. How could they have, amidst the senseless massacre!

Abhimanyu drove back to the hospital after consigning them to flames, till his motorbike skidded on broken shards of glass at a turn and betrayed him. He dragged the reluctant metal beast, his strength sapping in what became the longest walk of his life. Every nook and corner of the city haunted him, mocked him for being a coward. His mind was fixed on Jaspreet's daughter who lay peacefully in the nursery of the hospital.

November
1984

The shower cleaned off the grime and blood, but the pain lingered in his heart. He walked towards the nursery, and the nurse opened the door for him.

He finally held the baby in his arms, and held her close to her heart, resting her head on his shoulder. The tenderness he felt was out of the world, like a balm to the ravaged times he had lived in the past few days. She nestled in the curve of his neck, her breath a constant reassurance of life and a reminder that he would have to escape from the past soon. He would have to erase it if he indeed wished to make the beginning he desired for Jaspreet's daughter.

The memory of Jaspreet and the look in her eyes doubled his pain and he pressed the baby a little tighter to his chest, as if not wanting to let go. The baby moved with a moan, as if unhappy with his embrace.

And then he heard a gentle rumble; it smelt slightly funny too. Abhimanyu raised her and told the nurse, 'Sister, I think she has soiled herself.'

The nurse took the baby from him and started cleaning her. and he carefully watched the nurse in action. He noticed how the nurse lifted both her legs, joining the toes to each other first. He saw how carefully she first wiped the muck with a piece of dry cotton. Then she drew more cotton, dabbing it with water, and cleaned her very gently. This was the beginning of his training. He was after all going to raise Jaspreet's daughter.

Abhimanyu's mother rushed back to India when the madness had slowly evaporated and as things started moving towards normalcy. Abhimanyu had called her to India. Jagtar and his siblings had shifted back to their house in Tilak Nagar. Armed with Jaspreet's dying declaration and the hospital's discharge certificate, Abhimanyu brought the baby home. In a normal situation, there would be complications handing over the baby to someone like Abhimanyu, but there was so much chaos around that no one really cared. Jaspreet's mother was the only family of the mother he knew of and she had sunk into coma after learning what happened to the family.

When the baby arrived at Abhimanyu's house, there was an outpour of men and women from the entire block. There were many to pity the baby, sympathize with the luck with which she had arrived in this world. Then there were those women who volunteered to look after the baby. Everyone was bothered with the question – who would raise the orphan now?

Jaspreet's uncle called up Mr Saluja from his safe hideout in the Delhi cantonment area. Much later. In fact, he was expecting to hear that no one had survived, least of all the baby.

Mr Saluja had promptly called Abhimanyu and he had expected nothing from the phone call. 'We thought the baby won't survive, since Jaspreet was shot,' was what her uncle said. 'And a girl, is it? Are you sure? Of course you are! I don't know. We thought it would be a boy,' he mourned. 'Well, I don't know...we are moving out of this godforsaken country, and that too in a week. I guess Waheguru will take care of the child.' Correcting himself with a lot of hesitation, he said, 'I mean, I will be back later and make arrangements for the baby!'

But then Abhimanyu said something that sealed the decision for everyone. 'Jaspreet made a dying declaration that I take care of the baby. I will see what can be done. You don't worry about her. I know these are hard times for you. You please take care of your family.'

'Thank you so much, Abhimanyu! I promise I will be back. In the meantime, you have all my support and we assure you that there will be no problems from our side in case you wish to adopt the baby.'

Adopt the baby. The only deed that would bring him closer to Jaspreet even after her death. But he knew he would not be able to do it on his own. He was a single man and laws of adoption in India would not help. His parents too could not adopt; they had long crossed the age limit for adoption. But Abhimanyu was armed with Jaspreet's dying declaration. He had a witness too: the doctor who had operated upon Jaspreet. But that did not matter. He knew that no one would come to claim the girl. And even if they did, they would always raise her with the thought that the entire family was massacred on the day she was born. She would be called unlucky. And if that happened, Jaspreet would never forgive him. Perhaps she could foresee all this as she watched her baby from her half shut eyes, as her breath slipped away, as she saw her daughter lying next to her under the shadow of the man she could be with. Abhimanyu.

Abhimanyu's mother declared that it was the most beautiful baby she had ever seen. Much more beautiful than Abhimanyu had been. Holding the little angel in her arms, Mahima caressed her thick golden hair; the baby raised her head and made a sound. Something like a whimper. As if it was responding to her touch. A tear rolled down Mahima's left cheek.

While she fondled the baby, Abhimanyu told her how her immediate family had disowned her and how the child had nowhere to go. He told her how inconsiderate Jaspreet's uncle had been as she continued caressing the baby. He was preparing her for what he was about to tell her.

'Ma, Jaspreet left a dying note...and she wrote that she wanted me to take care of the child after she is gone. I won't mince words mom...I want to adopt this child. I want to raise her.'

Mahima didn't say a word; she just kept looking at her son. On the one hand, she was overwhelmed by the surge of emotions holding the baby in her hands. On the other, her son's outrageous desire.

'You want to...what?'

'I want to adopt her!'

'Go on! Why ask us? Have you bothered asking us anything in life? For everything that you have done.' Her face hardened.

'I need your help, Mom. It's not some personal whim; it's a life. I am answerable to a dead mother.'

'And what about being answerable to your own parents, Babu? The ones who raised you? The ones who are still alive? What about them?'

'Please let's not start—'

'No! Your father had this single dream in life, that his son becomes an engineer. And what do you do? You kick away something that people can only dream of! I have seen him crying silently. He doesn't say it, but he is still haunted by your refusal to join the IIT. You murdered that single desire he had. And now you come up with this desire to adopt a child? You are not even married. Forget that, you are barely twenty-five! And you want to adopt a child?'

'You don't get it Mom! Back then, IIT was not something I wanted for myself. It was thrown at me. But this...this is what I want to do.'

'Precisely! This is what I mean. Why do I have a son who is so different? Why does he not want stuff that other guys his age want? Why is my son so—'

Abhimanyu smiled, 'Weird?'

'What do you want me to do, Babu?' she said with a look of helplessness giving way to exasperation.

'I just want you to help me with my job. I can't raise this child all alone. I promise to do all the difficult work...being up in the night, changing her nappies—'

'So you think raising a child is all about changing nappies and being up all night? Is it? You are raising a life Babu. The future of a life will depend on how you mould it, how you raise it. And what about your marriage? No one will give you his daughter knowing that you are raising a girl. No one wants that kind of headache for his daughter!'

'And I don't wish to get married into a family that thinks like that.'

'Most families will. And they are justified if they think like that. You have no idea what you're getting into. And you're so passionate about your job; how will you manage that?'

'This is where you come in Mom.'

'So you want me to be *her* Mom as well. Is that it?'

Abhimanyu nodded.

'Aren't you ashamed of yourself? I am touching forty-five, and you expect me to—'

'It's just a couple of years Mom. I will hire a full day maid to look after her. I promise it won't be a burden. I just want you to be there, just look over her like her guiding angel.'

'And your father? How do you think he will react? Don't you have any pity on him?'

'What can I say Mom? This wasn't the life I chose for myself.'

His mother paused for a while and said painfully, 'You loved her so much, Abhi?'

Abhimanyu faked a smile and shook his head sideways as if dismissing the question. Keeping the baby on her crib, she moved ahead and held her son from behind, clasping him gently. And suddenly a painful lump came over his throat. Abhimanyu breathed out. He did not wish to cry...he knew he would. He was vulnerable and now with Mom hugging him, he knew that he would.

That evening, Mahima called up Abhimanyu's father during his lunch hour. She was on an international call, so she did not have the luxury of explaining everything. She used her experience with Ujjwal of all those years and broached the topic differently after asking of his well-being.

'Your son is adopting a child who lost her parents in the riots. An infant...not even a month old.'

Having put it like that, she had already blunted much of his ire. But that still did not take away the initial shock.

'But...how? He has a life of his own. He is hardly experienced in matters of parenthood.'

'We are way past that discussion...he needs our help. He wants me to supervise someone who could take care of the baby full-time. What do you say?'

After a long pause, Ujjwal said, 'Our son is different, Mahima... we did not raise him the way he deserved to be raised. He has this streak that makes him stand out from the rest.'

Ujjwal used the expression "stand out", which he had never used for Abhimanyu in the past. Mahima thought it was because he had enough time in London to ponder over his life. Particularly his relationship with his son. Although he was still hurt at Abhimanyu not joining the IIT, but he was at least prepared to visit Abhimanyu's premise on why he did so.

He also knew that no amount of coaxing or intimidation would work on him. Rather they had to figure out ways to ease it for him. They were after all his parents. Ujjwal and Mahima were still hoping that the matter would be sorted out in a few years when some relative comes ahead and claims the girl.

For now, it was decided. On Ujjwal's suggestion, they requested a poor and widowed distant relative of theirs to come to Delhi from Santpur. Seeta mami was alone and needed a home, and had also helped Mahima in the initial months of her motherhood. Moreover, she liked the Sharmas, thanks to all the help that Abhimanyu's grandfather had offered for her sustenance. Mahima knew Seeta mami would cherish the responsibility of raising a child and shoulder it till her last breath. They booked a train ticket for her and assigned their housekeeper at Santpur the responsibility to ensure her safe departure.

Later that day, almost around midnight, Mahima and Abhimanyu were watching her sleep peacefully. She would occasionally startle like infants do, open her eyes, look around and then lick her lips and doze off again. Abhimanyu would caress her forehead with his thumb and that would put her to deeper sleep. As he did so, he looked at his mother and asked, 'What do we call her?'

Till that moment, she had enjoyed many nicknames – Guddi, Dolly, Sweety – but now they had to find her a name that would be her identity for the rest of her life.

'She is ultimately a Sikh and I have always loved the name Simran. It's so pious; it means remembering the Almighty, like invoking Him with the purest heart.'

Abhimanyu smiled at his mother and knew that the little one had found a name. Simran. The most important name in Abhimanyu's life from that moment onwards. The name that would kiss his lips a thousand times every day. It would be his religion. The religion of a radical.

In a week, Abhimanyu received Seeta mami from the New Delhi railway station as the Gondwana train docked at platform number eight. From then on, everyday would begin under Mahima's watchful eyes as Seeta mami stretched Simran's legs and hands, and gave her a soothing olive oil massage. This was followed by an oil massage on her thick tresses. Abhimanyu watched the short, stout Seeta mami give Simran a bath carefully. He saw her stretching her own legs and placing Simran between them, the head resting on Seeta mami's knees. She would then carefully pour lukewarm water on the baby without startling her. Later, Abhimanyu would change into shorts and place Simran in an identical posture. But somehow, Simran could sense his discomfort and clumsiness in handling her. This would immediately be followed by a shrill wail and embarrassed, Abhimanyu would look at his mother and Seeta mami for help. Seeta mami would shake her head and tell Abhimanyu how she used to give him a bath as a child and how he was such a noisy kid. Abhimanyu, imagining being placed on a younger Seeta mami's thighs would turn his head away, as the women of the house laughed their hearts out.

But Abhimanyu kept his word. He would be up all night if Simran was unwell. He would gently press her to his chest and roam around the house all night humming his favourite lullaby, *'Surmai akhiyon me nanha munha ek sapna de jaa re'*. Even on normal days, he would put her to sleep, the lullabies alternating between *'Aa chal ke tujhe main leke chalun'* and *'Nanhi kali sone chali, hawa dheere aana'*.

There were times when he would be standing, holding her next to the window, the pristine light of the moon kissing her face. Abhimanyu would endlessly watch her face and occasionally kiss her gently. There were moments when Simran would gently open her eyes with an amazing glow emanating from her face. She would look back at her saviour and smile, yes smile. Abhimanyu was stunned when Simran did it for the first time. But soon, he realized that maybe this was Jaspreet's way of touching him from the world she was in now.

Because in those brief moments when Simran opened her eyes, she looked exactly like her mother. She smiled exactly like Jaspreet. The smile that was meant only for him. That smile he would never forget. It was surreal holding Simran under the moonlit sky next to the window and from there watching the spot where he and Jaspreet had met a year-and-a-half ago after India won the World Cup. He wished he had grabbed that moment with both his hands. Because if he had, Jaspreet would still be alive. He would often wonder if he had tried hard enough to save Simran's parents. To save Jaspreet's life. Maybe he should have reacted sooner and blocked the force of the bullet hurtling towards Jaspreet.

It was one such night as he stood next to the window holding Simran who had just fallen asleep. Thoughts from the past kept crashing on his mind like the force of an angry wave. Like a never ending trailer, the past kept replaying over and over again. The meeting with Jaspreet on that night, followed by that date at India gate, her marriage, her confession, the first sight of a pregnant Jaspreet, and then the cry. The cry from the roof with her hand stretched out. The journey through hell and finally the end. The half shut eyes and half a smile, even in the face of sheer helplessness. He was so disturbed that tears started streaming from his eyes.

And then, like an act of God, Simran raised her tiny right hand and placed it on his chest. Gently startled, Abhimanyu looked down. Her eyes were still shut, but her right hand was firmly placed on his heart. As if telling him, "I feel your pain, just as you felt mine. You rescued me, and in time, I shall rescue you."

And then someone spoke, 'Babu, beta go to sleep. Why are you still up?'

Abhimanyu wiped his tears and mumbled something like, 'I will!'

'Are you...?' She moved ahead and looked carefully at his face. Visibly embarrassed, Abhimanyu forced a smile and tried turning his head away, but could not. Mahima gently patted his back and Abhimanyu stood holding Simran in his hands, his eyes still fixed at that spot on the pavement.

Mahima knew he won't open up to her; she had tried numerous times. So she tried to distract him, 'What will Simran call you when she grows up?'

Abhimanyu was surprised at the question, 'I don't know. Never thought of it.'

'What about Babu?' Mummy smiled with a twinkle in her eyes. 'My all-weather friend?'

In years to come, Abhimanyu realized how prophetic his mother's words indeed were. He never desired to take the place of her parents. In fact, he had even retained her father's surname: Gill. The name in her birth certificate would be Simran Gill. He would rather be a friend, her Babu.

Simran brought out a facet in Abhimanyu that he or anyone who knew him, never thought existed – his vulnerability, his emotional side. When Simran was a month old, Simran would scratch herself and Mahima advised that maybe it was time to cut Simran's nails. It was a delicate job, as Simran was a restless kid every time she felt restricted or stifled. Once when Abhimanyu was cutting her nails, with little Simran on his lap, he was halfway down the nail of her middle finger when Simran suddenly jerked her hand. The edge of the blade poked her tender skin and a red dot suddenly appeared on the point of impact. The red dot started swelling as the blood started oozing from the minor cut. Abhimanyu gasped in horror. He looked at the cut and then Simran's face. She looked confused. It was her first exposure to pain, however little it might be.

'Mummy!' he shouted. 'Simran's bleeding. Mummy, she is bleeding!' He was panic-stricken and his hands shook.

Mahima ran towards Abhimanyu and saw the wound. She calmly said, 'It's a minor cut Babu.'

'No!' He shot back. 'The bleeding isn't stopping. We have to rush her to the doctor.'

'You get the first aid box and let me hold her!' He got up and started walking towards the cupboard to get the first aid box. Simran, though confused at the chaos, looked absolutely calm. Her eyes were following Abhimanyu as he rushed to get the cotton and then dabbed it with Dettol. Mahima suspected that Simran was amused by Babu's behaviour. It was only when Abhimanyu dabbed the cotton to the cut that Simran was startled by the sudden sting and then let out a feeble cry.

Abhimanyu said, 'Look Mom, she is crying. It must be hurting her a lot. I think she has ruptured some vein in her finger...'

Mahima shook her head and said, 'Abhi, you are panicking unnecessarily. You need to calm down.'

'Calm down? How can I calm down? Don't you see the blood? What if she catches an infection...she is a little girl... how can you be so casual about this?...'

'Abhi, shut up and look here!' Mahima finally raised her voice.

Abhimanyu looked at his mother and she pointed towards Simran who was now trying to curl her lips in a pout and cooing. Her eyes were fixed on Abhimanyu's face and she continuously kept making sounds, as if trying to have a conversation with him to calm his nerves. Yes! She was trying to talk to her Babu. She was trying to reassure him that as long as you are with me, nothing could go wrong. And she was smiling, as if amused at his behaviour.

'This definitely can't be the face of a child in pain, Babu,' Mahima smiled, gently patting Abhimanyu on his head. 'Look at her eyes!' Abhimanyu realized that Simran's eyes were exactly like her mother's. Blue. Her eyes that always reminded Abhimanyu of the mysterious ocean. Abhimanyu tilted his head and looked intently at Simran. Her eyes kept following him as he moved sideways. He was captivated by her eyes as God looked back at him. But she just didn't stop smiling.

Jagtar had moved his brother and sister to London within a month of the fateful carnage. They were safe with his widowed aunt in Southall who needed someone with her in her twilight years. But Jagtar had stayed back, still indecisive. He did not even know what he was latching on to, perhaps Abhimanyu. Or maybe that one trickle of hope that everything would be fine soon. Deep down, he wanted to hang on to that hope. But he was bitter, angry and ready to rubbish everything that was sacrosanct to him. Ironically, he was ready to rubbish even the bond for which he was latching on to India. The purest and the strongest he had known in his life.

Abhimanyu called Jagtar up, asking him to meet in Woodland Park. Abhimanyu thought it would help erase some bitterness from his heart. But Jagtar was unusually quiet, and understandably so. The deafening silence was the prelude to the storm which was raging at the horizon. This place meant something to the duo. It was a collage of memories; a ride through nostalgia for both of them. And that is why they would come back to this place over and over again. But today, Jagtar was barely recognizable to this place. The old memories came back, but only to haunt him. They were screaming to be heard, and Jagtar wanted to smash them to oblivion. In fact, something strange was happening to him today. He was uncomfortable with the man who had been his strongest hope for more than a decade. He did not know why, but he felt irritated sitting next to Abhimanyu.

Staring at a beetle trying to find its way through the foliage of grass, Jagtar said, 'Avinash Thakur!'

'What?

'The name of the Congress leader who led the mob that killed my father.'

'Are you sure?'

Jagtar smiled sarcastically, 'You should have given me this information, Abhi. You were the one to witness my father being torn apart. Instead of just reporting on that event, you should have named Avinash Thakur in your report. How did you miss out on this bit of the news, Mr Ace Reporter?'

'I was too shocked, Jagga. Why I could not save your father is a question that will haunt me for the rest of my life. But if Avinash Thakur was indeed there, I would have reported it. He must have left before I reached.'

Jagtar suddenly stood up, enraged and fuming, 'The whole world knows he was the one who provoked the entire crowd present there. How come you, my best friend, could not even give a small hint in your report?'

'That's because reports are based on the truth. And I did not have facts to support the claim. I spoke to many people, but none of them would come on record. Murmurs in a dark street don't make the truth, Jagtar. None of your so-called witnesses had the guts to come out and speak...'

'You and your hollow words! This is the least you could do for me.'

Abhimanyu could feel shame and heat rising inside him at the same time. Wasn't Jagtar being unfair to him? Did he not save his family's life? Should he not have been grateful to him for that? Did he not realize how his personal life had turned upside down with the arrival of Simran? Such thoughts would never have occurred to him some years ago, but things had changed now. They were not boys anymore; they had become men. And men say means things to each other.

And in a fit of rage and guilt, he said something he should never have, 'And you know well that you father had this coming.'

Jagtar hissed after a moment's uncomfortable silence, 'What?'

'You heard me, bro. He had it coming! You think a Sardar goes on distributing sweets after the assassination of Indira Gandhi and no one would notice him? He was asking for it!'

'Don't you dare speak a word—'

'Why? The truth hurts? Now do you realize how it feels?'

'No! *You* will never realize how it feels,' Jagtar roared. 'You will never realize what it feels seeing the mutilated body of your father. You will never realize what it feels when you haven't got over mourning your father's death and you lose your mother too. That is the hell that I am undergoing every moment, every bloody moment of my wretched life. I am so pathetic and helpless that I can't even kill myself because I have to raise my brother and sister. Damn them for being in my life! I wish I could join the Babbar Khalsas and my brothers fighting the brutality of the Indian state. I wish I could. But I don't even have the guts to do *that*. I see no hope in this country. Except for one! I was clinging on to this country only because of you. But today, by saying what you did, you have proved that you are no different than the others. I thought I would stay right here and get my brother and sister back when the time is right. But now, I know what every person of this country feels. Now that you have spoken, Abhimanyu Sharma.'

Jagtar left abhimanyu sitting there alone. The way it was to be for a long time to come. He just sat there with a mix of guilt and anger. He did not leave the park for another hour, and did not contact Jagtar for another week, giving him time to come to terms with his anger. It was only seven days later that he went to his house, not getting any response to his phone calls.

Abhimanyu had never seen the old woman who opened the door. He asked for Jagtar and came to know that he had left the country. 'Jagtar has not left any contact number or address. He said no one needs to know.'

Abhimanyu came to know that he had left India a couple of days ago with a plan to settle in Southall with his aunt. The old woman was Jagtar's relative from his village near Ludhiana. They had come just to sell off the property, the formalities of which had already been initiated by Jagtar.

Abhimanyu walked back to his motorbike, wondering if what he had said that day in the park was the trigger to Jagtar leaving the country. Probably Jagtar had been looking for an opportunity. Probably he wanted to demonize everything that was dear to him in this country, including his best friend.

The girl kept struggling endlessly. She threw her legs in the air in desperation, but he pinned her down in the mud, his strong body on her frail and weak frame. The grip on her wrists had finally stopped the flow of blood to her hands, and her fingers now lay anesthetized. Her lips were sewn together by black strings crisscrossing, piercing her lips, bloodied by the twisted imagination of the butcher who was now violating her. As she moaned in agony, he hissed. The guttural rasp of the predator. His hapless victim moaned in

anguish, and every time she tried to scream, blood oozed from the pores around her lips that were sewn together. It was a scene straight from hell. The butcher now dawned upon its prey and revealed himself. Shalini looked at him in horror. Abhimanyu smiled malevolently at his hapless prey...

Abhimanyu woke up startled. Shalini had revealed herself to him again. The girl who had been brutally raped in school in his presence. The one he had kept mum about. He was gasping for breath, his lips quivered, and his throat felt like the parched ground of a sun-scorched land. Every time he tried to suck in air, it hurt; the air passing through his throat feeling like a volley of needles. He stretched his right hand and reached out for the bottle of water. He gulped the entire water in one go, spilling it over his white T-shirt. He looked to his left. Her face bathed pristine by the moonlight, Simran was asleep, her head slightly raised and her hands clasped in a grip under her neck. Abhimanyu first raised his left hand to touch her, but then stopped midway. He bent down and gently touched the tip of his nose to her cheek.

The fragrance of innocence was an antidote to the worst possible nightmares. He moved closer to her and wanted to hug her to drown his fear. But he knew he could not. He could not risk waking her up. So he just lay next to her, hoping to exorcise his ghosts. Remembering the last time Simran had looked straight into his eyes, her assuring blue eyes whispering: 'You saved me, and in time, I shall rescue you back.'

1990

With tears lining her blue eyes, she looked at Abhimanyu and asked him, 'Babu, why does my mother never come for the parent-teacher meeting?'

It had been six years and Abhimanyu had been extremely protective of her on this subject. He had somehow sheltered her till now, but for how long? She had to face the world that would ask this question time and again to satisfy its ravenous curiosity. Her admission to the prestigious Delhi Public School at R.K. Puram was not tough, but what came with it, was.

The little girl with chubby cheeks and two pony tails had asked her in school that day, words coming out of her mouth in spurts, her eyes wide with curiosity, 'Why does your mother...never come for... the PTM?'

It was the first time that someone had broached the unnerving topic in front of the six-year-old Simran. Skinny and extremely fair, her pristine blue eyes had suddenly turned grim. She had wanted to answer, but stopped. Instead, she had pushed the lone golden strand of hair dangling in front of her eyes back to her plait.

'She's dead, isn't she?' A boy sitting right behind them with two missing front teeth and a lazy stream of muck oozing from his nose had interrupted suddenly, revoking the topic she wanted to escape. 'My mother said...Simran's parents died on the day she was born.'

'No! Babu said Waheguru needed them more than I did, so he called them soon!' she had wanted to say, but even she knew by then that it was a theory that was not entirely convincing. She could see the difference between her and the other kids. She could see mothers coming to pick up their children as their school buses stopped in front of their houses. She had Seeta mami. She would see children being kissed and spoilt rotten as their mothers carried them home. But her Babu would never reach home before 9. Other children would have their mothers take them to the park in the evening, and she had only the old Seeta mami for company.

The new Abhimanyu Simran had unlocked had nothing but love for this little gift of life. Despite being a senior correspondent with the *Times*, and travelling out of Delhi for special stories often, he ensured that he spent quality time with her. He even left office and dropped home in the afternoons on some days. That's when he would take her in his arms and prod her to tell him what all happened in school. Right from the grasshopper that stubbornly sat on the windowpane of her class; or the hapless tadpole in the puddle in the playground that Ishan grabbed with his bare hands and put in his water bottle. She would tell him things that the teacher taught them with animated expressions and Abhimanyu nodded in rapt attention. He would make it a point to have dinner with her and say a small prayer before having the first morsel. During bedtime, he would narrate to her stories he had made especially for her. She would listen to these stories wide-eyed. Abhimanyu had developed a trick to put her to sleep. And it worked without fail. As it struck 10, he would start massaging her forehead with his thumb. Simran's eyes would then start drooping, till she would fall asleep.

Abhimanyu was also religious about taking a day off, come what may. These were the days when Abhimanyu took her out to the zoo or the children's park or to a movie that she really wanted to see. He would also take her to his parents' place, who she fondly called Dada and Dadi. Her presence in the house filled them with joy that they had never felt. She was pampered and spoilt rotten by her "grandparents". But somewhere, the absence of the mother rankled. And it was increasing with her understanding of the world around her.

Abhimanyu sensed that she was a curious child; she also learned quickly. So he took to new ways of teaching her. He would devise games for her and spare no effort to bring her close to nature. At six, she had already been on a ten-day trip of Kerala, had been to the Andamans and Lakshwadweep, had roamed the streets of Pondicherry holding her Babu's hand bedazzled by the French architecture of the French quarters, had already been to a Safari in Corbett and Bandhavgadh and had already experienced her first fright on the beaches of Southern Goa as waves rose threateningly and her Babu held her in a tight embrace. She had even experienced the chill of the winters in Simla and had made her own snowman.

That day, it had been a nightmare as half a dozen children converged around her, firing bits of information that they had heard from the discussions of their own parents about Simran. The entry of the teacher after recess had saved her from the ordeal. In the afternoon, Simran walked towards Seeta mami with a blank but forlorn expression, in place of her usual scintillating smile. She never slept in the afternoon, but that day after having lunch, she went straight for the bed. Seeta mami had called up Abhimanyu out of worry, because Simran refused to utter a word.

Abhimanyu was about to go out for an assignment, but work always had to wait when it came to Simran. He had driven his second hand white Maruti car towards his house in R.K. Puram, wondering what could have happened to her.

Once home, Abhimanyu had come straight to her room. It had been instantaneous; just as he put his hand on her head, Simran had suddenly sat up, with eyes that had turned red and cheeks that had dark streaks of dried up tears.

Simran had buried her face in his stomach and just shook her head as she kept crying with a feeble whimper like sound. It wasn't dramatic but it was heart-rending for Abhimanyu who was baffled and shaken by possibilities of what could have happened. He started caressing her hair as he untied the knots of her plait slowly. He wanted her to cry her heart out before he started asking her questions. Abhimanyu could feel the grip around his stomach getting stronger as she dug her nails around his waist. Abhimanyu tilted his head and pressed his cheeks to her head, spreading his arms around her as she curled further inside her Babu. Like a baby inside a mother's cocoon, it was the safest and the most secure place for her in the world. The sound of his heartbeat reverberated across her senses.

'What happened, Simmy? My sugarplum...why are you crying betu? What happened?' he nudged her to raise her head and look into his eyes.

She shook her head, refusing to look at him. Abhimanyu had stopped caressing her hair by then. Irritated, she grabbed his hand and guided it back to her hair making a gentle grunt. Abhimanyu smiled and bent down to whisper, 'Do you know what we do to people who sulk?'

Simran whacked Abhimanyu's bum without raising her head. 'Ouch! That hurt sweetheart. Now I am not the one who is sulking, isn't it, sugarplum?'

Simran finally mumbled something that was barely audible to Abhimanyu, 'I am not a sugarplum!'

'Ok, so take your pick! What are you then, my chunkey apple pie?'

Simran dug her fingers in his waist, this time more strongly.

'Why am I been punished? I am neither sulking, nor am I being rude.'

With tears lining her blue eyes, she looked up at Abhimanyu suddenly and asked, 'Babu, why does my mother never come for the parent-teacher meeting?'

He had known it was coming, but wasn't prepared for it. She jerked him out of his reverie, 'What could be more important for my mother than being with me? Every child of my class has a mother... And you don't even let me call you Papa. Why?'

He was stunned by the child's innocent questions, now enmeshed in a sense of bitterness. She was not yet ready for the truth, for that would only multiply the bitterness in her. And this was not how he had planned to raise her.

He got off the bed and bent down on his knees, cupping her face in his hands. 'Now listen to me carefully Simran. Why your parents aren't there with you is a story that I will tell you, when the time is right...'

Simran interrupted, 'But why not now?'

'Because there is always a right time for everything. What did I tell you when you wanted to watch the movie *Tezaab?* That it isn't for children, remember?' She nodded. 'Similarly, there are stories that are not meant for children.'

He moved forward to kiss her on her cheeks. 'I promise you: when the time is right, I will tell you everything about your parents. Now do you trust me, Simran? Do you?'

Simran kept quiet for some time and then raised her head looking straight into his eyes. Her blue eyes were still scarred by tears. She mumbled something inaudible, but Abhimanyu knew it was a "yes". Abhimanyu pressed her tightly to his chest as his own eyes watered. Abhimanyu understood through Simran how children make one weak, even vulnerable. Because it is their vulnerability that haunts you. For life. Even when they become stronger, you still fear that they may fall or hurt themselves. And there are times they do. They get hurt and they seek emotional solace. That's what makes the bond so powerful.

Abhimanyu had a delicate and challenging task at hand. The last thing he needed was Simran filled with fear for school, because the questions would keep coming. He could not just barge in her school and ask her teachers to rein in the students. But he decided to speak to the teachers nevertheless, just to see if they could help.

It was unnerving for Abhimanyu to walk the corridors of Simran's school as images from his own past flashed across his eyes. The bleak and dark walk across the corridors of St. Mark's and the shrill sound of Matthew berating someone in some classroom. But here, it was different. It was brighter. Abhimanyu scanned the classes and realized that the teachers had grown younger over the years. They looked pleasant and smiled more while interacting with their students. He shuddered at the thought of leaving Simran with someone like Mrs Chaddha. He turned left at the end of the corridor towards class I-B and stood in front of the class. Simran was sitting in the first row, a picture of elegance and calmness. Her eyes were fixed on the teacher and even Abhimanyu's sudden appearance had not distracted her. The girl sitting next to her saw him and nudged Simran.

Simran looked at the man whom she trusted the most in this world. In years to come, she would realize that how this man dressed in a light blue shirt tucked in black formal trousers loved her so selflessly.

'Yes?' Mrs Bhatt asked Abhimanyu.

'Madam, my name is Abhimanyu. I wanted to have a word with you regarding Simran.'

Mrs Bhatt first looked at Simran and then trained her gaze back to Abhimanyu, 'Please wait for five more minutes, Mr Sharma. The waiting room is down the corridor, on the right hand side. We shall have the recess break and then I shall speak to you.'

He nodded and walked sideways to find the room. She appeared in exact five minutes.

'Mr Sharma!' Mrs Bhatt's strong voice echoed across the waiting room as she walked towards Abhimanyu. She was a well-built woman in her mid-thirties, immaculately dressed in a beige sari. Abhimanyu stood up seeing her, but she gestured him to sit down.

'I was expecting that I would meet you soon,' she said.

'You were?'

'Yes! I know why you are here. That day, I was standing outside the classroom hearing the conversation between Simran and her classmates; I knew this was going to happen.'

'So what do you think should be done?'

'What do you want us to do, Mr Sharma?' He looked confused, so she continued in an authoritative tone, 'The problem with such things is that the more you stretch them, the more they haunt you. I can't stand in the class and make an appeal to the students never to talk about Simran's parents. This will further accentuate the issue and isolate her. Instead, I think we need to tell Simran that it isn't her fault and she does not have to feel bad about not having a mother. It's also a challenge for you as a parent, Mr Sharma, for the years to come will test your parenting skills. The answers have to be with you. That day, I deliberately did not speak to Simran. I wanted to see how she feels and how you react to it.'

Abhimanyu weighed every word that Mrs Bhatt said. He was listening intently and she continued, 'I spoke to Simran this morning, and I am really happy on how she has taken the entire episode.' Her voice softened suddenly, 'You are doing a phenomenal job as a parent, Mr Sharma. Simran will be my student for a few years to come, and I assure you that I will keep an eye on her. But as I said, we can't be overly protective. She has to learn to take such things in her stride and become bold to face such situations...But you, as a parent, will indeed have to put in a superhuman effort to raise her. I am amazed how you actually decided to bring her up, knowing the amount of sacrifices you would have to make.'

Abhimnayu felt uncomfortable with words like sacrifice. It wasn't a chore or a sacrifice. Although it wasn't a decision made out of choice, but it defined him as a person now. Simran was the most important part of his existence. He found the talk of him having to make a sacrifice by raising Simran very patronizing.

He looked away and Mrs Bhatt realized that the talk was making him uncomfortable and restless. 'I am sorry to have raised certain uncomfortable issues, Mr Sharma, but if you seek a solution from me, then you will have to hear me out. And it's better that *you* feel the discomfort, rather than little Simran,' she said sternly.

'I am sorry, Mrs Bhatt, but I am as good or bad a parent as the others. She is no different to me than your child is to you. That's why I find this talk of having to make a sacrifice rather disturbing. I ask myself often: if not Simran, then what...what is the purpose of my existence? She completes me, Mrs Bhatt. That day when her parents were killed by a violent mob, it wasn't I who rescued her...it was she who saved me.'

Mrs Bhatt had been looking at Abhimanyu intently. She smiled and said, 'I am glad Simran has you. I have no worries about her future, Mr Sharma. None at all. He will watch over you,' pointing towards the sky she said, 'as you watch over her.'

On his way out, he waved at Simran from the door and she waved back with a hint of blush on her face. As he walked towards the school gate, he felt the restlessness dissipate slowly. The feeling of nervousness was diminishing gradually. He was driving towards Central Delhi, missing Jagtar so much. Wanting to sit next to him at Woodland Park and talk endlessly. He wondered what he would have said to him. He must have gotten married by now. Who knows, he must have a small child too. But did Jagtar remember him as he did? Every day?

The years that followed were tough for Abhimanyu, but greatly tumultuous in the history of the country. Abhimanyu reported the fires of the anti-reservation movement against the Mandal Commission that raged in northern India and changed the political character of the country forever. It spelt political doom for V.P. Singh, who gradually receded to political oblivion.

He also reported the re-election of the Congress party, that was preceded by an earth-shattering episode that brought back memories of the assassination of the former premier of the country Indira Gandhi and the riots that followed it – the brutal assassination of her son, Rajiv Gandhi. The man destined to become the Prime Minister for a second time was killed by a suicide bomber of the LTTE (Liberation Tigers of Tamil Eelam) in a political rally on 21 May 1991 in Sriperumbudur, Tamil Nadu.

As the news broke in Abhimanyu's office, he thought it was the handiwork of militants linked to the Khalistan movement. Memories of the anti-Sikh riots reared its ugly head again and he worried for Simran. After all, most people in his locality knew she was a Sikh being raised by a Hindu father. He was relieved when the truth was revealed. He was also relieved that there was no backlash against the Tamils living in the country. Perhaps the country and its people had matured after all, he thought.

But he was proved wrong once again. The patriarch of the right wing Bhartiya Janata Party, L.K. Advani undertook his most infamous Rath Yatra to rebuild a Ram temple in Ayodhya. This was where a structure called the Babri Masjid stood, built in 1528 by a Muslim King called Babur by felling a temple revered by Hindus. The country was on the edge again, and it finally culminated with the pulling down of the Babri structure on 6 December 1992. The riots that followed scarred the so-called secular nation and raised a new breed of radicals and militants amongst the vulnerable Muslim population of the country. The destruction of the Babri gave the ISI a new lease of life as it began its most sinister campaign in India by raising and building sleeper terror cells that remain its most potent weapon in scarring India over and over again.

As a repercussion, serial blasts hit Mumbai in 1993, carried out by the Muslim Mafia led by Dawood Ibrahim who would later become a strategic asset of the ISI, Pakistan's premier spy agency. This was war against India, from within, aided by the outsiders, much before the world saw its 9/11.

While the nation struggled, Abhimanyu moved from one riot to the other, from one terror attack to the other massacre, from one scar to the other wound – from one milestone to the other. But Simran was in the most important and formative years of her growing up too. Though she understood her Babu's unorthodox work ethic, she missed him when she saw other fathers play with their children. Babu would make it up by going on a long leave with her to a holiday destination. He would surprise her by turning up during the afternoon someday and taking her for a long drive. With Babu around, life was never a boring affair. And she had Seeta mami too.

1 November 1996

Simran's twelfth birthday! Abhimanyu left office early and was crossing the official headquarters of the Congress party at 24, Akbar Road. He was in a hurry to reach the birthday girl, but little did he know that the sight of something in his rear view mirror would change his plans.

He saw a man climbing a pole with a banner strung on his back. Nothing extraordinary about that; it was what was written on the banner.

> "WE WELCOME THE APPOINTMENT OF YOUTH LEADER AVINASH THAKUR AS THE GENERAL SECRETARY OF THE CONGRESS PARTY."

Avinash Thakur. The name hit him like 1000 volts of current. Like a powerful jab from an adversary who rises as you let your guard down. His head spun and things around him started getting blurred. He shook his head twice. And then again. He saw the banner again. He read the name. Again.

Avinash Thakur.

The man who led the mob in Tilak Nagar. The mob that killed Jagtar's father. The man Jagtar thought was directly responsible for his father's death. It was a chapter that Abhimanyu had erased from his life. Avinash Thakur had ceased to exist for him. But now, he had come back.

Avinash Thakur was climbing the political ladder of the biggest political outfit of the country, and very fast. Merely thirty years old, he had now become the General Secretary of the Congress. What were they rewarding him for, he thought. That too on the day they had killed Simran's mother? Suddenly a surge of restlessness and anger engulfed his senses. His eyes were fixed on the man climbing the electric pole. He had nearly forgotten that his car was in the middle of the road. His trance was broken by the continuous honking of an ambassador with a beacon behind him. Abhimanyu parked the car on the side and started crossing the road, his eyes fixed on poster with the bearded Avinash Thakur with folded hands. Even in that posture of humility, there was an unmistakable intensity in his eyes, a raw magnetic appeal. His sharp chiselled features accentuated the strength in his expressive eyes. As he entered the Congress Party headquarters, he saw a large group of political workers standing on the lawn to his left, surrounding someone who was sitting on a chair. Curiously, Abhimanyu moved ahead and raised his head to see the man surrounded by the large gathering. Just as he twisted his neck to have a closer view, someone patted his shoulder. Abhimanyu turned his head to face Samar Pratap Singh, the man who covered Congress for the *Times*.

'Kya Boss? Preying on my beat?' Samar smiled but could not hide the nervousness in his eyes.

'Oh, I don't have the discipline to cover a political party. I just came to check out this guy...Avinash Thakur.'

'Oh! You wanna meet him? He is right there,' Samar pointed to the man at the epicentre of the hubbub. 'But why? Anything special?'

Abhimanyu knew that Samar would keep pestering him till he assured him that he was not there to prey on his beat or at least give him a convincing answer about why he was there. He did not want to have a monkey on his back. So it struck him immediately.

'I...I am doing a special report on the rising youth political leaders, that's why!'

'Great! Then let me make your job easier. Though you don't need my introduction, but still...'

Samar pushed and shoved the men surrounding the chair and reached the middle of the gathering. There he was. Dressed in white kurta-pyjama with the sleeves pushed till his elbows. He was flipping the pages of a document that seemed like a list of prospective candidates in the upcoming elections.

'Hey Avinash!' said Samar.

Avinash Thakur raised his head and a wide grin appeared on his face. He stood up and raised his right hand to shake Samar's. Abhimanyu could see that the man was a couple of inches taller than him. He had big hands with long and strong fingers. Samar was short and looked like a midget standing in front of an overbearing Avinash Thakur. Abhimanyu realized from that distance that an air of haughtiness shrouded his face. He turned his eyes momentarily towards Abhimanyu, but he looked back at Samar without acknowledging his presence.

'Avinash, this is my senior colleague in the *Times* who wanted to meet you. Abhimanyu Sharma. He covers special assignments for the paper.'

Abhimanyu was amazed at how Avinash's expressions changed immediately. A few seconds ago, he had glanced at him and rubbished his presence as some non-descript friend of Samar. But now he had his intense eyes on Abhimanyu, an expression that wore the look of curiosity and deference.

'Of course. Mr Abhimanyu Sharma...our Government in Punjab wasn't too happy with your reportage on the so-called human rights violations in Punjab. But I was mightily impressed on how the radicals were brainwashing the peasants and using them as tools in their fight for a separate Sikh homeland. I am a fan of your reportage, Mr Sharma.'

Abhimanyu raised his right hand and placed it on his chest acknowledging his compliment and mumbled a feeble 'thank you'.

'But let's face it, Mr Sharma, if it weren't for the iron hand of our Government in Punjab, the Sikh militants would still be targeting our cities. Isn't it?'

Abhimanyu kept quiet and just smiled. Avinash Thakur raised his right hand, his eyes never leaving Abhimanyu's face and shook his hand. It was an intense grip. The palm had a rough feel, as if he had been working on the field for a long time. The grip bordered on intimidation. Probably trying to pin down a man whom he was meeting for the first time. Abhimanyu had absent-mindedly extended his hand and he could feel his bones sing under Thakur's powerful grip.

'So, what can I do for you Mr Sharma?'

'I am doing an article on the youth brigade of various political parties and I thought that it would be a great way to begin it with you.'

'Well, I am honoured and rather surprised. Because I have usually read your reportage from hostile areas.' Avinash smiled and patted Abhimanyu's back, 'Well, let me assure you...there is absolutely no hostility here.'

Samar let out a sycophantic chuckle as Abhimanyu nodded his head and said, 'A man needs a break, doesn't he? I have decided to—'

Thakur suddenly interrupted, 'Oh, come on! Don't say that you are now working for the features section. We would be really sad if journalism lost one of its cracking reporters. I hope you are not getting lazy.'

'I have always been lazy, Mr Thakur. Helps me, because my sources let their guard down when they are with me.' It was an honest confession that told of how Abhimanyu worked, but for some reason it appeared funny to Avinash.

Abhimanyu realized that Avinash was a charismatic man with an air of arrogance around him. He was appealing and loved to be surrounded by people, mostly his gang of sycophants. Avinash Thakur was feudal to the core, thanks to his landowner father in

Eastern Uttar Pradesh, his Zamindar ancestors in British India. He was always very close to the ruling class of the state. But Avinash had bigger ambitions: he did not want to start from the state. Rather, he wanted to make a mark at the national level. This is how he got into student politics after taking admission in Hindu College in Delhi. His father's links with the Congress made his entry in the student wing easier and the muscle that he carried with him landed him straight into the inner core of the students' politics of the University. His role during the 1984 anti-Sikh riots endeared him further to the bigwigs in the party. The important post of General Secretary in the Congress was just a matter of time.

That evening, Avinash, Samar and Abhimanyu went and sat in a hotel at Pandara Park. They ordered drinks over plates of tandoori chicken and mutton seekh kebab. Avinash Thakur did exactly what Abhimanyu had wanted: he let his guard down and spoke. Abhimanyu weighed each and every word that Avinash uttered about his family and his own rise in the Congress. At the end of two hours of conversation, he knew who he was dealing with. A good friend, but the worst enemy you could have.

It was only around 8 that he realized what he had done. It was Simran's birthday and he had totally forgotten about it. Cursing himself under his breath, Abhimanyu suddenly got up.

'What happened?' Avinash asked, more in the tone of a demand.

'I nearly forgot that it was Simran's birthday,' mumbled Abhimanyu.

'Oh, didn't I tell you, Avinash?' Samar interrupted. 'Abhimanyu has adopted a girl who was orphaned during the 1984 riots. Simran is like a daughter to him.'

'She is not an orphan,' Abhimanyu said sternly. His eyes were shutting and had streaks of red after a couple of drinks.

He repeated, this time forcefully, 'She is not an orphan.'

As he drove back to his house in R.K. Puram, he could sense a surge of anger inside him. Simran must have been waiting for him and he had made her wait for what? For the man who destroyed his best friend's world. The man who took away Jagtar from him, forever! The rage kept rising, and so did his car speed. It was only after he jumped a red light and nearly collided with another car that he realized he had lost control over himself. Just that one meeting with Avinash Thakur and he was on the verge of losing Simran and making her a real orphan. Abhimanyu slowed the car and parked it to the left. He was breathing heavily as a collage of thoughts struck his mind. The memories of the hospital where Jaspreet had lost her life, where he had seen Simran in a nursery for the first time came back. The last glimpse of Jagtar as he turned at the bend of Woodland Park, the last few moments of Jagtar's father as he frantically swayed his sword and the shot that took Jaspreet's life. And then he saw him. Avinash Thakur with his hands folded and the smile on his face. Abhimanyu clenched his fist and rammed it onto the steering wheel. It was already half past eight and he had failed in his promise to Simran.

When he reached the doorstep of his sixth floor apartment, Seeta mami was sitting with the door ajar. Her head rested on the palm of her hand, the elbow of which was placed on the bend of her knee. As soon as she saw Abhimanyu, she stood up with a grunt and walked towards the door.

'She just slept off a few minutes ago.'

'Where is she?'

Before Seeta mami could answer the question, Abhimanyu's wandering gaze stopped at the sofa where she lay. She wore the red salwar-kameez that Abhimanyu had bought a week ago. Abhimanyu walked towards her, his knees feeling weak with a strange anxiety that engulfed his entire body. As he bent down, he kissed her gently on her tender cheek smelling of jasmine.

Seeta mami whispered, 'Should I wake her up?'

Abhimanyu shook his head, feeling intense hatred for himself. How could he do this? How could he forget Simran's birthday for the man responsible for the mess in his life? Abhimanyu gently slid his hands under Simran and lifted her. He walked towards the bedroom, his gaze fixed on her calm face, her mouth slightly open with a gentle wheezing from her nose. His princess had slept off...waiting for him. What happened today was unpardonable. But what could he have done, he thought! How could he ignore Avinash Thakur? He felt as if someone was wrenching his heart. The restlessness was unbearable. He kept breathing in and out and kept telling himself: I have to get this man! I have to...at any cost! I shall not rest in peace till I have your head on a platter, Avinash Thakur.

Abhimanyu could feel a terrible vibe about the entire matter. The thought was disturbing, and something inside him kept telling him that the consequences could be disastrous. This was revenge after all. He looked at Simran and suddenly saw her expressions change. Her eyes were still shut, but a frown appeared on her forehead, as if having a bad dream. She moaned gently, as if in pain! Abhimanyu felt the turmoil in his heart now visible on her face. He suddenly got up and turned around to leave. But Simran's warm, tender and slender fingers wrapped around his wrist.

'You had promised me...' she mumbled, her eyes still shut.

Abhimanyu bent on his knees and hugged her, 'I am sorry, darling! It shall not happen again.' His eyes moistened, 'I had work and I could not wriggle out of it.'

Letting off the embrace and looking intensely into her eyes, he said, 'But it's not even 9. Do you want to come for a drive?'

Simran shook her head. 'I feel sleepy...very sleepy,' she mumbled. I have been waiting for you since four. I thought you would come early and then I drifted off to sleep.'

'Just forgive me this time darling. You know, nothing in this world is more important than you. But I just could not...'

Simran smiled and kept her right hand on his heart, the same way she had as an infant, 'You don't have to be sorry. You are the best Babu in the world. The best!'

That evening, Abhimanyu realized how much she had grown up. There was so much maturity in her eyes, the gravity, beyond her age. While she spoke, he felt the restlessness ebb away. He could feel her healing him from within.

'I wanted to say this to you had we sat in a restaurant, across the table...because I felt that you need to be told. But I want to say this to you now. I can see that you look distressed. Don't be! If I am the reason, let me tell you that no daughter in the world could be as lucky as I am. I am so lucky to have you...'

'Sshh,' Abhimanyu placed a finger on her lips. 'Don't say all this. We have a long way to go and we can do it together. Our journey has just begun.'

Simran moved forward and hugged him tight. Abhimanyu couldn't hold back his tears now. He stayed like that for what seemed like an eternity, and then...Abhimanyu heard gentle snoring. He gently laid her on the bed and tiptoed to the other room. After taking a bath and changing into his night clothes, he came and lay next to her, watching her sleep peacefully.

In a weeks' time, *The Times of India* published an article on the young Turks of Indian politics. Avinash Thakur was most prominent on the spread. The article would have never raised eyebrows had Abhimanyu not written it. He carried a reputation of filing reports from hostile spots of the country. So a feature, and that too bordering on profuse praise for Avinash Thakur, had to grab attention. In fact, a particular paragraph in the article created murmurs across the corridors of the party if Thakur had indeed gone too far this time.

> *On being asked if he saw himself as future Prime Minister material in a party that refuses to move beyond "the dynasty", Avinash Thakur said that anything is possible in a party that is dynamic and believes in changing according to times. He further added that they have survived as a party and have a legacy of nearly hundred years only because they have changed themselves according to the times. "It's too early to talk about being the future PM, but I haven't joined politics to be in the bottom rung of the ladder. I believe in giving my best and I feel that bigger the responsibility, the better you perform."*

No one could have dared to say that in the party, but then, Avinash Thakur was different. He was close to the right people. He was active as an activist when the martyred PM was alive. In fact, he was supposed to be with him in Sri Perumbudur, but a last minute change in plans saved his life. This is precisely the reason why he believed that destiny had grander plans for him.

For Thakur, there was nothing like a good massage to the ego, and the report had served its purpose. The Editor of the newspaper saw the article only after it was published and that too when brought to his notice by a peer in the industry. He was more curious than shocked. He reached office and called Abhimanyu to his cabin.

Lighting a cigarette and blowing the smoke from the window next to his chair, Pranay said, 'I just don't see the merit in this report. I can see that it has been published only because it was your report. Had I known about it, I would have never let it go. But you know very well that with my commitments, it is virtually impossible to keep an eye on each and every word that goes in the newspaper. So tell me Abhimanyu, what's the spin? Why have you filed this report?'

Abhimanyu smiled, 'There is always a spin. You know very well that things never are what they seem to be.'

'Particularly when it is you. So tell me, why?'

'You have to trust me on this one, chief. I assure you that I have a plan and you will get to know about it soon.'

'I don't care,' Pranay said sternly. 'I need to know what is that you are climbing at. I am your Editor after all.'

'Okay,' Abhimanyu paused for five seconds and then spoke, 'To put it brutally, I can say only one thing...entrapment!'

'Explain.'

Abhimanyu narrated his plan with the acumen of a strategic expert. Pranay was all ears and listened in to each and every word. It was the first week of November and there was already a chill in the air. It had struck 5 on the clock and a sudden darkness started swallowing the city. Pranay kept dabbing his cigarette butt on the ashtray as a black crow came and sat on his window. The constant cawing by the crow initially did not disturb Pranay, but then he banged his hand on the window and the black angel fluttered across to the building nearby.

It was now the waiting game for Abhimanyu. He had to wait for that phone call from Avinash Thakur and then make his next move. He didn't have to wait for long but the arrogant sonofabitch Thakur did not make that call himself. Rather, he sent across a message. The conduit was Samar Pratap Singh. Samar walked across to Abhimanyu and asked him if he was free in the evening as Avinash Thakur wanted to meet him and that they could have a few drinks like the other day. Abhimanyu refused. He did not want to have the monkey hanging around him. Samar Pratap Singh could be an irritant in his plans. So he said that he was busy. But he did make a call to the Congress headquarters. To Thakur's direct number.

'I guess my article hasn't left a very good taste in your mouth, Mr Thakur.'

Avinash laughed aloud, pleasantly surprised at the voice at the other end of the phone. 'I must say, you indeed have, Mr Sharma—'

'Don't call me Mr Sharma. You make me feel ancient like my father, and I don't like him much.'

Avinash laughed again. '*Khoob jamegi apni*. You are interesting, Abhimanyu.'

'I can only say the feeling is mutual. I would have never written what I have had I not seen what I saw that day.'

'What?' Avinash was curious.

'A spark...a brilliant one. But if not directed properly, could have disastrous consequences.'

'I am touched. I know what praise does to a man, but a genuine one is what I can make out. I think we have to meet soon.'

'I think Saturday evening would be great,' said Abhimanyu.

'Same place?'

'No, let's try something new! I am my boss's favourite and he is a member of the Aristocrat Club in Mehrauli.'

'That's a brilliant idea. But the treat is on me.'

'Not this time, Avinash. I am sure there are going to be many opportunities. Let me be your host this time.'

It was Abhimanyu's turf. It was his treat. That was the best way to disarm him. The prey was marked. The master of conspiracies was on an overdrive.

That Saturday, Abhimanyu was already there four hours in advance. He had to be sure that everything was in place and had been taken care of. Avinash Thakur arrived at thirty-four minutes past seven. Abhimanyu was waiting in a private room that oversaw the swimming pool teeming with children, and odd bodied aunties and uncles. As they walked in the pool water, their flab shook like jellies. Abhimanyu shook his head and a smile grazed past his lips. His eyes stopped at a nymph who had just stepped out of the pool. She had bronze skin and black hair. She walked at the edge of the pool wearing a black bikini and her cleavage shivered as she carefully placed her steps on the wet poolside. Men with fat bellies ogled at her, as some stretched their underwear with the slight tension between their legs. The women stared at her with jealousy. She looked unperturbed by the attention, yet the arrogance on her face suggested that she seemed to be enjoying every bit of it. She was exquisite, no doubt. She had a perfectly rounded bottom with not a bit of extra flesh on it. She occasionally licked her upper lip She sat with her right leg over her left one, glancing over her watch, seemingly waiting for someone.

Suddenly, a firm and powerful hand grabbed Abhimanyu by his shoulders, 'I see that you have an eye for detail and talent, Mr. Sharma.'

Slightly surprised, Abhimanyu turned around and saw Avinash Thakur in a black full-sleeved shirt and blue denim jeans.

Abhimanyu smiled and got up raising his right hand to shake Avinash's hand, 'So the Thakur is in a new avatar.'

'Well, the Thakur loves this avatar only. Just that occupational hazards do not give him an opportunity to slip into something like this more often,' Avinash proudly pointed towards his shirt and trousers in one movement of the arm.

'So what's it going to be Thakur?'

'The usual...whiskey - Royal Salute 21.'

Abhimanyu smiled as he shook his head, 'A feudal lord to the core; always wants the royal salute, doesn't he?'

'It's scary to meet people like you...who know you inside out.'

'Well, as you said, I have an eye for detail. But correct me if I am wrong Avinash, you reveal yourself only to people whom you like, don't you?'

'As I said, Abhimanyu, it's scary to meet people who know you so well.'

Abhimanyu said gesturing to the waiter, 'Maybe a little change will extend your innings in politics a little longer.' He turned towards the waiter, 'A royal salute 21 and vodka with orange juice. Sixty ml.'

'Just vodka? I mean, why such girly stuff?'

'Oh, I don't have a chauffeur, Mr Thakur. You have to sit on the back seat; I have to drive back myself. Moreover, it's your company that matters, not the drink.'

Avinash looked at the girl by the poolside and asked, 'So you are interested in girls?'

'Who isn't?' Avinash nodded. 'But yes, my interest is not like the Thakurs of yore, immortalized by Bollywood. Babes in choli-ghaghra running across the fields, and then a Thakur grabs and violates her.' He shook his head as he spoke.

Avinash gave a hearty laugh and said, 'You really believe in that characterization of the zamindars of India, Abhimanyu?'

'You know Bollywood! They end up dramatizing everything.'

'Not this for sure,' Avinash Thakur suddenly interrupted and Abhimanyu gaped at his face. He broke into a soft laugh.

'But seriously Avinash, do Thakurs actually do all that in their havelis?'

'Let me put this honestly to you. It's all about power. If I feel that violating someone makes me feel powerful, I will do it. It's all about that high that power gives, like no other. I mean, do you really think a beggar will enjoy fucking an apsara? There is no better aphrodisiac than power.'

'So you won't mind forcing yourself on a woman against her wish?'

'Well, if it gives me a high, why not? But hey, I am the people's representative. I gotta nip it in the bud, man! The elections need a clean image of me.' Another hearty laughter followed, and Abhimanyu laughed with him.

As the first round of drinks arrived along with two plates of assorted kebabs, the conversation drifted from politics to ambitions to sex. It veered around family and came back to politics again. It swerved towards education and then back to ambitions. Abhimanyu realized that it was the perfect beginning to the plan that was being carried out. The huge laughing Buddhas placed at every corner of the room stared blankly at the two, as round after round of drinks arrived, only to be consumed by Thakur's insatiable lust for power and praise. His eyes were bloodshot but not shifting; his hand was totally stable. His voice had lowered down and Abhimanyu knew he had to play it carefully now. Thakur was at his vulnerable best; the opportune time to strike.

'You miss the martyred PM, don't you?'

Avinash's expressions changed suddenly. He took yet another sip and said, 'Times were different then. I was with him in every tour that he undertook nationally. In fact, he even took me to an international tour once. But now, we need the family back. We desperately need it back. These idiots will finish off what is left of it otherwise.'

'Just curious. What endeared you to him?'

'Well, my father and his grandfather had been very close, and the association extends up to the freedom struggle. Our village is just sixty kilometres from Allahabad. Not far from Panditji's constituency. I was always politically inclined as I had seen my father dealing with these men of power. My father had raw power, but I desire something beyond that. I consider myself a polished man. This is where politics comes into play. This is why I shifted to Delhi, contested student elections and won!'

'And?'

'And what?' Thakur looked a little puzzled as Abhimanyu was raising the stakes.

'I mean there must have been some incident that put you in that inner core of people, the privileged ones.'

'Well...till Mrs Gandhi was around, I was confined mostly to students' politics. But her death gave an opportunity for me to step into Akbar Road. You know, in politics, we have conduits. They ease our way to the corridors of power. My role during the 1984 riots endeared me to these so-called conduits. Once I reached Akbar Road, I knew he liked young blood around him. But he never knew of the invaluable role that I had played during those times.'

Stunned at Avinash's utterance, many things were running through his mind. Thakur was clearly caught off guard as the Royal Salute 21, his truth serum, worked wonders. Despite wanting to, he did not say anything to counter Avinash. Rather, he changed the topic, but still did not veer too far from the one they were discussing.

'You really fascinate me Avinash. In you, I see the rise of an institution.'

Avinash brushed his hand, 'Oh, come on! Even a big head like me knows that you are flattering me.'

'No, listen to me! What I mean is, in you, I see ambition. I see a plan to meet that ambition. I see an urge, the hunger to achieve that goal, unapologetically and if you don't mind, unremorsefully. I don't see pretence in you, which is such a refreshing change. I think young blood like you will revolutionize Indian politics.'

'Oh, the sound of genuine praise is always so sweet, isn't it, Abhimanyu?'

'It is, indeed. I am really impressed at your theory about power. It's so simple, so honest. I mean, all of us feel it deep inside, but no one has the guts to accept it. No one, but you, Mr Thakur!'

While Avinash nodded, Abhimanyu turned his head towards the pool. The hot babe now had company. A young male who looked like her boyfriend, considering that he was suggestively caressing her waist. Avinash followed Abhimanyu's glare and said, 'Tonight they are gonna fuck like mad, like there is no tomorrow.'

Abhimanyu shook his head and smiled. He saw Thakur staring at the girl intensely. He breathed heavily and shuffled uncomfortably in his seat, probably uneasy at the desire raising its head. Avinash took a big gulp from his glass which was big even by his own standards. The impact was immediate: Avinash's head started spinning. He grabbed the arm rest of his chair and rested his head back. Abhimanyu watched him intently and waited for him to regain his senses.

In about three minutes, Avinash raised his head and his eyes met Abhimanyu's.

'I really want to know what happens when power is coupled with anger.' Abhimanyu left the question open ended, waiting for Avinash to do the talking.

'That is the biggest high a man can have, Abhimanyu. Imagine a mob of a thousand men at your call. Imagine your adversary begging for life. Imagine acting God. You know the best thing about revenge is when you have the ways and means to carry it out. When Mrs Gandhi was killed, it was like your mother being murdered. I am glad that I was able to get all those people who rejoiced at her death. I am glad...And it was such a high. It was my first lesson in mob justice.'

Abhimanyu was turning uncomfortably in his seat, sensing the blood rise within him. His ears had gone totally red because he knew he was on the verge of the breakthrough.

'How come we never met on the streets? Ha ha ha! You must be reporting then, isn't it?' Avinash was drunk, but could still think, Abhimanyu made a note.

'I never really got the chance to meet you. Alas! So, how did this anger manifest itself on the streets?'

'Well, the police had orders to stand by and not interfere…that much was clear. It only made the job easier for us. It was such a high seeing those sardars shiver in fear every time we entered one of their localities. I remember the first time I hacked a sardar. It was such a rush! But I still can't forget that one sardar on the terrace…'

Abhimanyu was all ears now, very attentive.

'Every time I am high on alcohol, and think about him, I have a hearty laugh. I mean it was nearly comical, how that sardar in Tilak Nagar was swaying his sword. It was great entertainment. Finally we got him. I still remember, on my way back to home, we kept laughing. The joy of killing him was double as we knew that he was a pro-Khalistani Sikh.'

Abhimanyu said, 'But you did kill many who were probably nationalists. I am sure you changed many who loved this country.'

'You know, Abhimanyu, I was young. I was raw. And I was angry. If you ask me, would I do it again if given a chance? No, I would not! But ask me if I am remorseful of what I did. I am not. I killed those sardars because of what I felt after Mrs Gandhi's death. I would never do it again because I know it changed many lives for the worse.'

Abhimanyu slid back in his sofa as he shook the ice at the bottom of his glass that once had vodka and orange juice. A smile appeared and vanished within seconds. He looked at his watch and his face contorted. Avinash gestured to ask him what had happened.

'I had to call up my Editor and thank him for letting me bring you here under his membership. Can I go and make a call, if that's okay with you?'

Thakur gestured with the sway of a hand.

Abhimanyu walked to the phone booth and dialled his Editor's direct number. 'Yes, I have him.'

He walked back to the cabin and saw Avinash pouring himself yet another large one. He could see from that distance that his hand was still steady. He was amazed at his capacity.

'My boss is elated to hear about you, and has been praising you more after the report I did. He would be joining us here.'

'So is that a signal for me to go?'

Abhimanyu registered that Avinash had clearly missed the 'us'. He was totally drunk. 'Come on, Thakur! You know what I mean. I would love it if you could join us for dinner.'

Avinash swayed his hand and said, 'No, not today. Maybe some other day! Enough of drinks now. Time for some flesh. Time for the feudal Thakur to do some hunting. But yes, I have to say that it was great talking to you. It felt as if I was unburdening myself. '

'On record?' Abhimanyu smiled.

'Sure, for you...why not?' He cackled. Abhimanyu smiled back.

Avinash Thakur sat there for another half-an-hour and then left. Abhimanyu had to wait for Pranay and others. It was a meticulous plan where not one, but a few more people were involved, the contours of which were about to reveal themselves soon.

In an hour, two men entered the cabin. One of them carried the laughing Buddhas one by one and the other slid his hand under the table to remove the wires. It was a sting operation, where not one, but two agencies were involved. Pranay and Alpana Kumar, a journalist with a private TV news magazine named *Kaal Shankh*, entered the private room where the laughing Buddhas were taken. *Kaal Shankh* was a weekly video news magazine and Alpana was a long time friend of Pranay Sengupta. It was Abhimanyu's idea to involve a television medium as well, for the impact of the sting operation to be maximum. He knew well that the government-controlled Doordarshan could never ever air this sting. So the private TV news magazine.

The report on Young Turks had been a set up to entrap Avinash. To ensure that he became comfortable with Abhimanyu. He knew the pressure points and what would work; what were the buttons he needed to push to get Thakur. Two Sony handycams had been fitted inside the stomachs of those laughing Buddhas. As a safety and precautionary measure, they had also bugged the table by placing a spy recording device that Pranay had procured from his friends in the RAW.

They planned to air and print the sting a day before the parliament was scheduled to meet. That would shake a government which was already riding on crutches and was in a minority. It was a political volcano which could impact other names that were often named in the anti-Sikh riots. It could result in a chain reaction that could engulf many more.

The recording was perfect, with no audio or visual glitches. Now was the crucial task of packaging and carrying it out in the most secretive manner because the government would leave no stone unturned to muzzle it. Avinash Thakur would leave no opportunity to see that it does not get aired or published. If revealed, he would turn into a rabid beast and would go to any limit to see that it does not get aired. But the D-day was still a week away. Till then, it had to be guarded, so that it did not get leaked out.

Samar Pratap Singh, the man who covered Congress for the *Times* was someone who could be described as a fixer in the lexicon of the world of journalism and politics. The bosses were aware of it, but he would also do the dirty work of the management. Hence Pranay Sengupta, in spite of having intense hatred for him, had to keep him in the job, that too covering the most important political party of the country. Samar also knew how to massage the Lala's ego, the proprietor of the company. He was the conduit who introduced the Lala to the bigwigs of the political parties. Hence, he served the purpose of the company in more ways than one. That's why he had access to every department of the newspaper.

That day, Pranay was not around and Samar was flirting with his attractive personal secretary Sonal. Samar was a harmless flirt, and the girls knew of his links with the Big Boss, so he always got an audience from the ambitious ones. Sonal was all ears to some random tale that Samar was narrating to her. Sonal's cabin was just outside Pranay's room. Suddenly, she heard a phone ring on Pranay's direct number. She got up to enter the room and attend to the phone call, and Samar playfully followed her inside. As Sonal entered the room followed by Samar, he saw this huge spread of newspaper cuttings on Pranay's table and lot of random documents. A curious one and to top it, a journalist, his eyes scanned the contents of the newspaper cuttings. His eyes kept moving from one newspaper cutting to another, one document to the other. The look of befuddlement grew as he saw more. There was only one thing in all these documents and newspaper cuttings.

Information about Avinash Thakur.

He moved ahead and had a closer look at the reports. Pranay had encircled a few lines in all the reports, which weren't many though! Samar grabbed his head and started rubbing the bald portion. Something was going on and he was not involved in it. A surge of restlessness coupled by rage filled his chest as he tried to exhale the hot air inside him. He was possessive about his beat and this was a clear violation of what he thought was a reporter's right.

Suddenly Sonal called out for him, keeping her hand on the mouthpiece of the phone, 'Can you please talk to this gentleman? He wants to speak to one of the reporters. I have to fetch a document from my desk. Will be back in five minutes!'

'Sure!'

'Remember, he is Pranay's uncle. An old man of 90. Just humour him till I come back.'

'Sure Sonal! You can relax....'

Sonal left the room and Samar took the phone. He sat on Pranay's chair, indulging the old man in small talk, though mostly with monosyllables. But his mind was on Avinash Thakur and the newspaper cuttings sprawled on the table. He looked at Pranay's drawer and wondered if it was open. He looked at the door and then reached out for the drawer with his right hand, ensuring to shut it when Sonal walked in. Samar grabbed the knob with trembling hands and slowly pulled it out.

Some documents. Some transcripts. Like a conversation.

Samar had a closer look and his eyes caught a glimpse of a part of the transcript.

Abhi: I really want to know what happens when power is coupled with anger.'
Thakur. That is the biggest high a man can have, Abhimanyu. Imagine a mob of a thousand men at your call. Imagine your adversary begging for life. Imagine acting God.

What the fuck is happening, he thought. What is this? Abhimanyu had done an article on Avinash Thakur recently. He had been curious then also, but this...this is something else. What does this transcript mean?

Samar moved his hand inside the drawer to have a closer look at the transcript but then, suddenly, Sonal walked in. Samar pushed the drawer inside, just in time to escape Sonal's view.

Okay sir, I have to go now. Sonal is here with the information you wanted...talk to you later sir.'

Samar gave the phone back to Sonal who whispered a thanks to him. Samar winked at her.

But as he walked back to his desk, all kinds of theories were floating in his head. A swell of emotions filled him. Mostly anger. How could they do anything on Thakur without telling him? He had a right over the party and particularly Thakur, who was a fellow "Thakur"! Samar shut his eyes and placed his head on his desk. But his mind was trying to figure out the mystery behind the transcripts. The newspaper cuttings and the documents. And then he raised his head with a jerk.

Abhimanyu only did special and investigative stories. He could never get involved in a story like "Young Turks of Indian politics" unless there was spin to it. And he probably knew what that was! They were up to something on Avinash Thakur. And he needed to know what.

Samar went back home and stood on the balcony of his fourth floor house in Patparganj. His mind was constantly on the documents and the newspaper cuttings that he had seen on the Editor's table.

Abhi: I really want to know what happens when power is coupled with anger.

Thakur: That is the biggest high a man can have, Abhimanyu. Imagine a mob of a thousand men at your call. Imagine your adversary begging for life. Imagine acting God.

 Acting God? Why would Thakur act God? What was the high he was talking about? A mob of a thousand men? What the hell did that mean?

Samar turned around on his left heel, angry at why they had left him out of whatever they were planning. And why? The Editor would never get involved with something that was at most a half page spread, if it indeed was! It had to be something big and Abhimanyu was involved in it.

He wasn't sure what he was to do. But the thought that was continuously haranguing him was: how could they leave me out of it? How the hell could they? He knew if he went to the Editor asking for answers, he would instead have to answer questions that could put him in a bit of a bother. But he had to seek answers.

Later that evening at the Congress headquarters, Avinash Thakur was on the phone with someone and the look on his face suggested that he was talking to a girl. In the corner of the room sat the fifty-year-old Bhaiyuji Maharaj, Avinash Thakur's burly 6'4" tall bodyguard. The thick white moustache and thick hands that could crush someone's skull were forgotten in his peaceful eyes. He had been Avinash's father's bodyguard till Avinash shifted to Delhi. Though Avinash was talking loudly, even lewdly, to this girl on the phone, Bhaiyuji's eyes were fixed on the door and his expressions stoic.

Suddenly Samar appeared and knocked. Bhaiyuji got up, but Avinash gestured for Samar to come inside. He sat on the seat in front of Avinash.

'Okay, we need to meet soon. You have to make me happy too. Why should I be spared from the pleasure!' He laughed loudly. 'Okay, I will hang up and will see you in the evening at my place. I have a visitor.'

'So Samar...what brings you here?'

Samar shifted in his seat, his eyes fixed on Avinash Thakur, still trying to figure out what may have happened. Still trying to figure out what those transcripts meant. Still in two minds whether he should speak to Avinash about the transcripts and become a 'traitor' to the *Times*. But he was burning with retribution and also had his loyalties towards 'the Thakur'. Plus, he had to repay him for all those 'favours'.

'I am not going to mince words. I just want a few answers from you.'

'What are you talking about?' Thakur's face suddenly became stern.

'Did you meet Abhimanyu recently? I mean did you speak to him about power or anger or mob justice?

As if struck by a massive blow on his chin, Avinash started feeling dizzy. He was drunk in his conversation with Abhimanyu, but the conversation was very powerful. Something that could never have escaped his mind. But he was shocked how Samar knew about it.

'I don't know what you're talking about. Why are you asking me?'

Samar looked towards Bhaiyuji Maharaj and said, 'Can we have some privacy?'

'No, we may not! Bhaiyuji is more than family. You may go on.'

Pausing for ten seconds as his eyes shifted from Bhaiyuji and Avinash, Samar moved ahead and spoke in a whisper, 'I have seen some transcripts on my Editor's desk where some conversation you had with Abhimanyu has been documented. We do it only when we sting someone...or if we have interviewed someone important. Now Abhimanyu had already interviewed you. So I don't see any reason for him to interview you again. And going by what I have seen, they are planning something really big on you. If it is just an interview, then it's okay. But if it is something else, I thought you should know.'

He could feel a panic attack unravelling inside him as Samar spoke. Blood rose and his ears turned crimson. He immediately knew what had happened. A senior journalist had stung a senior Congress leader during Indira Gandhi's regime and it was still fresh in his memory because the story itself had raised questions about ethics in reportage and whether journalists should cross the Lakshman rekha while reporting. And now he had been stung. Rather betrayed. By someone whom he had started liking. He was flattered to get the attention of a journalist like Abhimanyu. What he did not realize was that he was after all a journalist. Someone who carried the reputation of being an investigative scribe. How could he not see it coming? How could he bare himself like that? He also remembered how Abhimanyu had unknowingly warned him during the fag end of his conversation...'On record?'

For the first time in his life he felt like slapping himself hard. How could he be such a fool? How could he unburden himself in front of a complete stranger? He knew where this was going. He knew what Samar meant. He had realized that he had probably committed political suicide. And now, the self-loathing was changing into anger. Extreme. The quintessential rage that had epitomized the Thakurs of his family. The wrath that could crush adversaries and blow them to oblivion. Samar had told him what he wanted to know.

'Samar, thank you. I will never forget this favour. I know what you are trying to tell me. But I want you to leave now. I am afraid that I will not be my civilized best. I may say something that could hurt you...or I may hurt myself. Thanks Samar, you have been a great friend.'

As Samar left the room, Avinash Thakur clasped his hair and rested his forehead on the desk. He raised his head again, his eyes staring at the vacuum ahead but his mind focused on one man and one man alone. Abhimanyu Sharma. He wanted to focus all his anger, all his hatred for this man. His eyes were bloodshot and for that rare moment, his hands were shaking. For the first time, he could feel that he wasn't in control of himself. He surely wasn't. So he bowed his head again. Sensing his discomfort, Bhaiyuji moved ahead and started patting his hair. He then moved his hand gradually to the back of his neck and started caressing it gently as if giving a massage to small child who was in pain. This was Avinash's most potent memory of his childhood. This was Bhaiyuji's way of putting him to sleep when he was restless. But sleep today was out of question. He was not going to sleep for many nights to come. He had been done by an adversary who attacked him where he was most vulnerable. Trust. He had trusted Abhimanyu with the most damning incident of his life. He probably would not have felt this rage had Abhimanyu done it in the conventional way. But this was anything but journalism. This was personal. *Why?*

And then, he remembered. His adopted daughter. A Sikh orphan.

Avinash turned towards Bhaiyuji and said, 'Do you know what Abhimanyu Sharma's weakness is?'

Bhaiyuji said almost apologetically, 'No bachwa'.

'Simran, an orphan! Do you know where she studies Bhaiyuji Maharaj?' His tone had a cold menacing feel to it.

'I can find out.'

'DPS R.K. Puram!'

Bhaiyuji stared at him and he continued, 'And do you know what we do to enemies and adversaries who don't play by the rules of the game?'

He knew the answer to that question. Bhaiyuji Maharaj locked his hands, his eyes speaking of an unspeakable horror. The one that

Avinash wanted him to carry out. He was, after all, just playing by the rules of a game that Abhimanyu had decided – *Saam, Daam, Dand, Bhed*.

Abhimanyu was crossing the road just outside his housing complex, when he saw a truck coming towards him at a menacing speed. He was paralysed with fear at the resolve of the driver, who seemed to follow him, irrespective of which side he shifted.

Not very far off and not much later, Mrs Bhatt was taking the class when a burly, white-haired, white-moustached man knocked at the door of the class.

'Yes, may I help you?' She walked towards the man who stood at the door of the class.

'Madam, my name is Yashwant Sharma. I am a relative of Mr Abhimanyu Sharma, guardian of Simran. He has met with an accident—'

'What?' Mrs Bhatt cupped her mouth with her hand in horror and then looked back at Simran.

'Yes madam! He is admitted in Safdarjung Hospital. He was hit by a truck and Simran needs to be with him. I have come to take her.'

Mrs Batt turned, her eyes meeting Simran's. She must not have heard them, but that only made her task tougher. She was reminded of the cardinal rule in such circumstances; many would have forgotten that during such times of duress. She remembered that she needed to call up the phone numbers registered with the school to confirm the news before sending the child with a stranger, or at least send an escort with the child.

She said, 'I am afraid as a rule I will have to call up Simran's guardian...just to check! It does not mean that I'm doubting you. Not at all! Please don't take me otherwise.'

'It's okay madam. I understand,' said the old man.

Bhaiyuji Maharaj knew this was not going to be as easy as he had planned. But then, he had been in situations worse than this. He had kidnapped people from places no one could imagine.

Mrs Bhatt ran towards the administrative wing that had records of contact numbers. Back in Simran's class, Bhaiyuji Maharaj's eyes scanned the class. He did not know what Simran looked like. But that was hardly the issue.

In the administrative wing, Mrs Bhatt drew out a register with lists of students of VI-A. She turned the pages till she came to the alphabet "S" and then to Simran. Simran had three numbers in front of her – her residential number, her father's official number and the telephone number of Abhimanyu's parents. Yogita first dialled her residential number.

'Hello,' Seeta mami picked up the phone.

'Hello, I am calling from Simran's school. I want to know if everything is all right. I mean is Abhimanyu Sharma okay?'

Confused, she said, 'He has left for office...'

Not a very convincing answer. She said goodbye and dialled Abhimanyu's office number.

In Simran's class, Bhaiyuji Maharaj was getting restless. He knew time was running out. He kept looking at his watch and the corridor that the teacher had taken to go to the administrative block. His ears were tuned in to all sounds around him now. He glanced back to the class, moved in a few steps and said, 'Simran...Simran beta!'

Simran stood up. Bhaiyuji thanked his stars that there was only one Simran in the class. He walked up to her and said, 'Simran beta, your father Abhimanyu Sharma has met with an accident.'

Simran yelped a muffled shriek and tears started rolling down her deep blue eyes.

'You have to be there beta, he wants you to be there.'

Simran started crying. She asked, 'Is he going to die?'

'No beta. God is kind; He will take care of him. But he needs you. We are getting late beta.'

Simran came out of her desk and walked towards him. 'Let's go!' she said.

Bhaiyuji lifted her up in his arms and started pacing towards the exit gate of the school. He knew that he could not walk too fast as that might arouse the suspicion of the staff in the school, what with Simran's already teary eyes.

'Can I speak to Mr Abhimanyu Sharma?' Mrs Bhatt spoke into the phone again.

'Connecting you,' said the operator. Something inside her said that she needed to hurry. Time was indeed running out. After ten seconds that felt like ten days, someone picked up the phone.

'Abhimanyu here.'

'What?' Mrs Bhatt's heart sank. She felt that she would faint any moment.

'Mrs Bhatt this side. I was told you had an accident.'

'What?' It was Abhimanyu's turn now to feel fuzzy with shock.

'Yes, someone has come to pick Simran up, saying you had an accident.'

There was a painful silence as a barrage of thoughts hit his mind. He tried to make sense of what was happening. And then he shouted into the phone, stunning everyone in the news room around him.

'Stop that bastard! Now!'

Abhimanyu ran across the newsroom towards the car park, colliding with many in his way. He shouted across to one of his crime reporters, 'Someone is trying to kidnap Simran.'

Stunned, everyone saw him running as if his life depended on it. It really did.

Back in school, Mrs Bhatt scampered across the corridor shouting for help. She was incoherent as the school staff just watched her running like a woman possessed. She feared the worst and something told her that the man will not be there. She hoped he hadn't taken Simran along.

She saw the door of her classroom; she could see that the man wasn't there. She ran faster, still shouting incoherently, and teachers came out of their classes to witness the spectacle.

Bhaiyuji Maharaj was now nearing the exit gate. There was a guard who was watching him from a distance. The guard was supposed to take a written permission from people who had come to pick up their ward. He stood up seeing the old man walk towards him.

Outside the gate, a man sitting in a white matador with black glasses looked at Bhaiyuji Maharaj. A ghost of a smile played across his lips. Bhaiyuji Maharaj drew out a revolver from his inside his kurta.

Mrs Bhatt was like a woman possessed. As she turned a bend, she collided with the second guard who was coming out of the toilet door.

'What the hell are you doing here? You should be at the gate.'

'Madamji, I was...'

'Run, someone is trying to kidnap a child!'

The bulky guard ran slinging his rifle across his shoulder. He was some distance away from the exit where another drama was about to unfold. Bhaiyuji knew that the unarmed guard would ask for papers. So he started walking faster as he neared the exit. The guard sensed urgency in his steps and raised his hand to stop him. But to his shock, Bhaiyuji drew out a revolver and shot him in his thigh. The man fell on the ground. The shot reverberated across the ground and everyone stood stunned as it echoed across.

Simran gasped in horror; her mind could not fathom the pace with which things were unfolding around her. She saw Bhaiyuji putting the revolver back inside his kurta. She stared at him in mute shock, as if she had lost her voice.

The guard running towards the exit heard the shot and realized that the other guard was shot. He had the only gun in the school with him.

The man in the matador took the cue and revved up the engine of the vehicle. He drove it towards the exit gate and in no time, Bhaiyuji boarded the back seat of the matador with Simran next to him. He banged the door of the matador shut.

The guard ran towards the exit and saw his fellow guard down on the ground clasping his thigh. Without attending to him, he ran out. His fellow guard gestured towards the matador that was manoeuvring through the bends and other cars. He raised his gun to fire but held back because the shot could also hit the girl in the matador. Mrs Bhatt caught up with him. He turned towards her and his eyes said it all. She started running towards the matador in a futile effort to stop it.

They say miracles happen when you expect them the least. As the matador gathered speed, Bhaiyuji Maharaj slid open the black glass to spit out the tobacco in his mouth. As his head came out of the window, he turned it around in curiosity to look at the exit gate of the school. The guard saw this. He was not a marksman, but he raised his gun and aimed. And he shot.

The car had crossed a bumper, and Bhaiyuji Maharaj's head was still outside the window, albeit facing the driver. He had not seen the guard taking aim, and by the time he heard the shot, the bullet had found its mark. Bhaiyuji Maharaj's temple exploded and blood splattered to the front seat. The driver shrieked in horror, 'Bhaiyuji! Maharaj, my maharaj.' He cried in agony.

All this had been too much for Simran already, seeing a dead man beside her only added to her panic. Blood gushed out of his head as his eyes stared at her, motionless, yet ferocious. The driver was now shouting hysterically and his eyes were behind, looking at the burly Maharaj crumbling in the backseat. He clearly could not see what he was driving into – a huge banyan tree.

Bhaiyuji Maharaj was brought dead on arrival; the driver succumbed to his wounds five minutes after his arrival in the hospital. Simran had lost consciousness. Initially the doctors could not understand if the unconsciousness was because of the impact with the driver's seat or something else.

It was later that they realized that it was just shock. She had slumped under the seat after losing consciousness when Bhaiyuji Maharaj was shot, which was good in a way. She had been saved the impact of the car hitting the banyan tree. When Abhimanyu reached the hospital, she was still unconscious. He was followed by a barrage of press photographers and a few video cameras of the news magazines that existed during that time, including *Kaal Shankh*. An attempt to kidnap the adopted daughter of a journalist from a reputed newspaper was big news. And everyone wanted to know why. Information flew thick and fast. By evening, the reason was clear – the most dramatic sting operation conducted by a newspaper with tremendous ramifications. Everyone across the print world knew by now that it involved Avinash Thakur, the bright, young and rising star of the Congress.

Pranay Sengupta selectively leaked news about what the sting was all about. He knew that he could now no longer wait till Sunday to release the news. And the kidnapping attempt had provided an ideal platform for the launch of the news. The next day, every newspaper was splashed with the front page news of the attempted kidnapping from a reputed school and the daring effort by the guard to save the girl. There were also pictures of the guard, Abhimanyu and Simran. The newspaper reports also had a box item about the sting done by the newspaper.

A day later, the biggest sting operation of independent news was launched in the *Times*. *Kaal Shankh* followed suit. The entire market was flooded with bumper prints of the story. People, bureaucrats, politicians and the government officials rushed to buy the prints of the magazine.

It was political mayhem. There were widespread protests in Delhi and Punjab that extended up to the weekend. The only ray of hope for the government was that the sting did not implicate any other senior leaders who were often accused of leading mobs and killing Sikhs in those four days of carnage in 1984. The sting was more about one person – Avinash Thakur. The man in question was untraceable.

Mahima and Ujjwal had rushed to the hospital as soon as they heard about it. Mahima and Abhimanyu stayed at the hospital during the night and Ujjwal would go back to Abhimanyu's house in R.K. Puram which was walking distance from the hospital. Simran was discharged a week later and Abhimanyu's parents shifted in with him to take good care of her. It had been a week, and Simran hadn't uttered a single word. Even when they reached home, she merely stared blankly. She was scared. She would deliberately avoid eye contact with anyone. Initially Abhimanyu thought it was just because of the traumatic experience and that she would recover soon. But he was wrong. Simran was facing the biggest battle of her life and she had lost the urge to fight. She lay motionless, watching the fan and the ceiling till her eyes shut with sleep. She would not even go to the loo herself. She would urinate in the bed at times. It was shocking to see a twelve-year-old reduced to such a mess.

And the police discovered the man responsible for her state a week later, in an isolated farmhouse in Mehrauli. Dead. With tremendous alcohol content in the blood. He had shot himself in the head.

Abhimanyu and his mother were sleeping in the same bed, Simran tucked in between them. Simran slept as if in a cocoon; curled inside herself as if trying to shut herself from the world. The shot fired by the school guard still echoed inside her. The lifeless head of Bhaiyuji slumping at her feet kept striking her mind like a colossal wave. She had never seen so much blood, though her destiny was linked with it ever since she was born. Simran would get startled in sleep, her eyes would open and then wearily shut in a pattern. That night, she was unusually restless. Her body jerked and then calmed down. Jerked and calmed down. And then suddenly, she stood up.

She stared blankly at the darkness in the room, her eyes wide open. The expression on her face was not familiar. Her eyes wore a look of dementia. They kept shifting rapidly, and the fingers of her left hand froze in a gnarled way. Her right hand was perfectly stable. As if one side of her body had separated from the other. And then she slowly docked her head, locking her chin to her chest. Her right hand that was perfectly stable started shaking, and then as if in a rhythm, started patting the bed.

The thumping was light, but then she suddenly rose her right hand high and slammed it hard on the bed.

Thump!

The loud slam on the bed woke both Abhimanyu and his mother, who woke with a shriek. Abhimanyu immediately turned on the light and turned his head towards Simran.

It was the scariest thing he had seen. Scarier than any memory of his life. She looked possessed. Tears were rolling down her eyes, that otherwise seemed covered by a film of crazed calmness. Abhimanyu held her right hand that was still thumping the bed uncontrollably. With the other hand, he held her chin and raised it slowly. He was caressing her hair while Mahima held on to her shoulders. Simran turned her head towards Abhimanyu and her chest started heaving. Abhimanyu thought she was about to cry and crying was good. That would release a lot of pent up torment in her. But instead, she raised her other hand and swung it across Abhimanyu's face. Drops of red glistened across three lines on Abhimanyu's face – one across his eyelids and the other two below his left eye. She looked at him as if he was the most hated person in the world. Her eyes said it all. It was at that moment that Abhimanyu realized it – Simran was the victim, the price that he had paid for revenge.

How ironical! All the twelve years of her existence, he had tried to shelter her from the memories and the events surrounding her birth. In the obsessive desire to get the man responsible for the murder of his best friend's father, he had unknowingly pushed Simran back in time. Twelve years back. Simran raised her hands to strike at him again, but Abhimanyu clasped her to his chest and she kept struggling with cries that travelled to the other rooms also. Ujjwal and Seeta mami rushed to the room to find Abhimanyu holding a restless Simran to his chest and Mahima trying to calm her down by caressing her back. Tears welled in Abhimanyu's eyes and he wondered in horror at what was happening to Simran.

Ujjwal came and sat at the edge of the bed; Seeta mami stood at the door watching Simran in horror.

'I think we need to take her to the doctor,' Ujjwal said.

'What doctor? She is losing it, Papa...she is losing it.' The exasperation in his tone was distressing.

'Then maybe we need to meet a psychiatrist.'

Abhimanyu shifted his eyes from Simran to his father, his eyes accusatory. *He would never understand a child. She is not mad!*

'I know it sounds disturbing, but she needs help. The only other option I see is to wait...and hope that she is healed with time. But this is a move fraught with a lot of risk. It's a call that you need to take, Abhi.'

Abhimanyu looked at Simran who had buried her face in his chest. She was shaking and had tucked her arms under his shirt. Her cold hands trembled on his skin. Her pain was his to feel. Slowly but reluctantly, she drifted into sleep. But Abhimanyu could not.

He wondered if he had done the right thing by adopting her. He had desired a normal life for Simran, and this was not that. Had he sucked her into a vortex of fear and retribution, the one that was his, and only his to endure? He twitched his toes as numbness overcame them. As he pushed his shoulders back and moved his chest forward, a stinging pain ran across his spine. His eyelids felt heavy and his calf muscles hurt. A sense of déjà vu overcame him. He hadn't known this feeling for a long time now. But he hadn't forgotten it. The exact moment. That day when mayhem engulfed Delhi. That day when he lay on the bed. Stung by the viral. The day that changed it all.

'I know what to do Papa, but I need your help.'

'What?' Ujjwal suddenly became curious.

'What do you think Daddu would have done had he been alive?' asked Abhimanyu, knowing the answer to his question.

Ujjwal knew what Abhimanyu was thinking. 'You knew him as much as I did; maybe more, Abhi. He would have probably asked us to bring her to Santpur.'

From the look on Abhimanyu's face, he knew that this was what he had in mind.

'I really want to take Simran to Santpur. I don't know but something deep inside me tells me that it will work. I don't know how or why, but it will!'

He turned to his mother and said, 'I can't do this alone. I want your help and I promise you that I shall never ever bother you again on any other matter. Just this last time...'

'Shut up!' Mahima looked furious. 'Why do you speak to us like this? Do you get a high in shaming us? We are your parents Babu. We shall go and stay there till Simran is fine.'

With deep hesitation he said, 'The only option left is taking her to a psychiatrist and this is one thing I don't want to do. I don't want to walk that path. I don't want to believe that anything is wrong with her mind. I know it's going to be difficult, but I will not give up. I can't afford to. It will be like breaking her trust. Jaspreet's faith in me...'

There was an uncomfortable silence as everyone in the room stared at Simran who was now fast asleep. Abhimanyu had lost everything in Santpur the last time. He hoped to regain it this time. Not for himself, but for little Simran.

Abhimanyu was engrossed in his work the next day at office, when his phone rang.

'Is that Abhimanyu?' The velvety female voice on the other end had an air of familiarity.

'Yes. Who is this?'

'Someone from your past, dying to meet you. Can you please meet me in Connaught Place? I want it to be a surprise'

'I have no times for games, ma'am. I have had a lot of drama in my life recently to meet someone blindly like that.'

'I know, and I am sorry for that. How is Simran?'

'She's...err. I am sorry but unless you identify yourself, this conversation will have to be terminated. I am sorry for sounding so curt.'

There was complete silence on the other end. Abhimanyu said, 'Hello, are you there?'

'Hmm,' said the voice with a deep breath. Abhimanyu could feel that she was smiling. With a second's pause she said, 'Do you remember our last meeting at the airport?'

The cold breeze from the window open next to him suddenly got cooler. His head felt dizzy and that was surprising. The sounds around him got muffled.

'Shweta?!'

'I am impressed, Mr Sharma.'

'Where are you? And what are you doing?' There was a sudden urgency in his voice.

'I came back from London three months ago. I needed a change and my publishing house needed someone in Delhi, so I jumped in.'

'You're working in a publishing house? I thought you would be a writer. Have you written any books?'

'No, I could not. Life has kept me busy. Meet me for dinner,' she said. 'Rather, let's meet earlier so that I have more time with you.'

Abhimanyu breathed in and said, 'I wish I could see you this evening. I have to take Simran to a doctor.'

'Things are bad, isn't it? Well, if you do change your mind, I stay in Defence Colony. It's my dad's house. I stay there alone.'

'And your dad?'

'He is still in London.'

'Did you get married?'

'Abhi, I am not going to answer any of your questions now. Or else I might lose the small chance I have of meeting you, mister journo!'

'Why do you say so? You had left me high and dry.'

'Really? I don't remember!' she smiled.

'Why would you? I guess you got a kick out of it, didn't you?'

'We need to meet, Abhimanyu Sharma. You can then remind me of all my sins. I promise you that I shall atone for them...all of them.'

Abhimanyu kept listening to her and kept picturing her too. What must she be looking like now? What if staying in London had turned her into a fat English cow? He was curious but there was also a rush of adrenalin inside him. He was also getting restless. Life had been miserable for him in the past few weeks and he needed a break, but he had to take Simran for a check-up before they left for Santpur. Yes! They had decided to leave for Santpur in a week's time. But there will always be a tomorrow. There will always be a second time. She was not going to leave Delhi. He could always meet her later. Tomorrow. But a strange restlessness ran across him.

What should I do?

Simran's appointment with the doctor would only take a couple of hours and then he could meet Shweta. But then he would not be able to leave Simran after reaching home; she needed him while she slept. It was just one day and his parents could manage it just as well. But he also knew Simran had not slept without him ever since the incident."

'Are you still there?'

The rush of thoughts was suddenly broken by her silken voice. 'Yes I am!'

'Well you take your time Abhi and do let me know when you are in a position to meet me. There is so much to catch up. I would love to know about the extraordinary life that you have been living.'

Abhimanyu smiled, 'Trust me, I wouldn't wish it even for my enemy. But yes, looking at Simran, I am ready to play that in a loop for myself...forever. She gave me a purpose. Anyway, what's your number?'

The next call he made was to his home, and informed Mahima that he will arrange for a taxi to take them to the hospital and back. That he had some urgent work in office.

But soon after, a sudden surge of guilt overcame him. He felt his cheeks going red and his ears warm. With shame. He started pacing in the corridor restlessly. But the feeling just multiplied.

He thought of cancelling the date, but then realised he hadn't even informed Shweta that they are meeting.

Abhimanyu kicked the wall. Cursed himself on how easily he had ignored Simran for someone who at best was a relic of the past.

It was only around six in the evening that he made the call.

'Hi, it's me. Abhimanyu. Do you still want to meet?' He said with the pang of guilt refusing to liberate him.

'Are you sure? I thought you had work.'

'It got postponed.' He lied.

'Great! I know of this place near my house that serves great coffee and the garden restaurant is amazing. Very romantic. So, if you want to meet early, like seven-ish, we could meet up.'

'That sounds like a plan.'

Abhimanyu stood at the edge of the road in front of the garden restaurant. A valet had parked his white Maruti and he had decided to wait outside because the restaurant was empty.

He saw a black BMW approaching and it slowed down as it came nearer. The valet sprinted towards the car. He opened the back door of the car while the chauffer remained seated in front. His heart began racing, not sure if it was indeed her. The feeling of excitement had dwarfed everything else including the guilt that had enmeshed him not so long ago. He stared at the door of the car, but it seemed that the person sitting was taking more time than usual. And then she emerged, her eyes looking straight at him.

She walked towards him, and he realized that nothing had changed since that day at the airport. She still wore that air of arrogance around her. She did not look as tall as she used to, but then those were the times when he was shorter than her. Her open hair with curls at the end rested on her shoulders. She still had the bronze skin, the first thing he had noticed about her in the principal's room. She wore a long flowing dark coat and dark trousers with a V-cut white top. She ruffled her hair as she walked towards him. And then a smile appeared on her face, just like that day at the airport. Shweta expected that Abhimanyu would make the move of either hugging her or extending the hand, but he stood there. Her face glowed as the light from the lamp post kissed her face. She had the same eyes, proud, with a hint of fatigue. Her lips... yes he remembered them and as he stood in front of Shweta that evening, a whiff of strawberry teased his senses. The taste was still so portent inside him. There was something new in her. A hint of tenderness in her eyes, perhaps.

'Am I just going to stand here like that, or is somebody going to hug me?' she said. Her silken voice had a prominent British accent.

Abhimanyu moved ahead and hugged her, and the fragrance of her hair filled his senses. Even in that chilly December evening, he felt warm. She raised her head and gently kissed his cheek. It was electric. The touch of her tender and sumptuous lips to his cheeks ignited memories of the past. He felt a pleasant tension between his legs, and was embarrassed.

'You still smell the same,' she teased him.

'And you still look like a dream.'

She smiled and gestured for him to walk inside. They entered the restaurant nestled between thick foliage of various trees and Abhimanyu was pleased by what he saw. 'I have never been here, and I must accept that it is beautiful place.'

'I am still finicky about taste, places, food...and men.'

'Really!' Abhimanyu paused in his stride.

The expression on her face suddenly became serious, 'I appreciate what you're doing, Abhi. It's indeed commendable.'

With a hint of irritation on his face he said, 'I did not want to make it public...but it was unavoidable, I guess.'

With a tender fondness on her face, Shweta kept looking at him. Embarrassed, Abhimanyu bowed his head and looked at his own feet. Like old times.

'You haven't changed Abhimanyu Sharma, not one bit! You are still the boy from St. Mark's, only more handsome.'

Abhimanyu sensed he still had the ability to blush. Or it was just her effect. They walked towards their cosy table and he realized that she was indeed such a dream, the perfect woman. But a high maintenance one.

Abhimanyu's gaze went to her perfectly manicured slender fingers with a skin-coloured nail polish. They were slim, yet not frail. Those were the fingers of a woman who knew her mind and who did things by her rules. As she jerked her head back, the V-shape blouse revealed itself further. The light from the bulbs above the trees caressed her cleavage and she noticed him checking her out. Shweta smiled. And Abhimanyu knew why. He bowed his head and bit his lower lip.

Raising her right hand and ruffling his hair she said, 'You are still a boy, the boy I left behind. I should have taken you with me.'

'You should have, Shweta. It would have saved me from so many nightmares.'

Shweta crossed her legs, her face a mix of many emotions. Abhimanyu realized that time indeed hadn't changed her. This lady had sat on the teacher's chair like a queen, her legs crossed and her toes caressing each other in her black stilettos. Shweta had taken off one of the stilettos and curled the toes that looked tantalizing and sensuous for a miserable Abhimanyu.

She did the same again: she gently stretched her toes as if easing off the pain in them, after removing one of her black bellies. And this time too, she saw him staring at her feet.

'Why can't you stop checking me out, Abhi?'

'I am sorry. It's nothing.'

'Come on, tell me! I know you better than that.'

'Just memories of another day. Remember that classroom on the day of your farewell party? Each and every moment is so vivid in my memory.'

'Wow, I am surprised. But except for a few dramatic moments, I don't remember much,' she said.

'Weren't most of the moments we had dramatic? Right from snatching the chance to represent the school in the story writing completion—'

'I loved doing that, I loved your misery then, though on second thoughts, I do remember apologizing to you, albeit half-heartedly.' This time she smiled laden with mischief. 'But tell me, Abhimanyu, you never found a woman for yourself?'

'Hmm, I have been on and off women. But nothing concrete. You?'

'Well, I am not into women.' She laughed, her head rocking back.

'You know I did not mean that.'

Shweta raised her right hand and cupped her right cheek in it, her elbow resting on the table and her eyes digging deep into

Abhimanyu's. The playfulness disappeared from her eyes; she started looking pensive.

'My father left India for the woman he loved. He discovered three months later that she was sleeping around with someone. It broke his heart and he took to the bottle in a big way. I was helpless and he did not care. It was a nightmare. It was only when I had an accident in which I fractured my leg that he realized he was punishing me and not that bitch for breaking his heart. He paused on the booze, but it did not heal his heart. Five years later, he had his first heart attack. That left both of us shattered. I grew up looking after him and he...looking for a cure for his broken heart. My father was a wealthy man and financially we were never in a difficult spot. My dreams of making it as an author just vanished. I mastered in languages and studied Chinese and French, which meant working for Consortiums and companies and earning big bucks. This is where I met Yang!'

Abhimanyu was drawn to each and every word she spoke and as she mentioned Yang, her eyes turned bleary. Abhimanyu did not know why, but he extended his hand and held hers.

She said, 'Yang was traditional, Chinese to the core. It was an amazing time in my life. Dad and Yang really started liking each other. It was one big happy family we had. And mind you, we were still not married. And then one day, he had to go to Chicago for a business meet. I was supposed to go along, but was held back due to some urgent work. He left for Chicago a week later, but not before proposing to me. It was the happiest day of our lives. And then...'

She paused and looked straight into Abhimanyu's eyes.

'I received a call from a common friend in Chicago that Yang had a brawl with someone in a strip club and that he was admitted in a hospital. I rushed to the airport and just before boarding the plane, I called up my friend to ask about Yang.'

The tear entangled in her fine eyelashes dripped on her cheek. Abhimanyu intertwined his warm fingers around hers and she felt comforted.

'He had breathed his last two hours after they brought him to the hospital. When I reached Chicago, I stared at his corpse blankly, wondering that even if he had lived, this would have been the end of the relationship. I was told by the police that he was drunk and had he insisted on having sex with the stripper. She refused and her boyfriend intervened. I didn't even know he used to drink. I could not believe it till I saw the post-mortem report myself. I had already seen dad drinking himself to a heart attack, but couldn't understand what was Yang's provocation. And most importantly, he could force himself on a woman? Molest her?'

Shweta withdrew her hand from Abhimanyu's and wiped the tears off her face. 'That was two years ago.'

As the waiter served the soup and the appetizers, the conversation gradually drifted towards other issues. Abhimanyu narrated his own tumultuous tale after she had left for London. They were amazed at how much drama their lives had endured. They hoped that they would emerge out of it soon. As they sat together with their fingers intertwined, they could feel the rising warmth between the spaces of their fingers.

'I would like to be hugged,' she said with an expression that bordered on desire and vulnerability.

An hour later, they stood in front of each other in her first floor apartment in Defence Colony, in front of her door. Abhimanyu held her slender waist and gently pushed her towards himself. Shweta rested her head on his chest. She clasped his back, and held him tight with both her hands. The smell of her hair coupled with the warmth of her embrace and the chill in the air was intoxicating. His fingers felt the warm skin between her back and her perfectly rounded posterior. He was gently rubbing his ring finger on her skin; she was digging her fingers into his back. The gentle moan proved to be the perfect start to what was turning out to be a sensuous evening. Shweta raised her head, her eyes locked into his. His gaze shifted from her eyes to her lips, as they opened up slightly.

'You remember them! Don't you?'

Abhimanyu moved closer, smelling her cheeks and teasing her neck with the tip of his nose. Shweta's lips longed for his. Abhimanyu relished every moment of the touch as he filled his senses with her fragrance. And then as his upper lip touched her lower lip, they froze. As if time had never moved from that time in school.

Abhimanyu whispered just before he drowned his lips in hers, 'Don't run away this time...'

Shweta gasped as he slid his hand inside her blouse feeling the warm bronze skin of her back. She clasped his hair with both her hands and their lips got entwined in a passionate embrace. Abhimanyu's hands moved up. With his thumb and forefinger, he unhooked her bra and traced the lining as it slackened. The tips of his fingers were teasing the lower part of her breasts while his lips drank from hers. His fingers moved up, and Shweta moaned loudly. He could feel her nipples taut with arousal. Shweta started unbuttoning his shirt as the embrace of the lips got even more passionate. She raised her hands and he removed her blouse; what he saw was a perfect specimen of a woman's body. He paused for a while he looked at her breasts. His breath was still uncontrollable and his gaze shifted from her breasts to her eyes. Strands of her dark hair with streaks of golden lay scattered across her forehead and eyes. She was breathing heavily too. But that momentary pause was as sensuous as the passionate embrace.

Abhimanyu smiled and saw desire in her eyes. 'I want to taste you, relish every part of your body.'

He carried her in his arms to her bed, memories of that day in senior wing playing in his mind over and over again. The memory coupled by the chemistry between them made that night, made loving her, the most amazing experience of his life. They climaxed together for the first time that night, and they did not lose sight of each other. She had promised him that she would not leave him this time. So she looked directly into his eyes till that final burst when she jerked her head back and moaned sensuously.

That night, they made love all over the house: the bathroom, the kitchen, the storeroom, and even the balcony as traffic zoomed past the inseparable bodies. The chill of the night did not matter as they lived the moment over and over again.

It was only at five in the morning that they dozed off. A couple of hours later, Abhimanyu woke up with a startle.

'I have to go,' Abhimanyu got into his clothes.

'Now who's leaving me?' she smiled.

'This is the first time I have been away from home, away from Simran since that day.'

'It's okay Abhi...you don't have to explain. I understand,' she smiled.

Abhimanyu bent down and kissed her forehead and then her lips. Shweta spread her arms around him and hugged him tight one last time that day.

'Just pull the door outwards and shut it. I don't want to be raped by the milkman,' she giggled.

Abhimanyu first frowned and then shook his head at her attempt at dark humour.

Abhimanyu got into the car and drove towards his house. His mind was still remembering the moments from last night, and then Simran. A sudden pang of guilt overwhelmed his senses. Suddenly, the beautiful moments of the night before started vanishing and the thought of Simran drove a wedge through his heart. He pushed the accelerator and drove like a maniac towards his house. When he reached his house, he saw his father pacing frantically in the balcony. Something was definitely not right.

Abhimanyu scampered towards his house with all kinds of weird thoughts striking his mind. The door was open and he looked around for Simran. He saw her lying in Mahima's lap, clasping her tight, her eyes shut, cheeks stained dark with dried up tears.

'Where have you been all night?' Ujjwal's voice was barely a whisper, but had an edge to it.

'I was at work. Why?' he lied.

Ujjwal rose and walked towards the bedroom gesturing him to follow. Abhimanyu's eyes were fixed at Simran whose eyes were shut tight.

Ujjwal shut the door behind them and shouted, 'I searched for you all night. I went to your office, I spoke to your colleagues, I even visited the police station. I visited the bloody morgue...' Abhimanyu noticed that his father's eyes were bloodshot; he hadn't had a wink of sleep.

'Just to see if my son is alive,' his voice started breaking. 'Last night we saw hell...we saw Simran wailing as the most important man of her life was nowhere to be found. And now that we have found him, he lies. Shamelessly!'

'What happened, papa?'

'What happened! She kept waiting for you, she would not sleep till you came, that's what happened. We kept telling her to sleep, but she would not. Finally she dozed off at 11. Only to wake up again at an hour later. And you were still not there. I have never seen something as painful as that; the cry of that girl was heart-wrenching. She kept telling us that even you have left her, that even you have abandoned her. Just like her own parents. She kept banging her head on the wall...she vomited half a dozen times through the night. She even lost consciousness once. Mahima had to rush her to the hospital as I was away finding my son. She had to take an auto at 2 in the night because *you* were *working*. Thank God the auto-wallah was a decent chap. Thank God that after administering her medicine, the hospital dropped your mother and Simran back. But you know what? She still could not sleep. The medicine did not work. It did soothe her nerves, but not her heart. The heart that you broke, mister Abhimanyu Sharma!'

Abhimanyu dug his knees in the floor and bent over, hiding his face in the cup of his hands.

'I am not questioning you. You are an adult and have a right to live life on your own terms. But she does not understand this. You can punish us, but you cannot do that to her. Not even unknowingly.'

Abhimanyu raised his head, his eyes bleary and red. He saw pain in the eyes of his father for the first time. He wanted to get up and hug his old man. He should have. It would have erased the past. But he did not. He rose and stood in front of his father who wiped the tears in his eyes. He desperately wanted to hug him. He knew that his embrace would have erased the tumult of the night gone by. Maybe Ujjwal was also waiting as he stood in front of him. But an uncomfortable half-a-minute later, Ujjwal walked towards the door.

Abhimanyu turned around and said, 'I am sorry, I really am. I have no right to do this...'

With his back to his son, Ujjwal waved his hand in the air implying that it did not matter.

Abhimanyu could not get rid of the burning sensation of guilt from his heart and he knew that it would be erased only if he could indeed rescue Simran. It was going to be the biggest challenge of his life.

When he entered the drawing room, Mahima looked even more unforgiving. She pressed Simran tighter to her bosom and turned her head away from Abhimanyu. He raised his hand to place it on her shoulder but stopped. Instead, he placed his head at the edge of the chair and broke down. He kept crying softly and inconsolably. His mother had never seen him cry like that. Never.

Abhimanyu didn't call Shweta for two days after that. He felt bad about ignoring Simran, but not about that night. Knowing that it would reflect very badly on him if he ignored her, he dialled her number. She confessed that she was hurt, but that was only for a while. He told her how he lied at home to be with her that night and how hell had broken lose. She apologized. For the sin he had committed, as she was unknowingly as much party to it as he was.

He told her that he was going to Santpur soon and would meet her once back. Deep down, he wanted to give love one more chance. He wanted to let go of Jaspreet. He did not say it, but she knew what he meant. She too was ready to let go of the past, only for Abhimanyu. She told him she would wait for him. She hoped that Simran will be cured. She was confident that she would be fine.

Abhimanyu knew that this time, he would have to weave a conspiracy to fool destiny to save her life, to save the twelve-year-old girl with a turbulent past.

The caretaker of Daddu's house in Santpur, Brij kaka, had come with a bullock cart to pick them up from the main road. It was half past five in the evening and the sun was already smarting after an assault by the approaching winters. It was getting darker and the sky was filled by a crimson and orange tinge that engulfed the sugarcane fields spread wide across. Simran had been curled next to Abhimanyu, clasping his right hand throughout the journey. For the first time, Simran raised her head and her eyes looked interested, as she saw the bullock cart. This was her first actual exposure to one after reading and looking at pictures in her textbooks. This was the first time she was about to enter a village.

The bullock cart was dragged by two black oxen, and it wobbled and jumped on the rock-strewn track. Simarn's gaze followed the lush green fields around her. Her senses were picking up interesting smells and fragrances. For the first time in her life, she did not shrivel her nose to the smell of cow dung. The sight of sugarcane in its lush avatar and its natural habitat was a revelation for her. She had till now eaten it as sugarcane cubes. This is where it came from, she thought. Abhimanyu noticed that though her eyes were still scarred by the melancholy of the recent experience, they seemed curious for the first time in many days. The sight of Santpur always filled Abhimanyu's heart with hope; this time, the emotion had a special meaning. His gaze was fixed on Simran's face who was exploring the view, albeit with a bit of hesitation.

All this while, Abhimanyu did not realize that he was about to face his own moment of truth. As he gently caressed Simran's hair, the bullock cart took a left turn. The road was still as rocky as it had been eighteen years ago. As they got deeper inside the village, Abhimanyu realized that though the village looked dramatically different from outside, most of the houses inside were still the same. The fruits of prosperity had percolated to some houses but most were the same: thatched roof, wood and brick houses, coated with cow dung.

Abhimanyu patted her head, and his gaze slowly shifted from her face to the muddy and rocky road ahead. At the end of the road, as it curved to its left, was the house that belonged to Daddu. For a couple of seconds, he thought that something was terribly amiss. It did not take him much time to realize what! Daddu was not there to receive them. Like he had always been. The bullock cart stopped in front of the house and Brij kaka jumped out and rushed towards the door, drawing the keys from his pocket. They stepped on the veranda of the house, realizing that the floor of the house was freshly coated with cow dung. Over those eighteen years, Brij kaka had done a good job in retaining the house in its pristine glory. It was clean and nothing had been touched or moved from that fateful summer of his discontent. Simran had dozed off while travelling on the bullock cart and Abhimanyu carefully lay her down on the bed. Abhimanyu's mother lay down next to her and he moved to the far end of the house. He first crossed the room where he had last seen Daddu. His body shrouded in white. He sidestepped the place where they lay him all those years ago. A sudden surge of emotions filled his chest. He walked on, his eyes fixed at the far end of the house. Daddu's study room.

The book rack was untouched, though without a single speck of dust anywhere. In the middle of the room was Daddu's freshly garlanded photograph. His eyes looked at him with the grace of a proud man. No one could match up to him; neither his sons, nor his grandchildren. His eyes shifted towards the book rack. Between pages of *Great Expectations* lay his dream. The one that never made it. Abhimanyu moved towards the rack but then something stopped him in his steps. He moved to his Daddu's garlanded photograph and caressed the frame. He paused when he touched Daddu's eyes. His feet went numb and he felt a lump in his throat. The fragrance of Daddu's warm hug filled his senses, and it was so powerful that he could feel his presence all over the room. He felt good, but it made him restless too. It brought back memories of that fateful summer vacation that culminated with Daddu's death.

Breathless, Abhimanyu rushed out of the room and locked it. He paced back to the bedroom where his mother and Simran lay. Ujjwal was standing in the veranda with Brij kaka and going by the sounds that reached him, they were probably talking about the state of the crops that year and the rain.

Abhimanyu sat at the edge of the bed, startling Mahima.

'It's just me, mom. Keep sleeping!' he whispered. 'It's been tiring for you, I know.' He patted his mother's head and she shut her eyes with a smile on her lips. He stared at the two most important women of his life. It was a chilly December evening in Santpur and Abhimanyu pushed the quilt till Simran's neck. The distant sounds of bells tied around the necks of cows and buffaloes returning home and the barking of a dog pack broke the shrill silence of the dusk. The birds were also getting noisier now. In a few hours' time, dinner would be served and the dinner table would unwrap a few more memories for Abhimanyu.

Simran sat between Abhimanyu and his mother silently, her eyes still sleepy. His father sat in front of them and they all ate quietly. Mahima would often prod Simran to eat as she would get lost while stirring the dal on her steel plate. Abhimanyu would gently pat her back to reassure her. He could already see some improvement in her but that was obvious. They were now at a new place and memories of the incident in Delhi were behind them. But they had to wait to see how she behaved over the days to come.

Simran scanned the walls of the dining room. It had black and white photographs of the family. A younger Ujjwal, an infant Abhimanyu in his grandfather's lap. The time when Ujjwal got

Mahima home after marriage. Daddu's photographs with his wife looking away shyly from the camera. Ujjwal with his brothers and their wives. But she could see that Abhimanyu was a clear favourite of her Daddu. He could see Abhimanyu's photograph right from infancy till he was twelve. But nothing beyond that. Time had stopped since then.

All this while, Brij kaka was monitoring the cook who kept serving them warm chapatis. The stunned silence in the room was discomforting till someone finally spoke.

'Why are we so quiet?' said a weary Simran, her voice drained in exhaustion.

Simran's sudden interest in her surroundings caught everyone unawares. They started gaping at her and then spoke at the same time, as if trying to reassure her. Three voices struck each other and then two went quiet. Abhimanyu continued, 'It's not that baby. We have been worried about you. We hope that you feel better here.'

Simran bowed her head and Abhimanyu gently pressed her shoulder. And then as if on a cue, Mahima spoke.

'Do you know Simran that your Babu got lost in the jungle nearby when he went to play in the fields? He was just eight years old. It took us nearly three hours to find him.'

Simran turned towards Abhimanyu and asked, 'But how did you get lost?'

Abhimanyu shook his head as each sound and fragrance came back to him. 'I was just walking at the edge of the fields and became curious when I saw the forests. I kept walking...I clearly remember, I just kept walking. It was so beautiful. The whisper of crushed leaves under my PT shoes, the unending sound of a koel in the jungle, the bite of the thorn infested shrub as it brushed against my skin, the sudden gust of wind through the trees that were conjoined through the branches. It was so calm. I sat down after walking for nearly one hour. Initially it was beautiful, but the trouble started when the light started fading.'

'Did you not see any wild animals? Like a tiger?' Simran was listening to him in rapt attention.

'I guess I was lucky. But I did see a hyena. But I was lucky again, I guess.'

'What happened?' Simran's eyes widened in anticipation.

'I was sitting under the tree. It just emerged out of the bushes and stood in front of me. Initially, I think it was as confused as I was. But when I got up with a jerk as my confusion transformed into raw fear, it backed off. Only to growl and bare its teeth at me. This was the time I thought it was all over. But I didn't realize that it was also scared. Only that his growling was more out of its basic animal instincts. I looked around for a stick or something to defend myself.'

It was not just Simran, but Mahima and Ujjwal also who listened in rapt attention. Brij kaka stood at the door, frozen.

'I could feel that its confusion had changed into fear and then it started sensing my fear too. You know, they say that animals can sense fear. So it started circling me as I stood under the tree. And then, I took a step back. I stepped on a twig that crushed with a sound under my shoe. Though startled, the hyena became even more aggressive. It saw me stepping back, and started moving towards me. But just then, something happened.'

'What?' Ujjwal asked wide-eyed, staring unblinkingly at the storyteller.

'As I backed off, a strand of a creeper weed that hung on to the bark of the tree poked my nostril. I first shrivelled my nose and then...I sneezed. The hyena crouched and ducked, as if saving itself from a surprise attack. It growled again, which was more like a whimper. The creeper was a dusty one and I do have this allergy to dust. So I sneezed again. This time louder. The young hyena backed off and yelped. The fear was back in its eyes. I sneezed for a third time, louder, crashing onto my knees. The hyena was so scared that it turned back and vanished into the bushes.'

Suddenly, the rare smile reappeared on Simran's face, 'You scared a hyena by sneezing?'

Ujjwal and Mahima started laughing and Brij kaka and the man serving chapatis joined in. Abhimanyu smiled as his ears turned a shade red. But Simran...she was so amused at Babu's brush with the hyena. Her eyes, though sleepy with exhaustion, suddenly shone and she joined in and giggled, gently slapping the dining table.

Abhimanyu looked at Simran. He could still see the scars of that day in her eyes, but through them he also saw the dawn of hope. He put his arm around her shoulder and pressed her towards him. As he gently kissed her hair, his eyes became watery. Mahima raised her hand and clasped her son's. Her eyes said it all: It's just a matter of time and we will be with you till the end.

In the quiet of the village as faint sounds of crickets and other creatures of the night permeated their ears, Mummy asked, ' Babu, did you really encounter a hyena that day?'

'No mom! I just made it up. But look at what it did to our Simran. I am ready to speak a hundred lies for her. I am ready to barter my soul with the devil if I have to, for that one smile on her face. I would sell a hundred lives to the Satan if I had to. If she turns into a freak because of this incident, I will never be able to forgive myself.

'A hundred lies for you Simran...and a hundred lives for you.'

The next morning, Simran woke him up. Abhimanyu thought that she would sleep till late, but perhaps the chirping of birds had woken her up. Not just that, she also wanted to go out for a walk.

So, while Mahima and Ujjwal slept, Abhimanyu wrapped Simran in woollens and held her hand as they walked out of the house.

Dressed in blue jeans and a red sweater with a white muffler around her neck and a woollen cap to cover her head, a slender Simran walked next to Abhimanyu. In the cowshed, the herdsmen were untying the cows and the buffaloes who stared with a wide and bemused gaze at the new visitors in the village. Simran clasped Abhimanyu's hand tighter while crossing a buffalo who stuck her neck out to sniff Simran.

'Don't worry, they are harmless. They just want to know who has come to see them.'

Simran moved closer to Abhimanyu. As they exited the shed to the open skies, a pang of nostalgia pricked Abhimanyu's heart. It was his first walk towards the fields after the one he had taken with Daddu. Each step felt heavier than the previous one. Abhimanyu remembered how Daddu would carry a stick and rustle the leaves to check for snakes. He immediately reached out to a tree and broke a branch. He would use it to check for any hidden snakes in the dry leaves. The crunching sound of the leaves under her white shoes and the fragrance of the mogra flowers ensnared her senses. Her eyes were wide open to the beauty around her, and after a long time, the red streaks in her eyes started fading. They carefully placed their feet across the bed of leaves, through the narrow water canals and then to the fields, while the sun rose from the east and the mist started clearing. The workers were in full force in the fields and they stared at Abhimanyu and Simran with curiosity.

'You want to take a tour of the jungle?' he asked.

'No! What if the hyena comes back?'

'Oh, the poor thing must have died years ago.'

'Don't say that Babu.'

'Why Simran? What happened?'

'No, the hyena must be someone's father and have a small baby too.'

Abhimanyu smiled and shook his head. He ruffled Simran's hair, but she looked back at him in mock irritation. They walked across the fields, but Abhimanyu's eyes were fixed at the mango tree at the far end of the field. The machan where he and Daddu used to sit was not visible from that end. They must have dismantled it, he thought. Why would they keep it anymore, now that the grand old man was not alive. He started walking faster towards the mango tree. Simran could feel the sudden spurt in his walk. She was surprised and as her eyes followed his gaze, she could see that he was looking pensively at the far end of the field. There was a strange restiveness in his eyes.

She dug her fingernails in his hand and said, 'Slow down Babu. I can't walk fast here.'

'I am sorry love. Just curious if the machan is still there. Daddu had built one, especially for me.' The radiance on his face brought a smile on Simran's face. She shut her eyes for a while and prayed that Babu's machan would still be there. What would she not give to preserve that smile on her Babu's face!

As he stood in front of the mango tree, he heaved a deep sigh. The smile on his face grew wider when he looked at the machan and then at Simran. She smiled back, though a bit amused. It was as if he was the twelve-year-old.

'You know, I think they have shifted the machan down. It used to be higher. I mean, the stairs look shorter to me.'

'It's quite high for a child my age,' she said with a twinkle in her eye. 'Isn't it common sense, Babu?'

'Oh, your Babu is so dumb. I was so small then,' he retorted playfully, gently pulling her cheeks.

Both of them went up the machan, and she lay with her head in his lap. She saw the vast expanse of the mustard fields and the sugarcane plantations beyond that. She saw the jungles beyond, that were still covered in a thin layer of mist. The sun rose higher with all its shenanigans. Simran snuggled up to Abhimanyu, and he looked around like a man in trance, gently caressing her hair. The cool air, the comfort of Babu's lap and his warm jacket around her was pushing her towards the threshold of sleep again. She kept fighting it, finally giving up. In a few seconds, Abhimanyu could hear her gentle snoring.

He looked down and whispered in her ears, 'Simran, wake up beta! Look at the splendid view around you. Look, how God smiles back at us.' His voice trembled and he felt a lump in his throat, with the realisation that he had now taken his Daddu's role upon him. The old man had kept him going, and he was to do the same for Simran, as if to repay Daddu's debt of love.

About an hour later, he headed back home, holding Simran in his arms. His heart felt heavy, yet a comforting feeling filled his senses. A very powerful and reassuring one. The smell of betelnuts and rain soaked soil. He turned around to see if...if he was indeed around.

He mumbled under his breath, 'You should have made it Daddu, you should have.'

As he crossed the now empty cowshed, he saw an ambassador car parked right in front of his house. He could hear Ujjwal chatting with someone. The other male voice did not sound familiar. When he reached the veranda, he saw his father sitting on the charpoy. Suddenly his heart started racing, anticipating something dramatic. The beard had got thicker. The girth had increased and he had a few extra pounds around him. He was no longer the slim guy he used to be. He was wearing glasses, but even through them, he could recognize the eyes. They were still the same – brown, comforting and intense. When Jagtar saw Abhimanyu, he stood up.

Instead of an emotional reunion, it was awkwardness that defined the moment of reckoning. Abhimanyu moved a few steps ahead and paused. Jagtar moved ahead and hugged him. Abhimanyu responded with unease and Jagtar could sense it. It wasn't a cold response, but the discomfort was evident.

Simran woke up with the hug, and was staring at the new member with curiosity. 'That must be Simran. God, she was so small when I saw her last,' Jagtar gently patted her cheek and she blushed.

He wanted to say that she has her mother's eyes, but restrained. Abhimanyu's unexpected reaction to his arrival was heart-breaking for him. It was the Avinash Thakur episode that had brought him back to India. Avinash was dead and Abhimanyu had avenged his father's death. But Jagtar knew very well that he himself had killed that moment at Woodland Park, long ago.

Simran walked inside the house, and Abhimanyu gestured Jagtar to take a seat. He stood there stunned, unable to express himself in words. He was confused about his feelings at that moment. Nervous energy swirled inside his chest. The air suddenly turned thick and it became difficult for him to breathe. Thankfully, Abhimanyu's father broke the ice.

'So Jagtar, tell me...what have you been doing? You have a family now?'

'I have a four-year-old son. I married a British born Sardarni there. She works with Barcalays. I work with Lloyds TSB, another major bank in London. My younger siblings are settled too. My brother runs an Indian restaurant in Soho and sister got married to a businessman. She is expecting her second child.'

'That's brilliant! It must have been quite a struggle to make it big, considering what happened in 1984. I mean even Abhi did not tell us about you after that.' Their nervous looks made clear to Ujjwal that he had probably broached an uncomfortable topic.

'Well, let me ask the cook to make some tea and lay breakfast for Jagtar. You boys catch up.'

Abhimanyu and Jagtar sat in front of each other. Jagtar scanned the surroundings, with nothing to break the ice.

'I miss Punjab, and my village near Jalandhar. I guess it's time to pay a visit there too. I have been away too long. Things have changed here.'

'No!' There was a sense of confrontation in Abhimanyu's tone. 'Nothing much has changed. People still get crazy on the slightest of provocations. A couple of years ago, this country witnessed its biggest shame, the demolition of the Babri, and the massacre of innocents after that. We have been finally exposed to new age terrorism that would plague us in the years to come.'

Jagtar could sense hostility in his tone. He had been expecting warmth from the friend he had abandoned. He should have known better. This wasn't the boy he had abandoned; here was a man. And men don't forgive easily. Abhimanyu, moreover, had a grudge. A serious one.

'You never got married?'

'No!'

'Never felt the need to...'

'I get a fuck whenever I want to. There is absolutely no reason for me to get married.'

'I did not mean that, Abhi. Why are you getting irritated?'

'I am not.' Abhimanyu raised his eyes and for the first time, they were locked directly into Jagtar's, as if challenging him. 'I certainly am not! I mean, I am sick of this conversation about getting married.

Why do we have to get married? Honestly speaking, I don't give a damn.'

Jagtar thought that it was just a matter of time. Abhimanyu could not stay mad at him for long. He wanted Abhimanyu to speak and pour his heart out, like old times. They sat in the dimly-lit veranda, where the cook served tea and some snacks.

'I know that I overreacted when I blamed you for the murder of my parents. I know I did! God knows that I have repented every day of my life since then. But I wanted to sever every bond with this country, every link. And you Abhi...were the strongest one! I never meant it...'

Abhimanyu shook his head with a look of disdain, 'I know Jagtar. You don't have to apologize or justify your actions.'

'So why can't we talk like the friends that we were?' Jagtar spoke and his voice cracked.

'What has changed from the day you left Woodland? Why have you decided to pardon me?' Abhimanyu retorted.

'I told you I overreacted.'

'Don't insult my intellect by saying that, Jagtar. You came back because I avenged you...because Avinash Thakur died. Now tell me Jagtar, would you have come back had Avinash Thakur still been alive?'

'Listen Abhi—'

'Cut the crap, Jagtar! Just answer my question? Would you have come back had I not avenged you?'

Jagtar kept quiet, stirring the tea with a small spoon

'You thought that after taking *your* revenge, I would be dying to receive you with open arms. You thought that maybe I would trace you and tell you – hey look! I screwed the guy who murdered your family. You thought that all these years I was dying to meet you.'

'Why can't we move on? We have lost ten valuable years. Let's not...'

'Hold on! You ask me to move on? I am still standing where I was standing two decades ago, Jagtar. Two decades ago. I was blaming myself for the death of my grandfather...I still do! And now in the year 1996, Simran might end up being a mental wreck because I was consumed with the obsession of avenging my best friend. Don't you see the irony of it all, Jagtar? You ask me to move on, because you can afford to. Your ghosts have been buried and someone else did that for you. But what about *me*?' Abhimanyu's voice rose alarmingly and Ujjwal came out to ask if everything was okay. Abhimanyu nodded and he went back in, knowing well that it had been long overdue.

'I played with the life of a twelve-year-old who is my responsibility. Drama is the last thing I wanted in my life after what happened in 1984. But I grabbed her hair and dragged her into hell. My own hell!' Abhimanyu gestured with gnawed fingers and gritted teeth, 'Who is going to exorcise my ghosts?'

Before Jagtar could answer, Abhimanyu butted again, 'Just answer this question and truthfully. Would you have come back to me had I not avenged your father's death?'

'Abhi, please yaar—'

'Just answer my bloody question!'

With a tear on the verge of falling out, Jagtar bit his lower lip. He turned his head away. Abhimanyu got his answer.

'Thanks bro!' Abhimanyu rounded his lips at the mention of bro, as if taunting him.

'I can't forgive myself for dragging Simran into this, and every time I look at your face, I shall be reminded of my recklessness. Jaspreet had trusted me and look what I did! I have no one else to blame, but me. I can easily wallow in self-pity like the pig in the muck, but I am way beyond that now. No one else is to be blamed for what is happening in my life. It's not fate, it's not destiny...it's just bad decisions.'

Jagtar could sense that Abhimanyu was indirectly blaming him for what had happened to Simran, yet he wanted to crucify himself for the bad decisions that he took in life. Abhimanyu called out to Ujjwal, informing him that Jagtar was leaving and he would be back from the village in an hour.

Jagtar hung his head and walked back to the car, driving off without a word. Abhimanyu walked away from the house, knowing well that it was a harsh call, and the only one he could take at that moment.

Even if he could hide the slight wobble in his walk, he could not hide his bloodshot eyes or the reek of cheap alcohol that was nauseating.

Ujjwal took him to task, 'You stink of alcohol. How dare you enter the house like this when Simran is in such a state?'

Abhimanyu turned around and forced his eyes wide open, speaking with a slight slur, 'Yeah papa, my apologies again.'

Abhimanyu walked in, and Ujjwal followed him in with a slight intimidation in his tone, 'That does not answer my question!'

Mahima and Simran saw the two, a bemused look written all over their faces.

He sat in front of Simran and his mother, but could not dare to look into their eyes. He could smell the cheap liquor in his skin. Mahima held Simran's hand and walked her out of the room; Simran kept looking back at Abhimanyu, wondering what was wrong.

Ujjwal felt beaten to see his son in this state, 'How do you feel walking into this house that your Daddu built with the stench of alcohol all over your body? Do you know he would not allow even guests in his house who had alcohol, even if he traced a whiff of it...'

Abhimanyu remained silent, and Ujjwal continued, 'I should have put my foot down! I should not have let you adopt Simran. This is not the future she deserves.'

It was at this time that Abhimanyu raised his head, his eyes filled with rage. His father had no business to cross that line. But the overwhelming sense of shame was stopping him from retorting.

'You have lived life on your own terms. You have just frittered away opportunities on a whim. On some stupid whim! It should be crime for people like you to adopt children.' Ujjwal's voice kept rising as he spoke. Abhimanyu looked like a volcano on the brim.

'I should have known you won't be able to take care of Simran—'

'You are so ashamed of me, dad. You always will be. I cannot take care of Simran, and she feels disgusted with her Babu coming home drunk. But how do you think the thirteen-year-old boy felt when he heard his father saying, "I wish we had the courage to have a second child!"'

I wish we had the courage to have a second child!

Mahima had tucked Simran into bed and came into the room just then.

'What are you talking about?' Ujjwal looked confused.

'Yeah! It's rubbish now, isn't it?' He turned towards his mother, 'Don't you remember, mom? Or do you also have this selective amnesia. That night when I brought the biggest news of my life... telling you that I have been selected to represent the school in a competition! What did he say, you remember?' He turned back to his father, 'Remember papa?' The alcohol in his blood stream was now doing the talking.

Both looked at Abhimanyu, stunned.

'You demean every moment of my life I felt happy about. You make me carry the burden of Daddu's death, and I am still carrying it on my shoulders. Do you realize what that means? You insulted me in front of my cousins. I was always a disgrace for you. Do you realize how it feels when the entire world gangs up against you and the people whom you expect would back you are the ones who push you in the cauldron? I was your son, dad...I needed your support when I was down. Instead, you continued whipping me. As if I was symptomatic of everything that went wrong in your own life. And then these words.'

Ujjwal and Mahima realised what a few words said in utter frustration had done to their child. What they had done to their relationship with them. Ujjwal was still trying to understand it all when Abhimanyu dropped another bomb on him.

'And all this time you thought my not joining IIT was some whim, some misplaced sense of priority? It wasn't! I just wanted to prove your theory right – you should have had that second child. I wanted to get even with you. I wanted to avenge that night, those words and...Daddu.'

Ujjwal looked at Abhimanyu with a look that bordered on shock and confusion.

'Tell me how does it feel now? That your son did not fulfil your biggest dream because he wanted to avenge that night and many after that.'

There was complete silence in the room, barring the village sounds that permeated the dimly-lit room. Abhimanyu went back and sat on his chair, crestfallen and tired. Ujjwal stood where he was, staring blankly at the space ahead of him. Mahima's shock was more animated as she held her mouth with her hand.

Abhimanyu spoke slowly, barely a mumble, 'And all I have earned through revenge is more turmoil in my life. And the life of others.' His voice started breaking.

Abhimanyu looked up, then slowly got up and walked towards his father. 'I know I reek of alcohol, I stink of your mutilated dreams... but today I speak with the utmost clarity papa...' His voice crumbled further, 'I am sorry. Forgive me for the unpardonable. I don't know what else to say.'

While Abhimanyu fought hard to stop those tears from rolling down his cheeks, Ujjwal held his hands and raised them to his eyes. He buried his face in his son's hands and started sobbing uncontrollably. Abhimanyu had never seen Ujjwal so distraught and vulnerable.

Abhimanyu hadn't expected this, and seeing his father, he broke down too. 'Please papa, don't cry. I can't see you crying. You are the only image of my life that is unbreakable. Don't cry and make me feel even more miserable.'

Abhimanyu hugged his father and buried his face in his chest, sobbing even more vigorously. Mahima moved towards them and put one hand on each of their shoulders.

'Why didn't you come to me? I am not a demon, Abhi. I would have apologized. Ask your mother, I did that night too. You could have told your mother. It wasn't the price worth it. I am sorry, son. I am so sorry.'

Ujjwal looked like a man who had been robbed of the singular pride that he had possessed. His tired eyes bore a thousand questions and every question tormented his soul.

Ujjwal sobbed, 'And now, you slap this on my face nearly two decades later? I have been haunted by that moment of your refusal to join the IIT. I have been wondering why? All this...just because of one utterance?'

Abhimanyu bowed his head, as he could feel an intense throbbing inside. He was feeling sick. He wanted to throw up and detoxify himself of all the turmoil that had plagued his relationship with his father.

'I am sorry, dad. I never felt comfortable talking to you about it—'

Ujjwal shook his head and said, 'How far did I push my son! You could have spoken to your mother.'

Ujjwal shook his head as he got up from his chair with a painful grunt, 'And now I shall have to live with this thought for the rest of my pathetic life that my son destroyed his life just because of one utterance. Something that would have been just been a lost memory had he come and confronted me. Or his mother. But you chose not to...because he was uncomfortable! Great...'

His shoulders drooping, Ujjwal started to walk away, his mind numb. At the edge of the door, he paused and turned around. 'But Abhimanyu, you are the pride of any parent. You are the son any father would dream of having. And I am sorry that I realized it so late.'

Mahima had been quiet all this while, just like she had been a quiet witness to the father-son saga for over two decades. She couldn't restrain any longer, 'And you would fritter away yet another chance that life has thrown at both of you?'

Stunned, Ujjwal and Abhimanyu turned their gaze towards the lady of the house. Mahima's hands were shaking, as if she had just uncorked years of bottled anguish. She wished she could break free of her roles back then as the dutiful mother and the faithful wife. She should have put her foot down. She should have drawn them together.

Turning towards her husband, she questioned, 'Can I ask you when was the last time you sat with him, put your hand on his shoulder and tried asking him what bothered him? When? When he refused to join IIT? You slapped him and pushed him further away. And he should have come to you.'

Turning her head towards her son, she said, her voice now breaking, 'Stop romanticizing your victimhood, Babu, stop it! Don't think it only affects you. We don't lead lives in isolation. Even if someday, me and your father perish and God forbid you are left alone, don't think that your actions would not impact the person next door or the random person walking next to you on the street. We are all strung by an invisible cord that binds us. Look at what has happened to Simran! The last thing you wanted for her was pain. And look what your reckless act of revenge has done to her. Do you expect her to lead a normal life soon? That day, she got saved just by sheer dumb luck. God forbid, that security guard had not found his target. What if he had missed? It was sheer recklessness that you crushed your father's dream, which was your misplaced idea of revenge and now you brought this on Simran...'

Abhimanyu crashed on the chair clasping his hair. He raised his head to the left and saw his father walking slowly towards his room, vanishing at the turn to his room.

The voices haunted by the past and thirsting for catharsis carried to the other room to Simran. For the first time in her life, she came to know who her Babu was. She now knew his pain; she knew the tumult that engulfed his life. Simran shut her eyes and prayed. She prayed hard that her Babu finds his peace with his father. She implored her Waheguru to heal their relationship.

The jingle of the cowbells woke Simran up early the next morning. She saw Mahima sleeping next to her, and Babu was nowhere to be seen. Her teeth chattered gently with the morning cold as she sauntered towards the far end of the house. She wanted to look for her Babu to ensure he was fine. As she reached the far end of the house, her eyes paused at the door of Daddu's room. She stood in front of the olive door, wondering if she should walk in. No place in the house was out of bounds for her, just that she had not explored it without Babu. She drew her left hand from under the warmth of her arm and then pushed the unlocked door that opened with a slight creek. She stepped inside, carefully crossing the wooden threshold of the room; a peculiar smell caressed her senses. Like the fragrance of dry mud, like the whiff from the pages of an ancient book, like the heady scent of crushed betelnuts. It was the scent that Abhimanyu identified with his Daddu. It was for Simran to feel now.

Her eyes paused at Daddu's photograph and she remembered that Babu had brought her to this room once. She had fleetingly glanced at Babu's favourite man then. This morning, she stood in front of the wooden portrait observing each and every tress and wrinkle of the grand old man. His graceful eyes with a touch of pride filled her heart with warmth. She stood there mesmerized, a hint of a smile on her morning kissed face. How many times had Babu spoken about his Daddu! And today, she stood in front of him. All alone. All to herself. This was her moment with Babu's grand old man.

Simran raised her right hand and touched his face. Simran cursorily looked at the book shelf on her left and started moving towards it. She stood in front of the shelf, taking in the collage of titles she could see: *To Kill a Mocking Bird*...*Malgudi*...Khushwant...Oliver Twist *Tale* Nabakov,...Premchand...*Godhuli*...Mahashwetadevi... Wordsworth...and...*Great Expectations*."

Impressed by the neatly lined up books without a speck of dust or dirt, she raised her hand and touched the edges of the hardback books. She had never seen such old books. Looking at the pale and faded yellow colour of the books, she wondered if these must be one of the oldest editions available. She had read most of them, except of course Nabakov and Khushwant. Mostly the ones Babu brought home. She never made any demands ever for any specific books, so her collection included only the ones that Abhimanyu got for her. As her eyes moved from one book to the other, her eyes paused at one. What intrigued her was a slight fold in the volume of one book.

Great Expectations.

She thought why Babu had never brought home this all-time classic, though she had an abridged version of the book as the part of her course in school. She decided to ignore the fold at first, but then moved a step ahead. She raised her hand and stretched herself, now virtually standing on her toes, trying to reach *Great Expectations* placed on the topmost shelf.

Settling on the reading table next to the shelf, Simran turned the pages of the book. She had never seen a book this old. The smell of the old pages was comforting.

And then, after nearly two decades, Rupali revealed herself to Simran.

Rupali stood at the wooden door of her hut and her eyes searched for someone. The fifteen-year-old girl with her hair tied in a plait scanned the neighbouring huts. Her vision was hazy owing to a thin film of tears across her dark eyes. A rock and pebble strewn dusty road run in front of her house. Rupali's heart felt heavy. She knew this would happen someday. It was just a matter of time. But now her mind was wandering towards the dark and bleak immediate future. It was lonely, uncertain and hostile. And then suddenly, the tears crossed the threshold of her eyelashes, accompanied by her muffled sobs. She wiped them with her long, mud-stained fingers, but her sobs were now getting intense. With trembling fingers, she clasped her chest, which was heaving rhythmically with her sobs. 'Ma', she whimpered.

A sudden panic engulfed Simran's heart as she looked at the old and pale white papers torn out of a school notebook. The hand writing was a bit familiar, but not familiar enough. She was curious. So she turned the pages, all three, one by one. She reached the third page and saw the name of the author.

Abhimanyu Sharma
9th B
Roll number 11
Story: The Girl by the Hut.

Simran smiled and a rush of emotions filled her. The thought that her Babu was just a couple of years elder to her when he had written the story amazed her. It tickled her no end that Babu was standing next to her...as a gangly boy. She was holding his story in her hand. But there was something else too. The story of Rupali. She had read a few lines, but there was so much anguish in her. The pain! She turned over the pages as her eyes paused on the last line she had read.

'Ma', she whimpered.

It was this pain that found an echo in Simran's heart. The pain for the mother who had abandoned her twelve years ago. Simran was curious. She wanted to know more about Rupali. So she started reading further.

She peeped inside her hut and then came and stood on the edge of the street. She could hear distant chanting, which was getting louder as the procession gradually approached her. The prabhat pheri, the procession of freedom fighters in that locality of Chandni Chowk. The year was 1946 and there was hope in the air. Not for Rupali, though. It was all over for her. Like a panic attack, pain engulfed her knees as she sat slowly at the edge of her hut with a painful grunt. The prabhat pheri procession at 4.30 a.m. had woken her up every day for almost fifteen years now. She would rub her sleepy eyes daily and look at the men and women chanting hymns and bhajans with the fervour of desire renting the air. Desire for freedom. As the procession neared her hut, Rupali buried her face in the crook of her arm resting on her thighs. The chanting of Mahatma Gandhi's 'Vaishnava jana tu tene kahiyeje' was getting louder and she could feel that they were now passing her hut. Rupali had memorized Bapu's swan song by heart because of the daily prabhat pheris. She would often follow them till the arch of the road ahead, but never beyond.

The sound was getting gentler in the chilly December morning, and as it gradually faded, Rupali knew that the procession had crossed the arch around the corner. She raised her head and rested her chin on her arm. It was quiet again, except the sound of her toenails scratching the soil and a distant howl of a dog pack. And then from the arch of the road, she saw a tall man walking towards her. The man was walking towards her. It was dark, but she could make out that the man was clean shaven and was wearing a mud-coloured dhoti kurta. Rupali looked at him confused, tears still caressing her cheeks.

Simran's heart suddenly sank. It was dark and a stranger was approaching Rupali. A surge of nervous energy filled her bosom.

The man spoke with a hint of an apology in his voice, 'I am sorry, but I could not stop myself...I was with the prabhat pheri and I saw you sitting at the edge of your house. I could see that you were sobbing....is everything okay?'

Who was this man, Simran wondered. What was he doing here? Why did he come back? What were his intentions? A wary Simran paused and wondered if Rupali should respond to this man. She wondered if her parents were around. She was curious if her mother would walk out and protect her vulnerable daughter. She was not sure if the man could be trusted.

Maybe it was the helplessness of the situation and her own vulnerability that the hint of sympathy in his voice sounded genuine to her. Rupali had been longing for solace since last night. But now that someone was standing in front of her, she did not know what to do. She buried her face in the bend of her left arm again and started sobbing uncontrollably. The man moved ahead and bent down, resting his right knee on the ground.

'What is it, please tell me... It was as if the vibe of your pain drew me to this hut.' Rupali was still sobbing, as the man raised his hand and reluctantly placed it on her head.

'I don't know what your pain is, but I am sure that there is some way out... There is some hope...'

It was at this point that Rupali stopped sobbing and raised her head. The pain vanished and a strange hardness filled her face. She wiped her tears and stood up.

'There is no hope...not for me...'

With a small pause, the man spoke again, 'I don't know what your story is, but this entire country is thriving on hope. Our prabhat pheris are all about hope. We hope that our words bring this sentiment back into the lives of nearly thirty crore individuals of this country. I am sure there is a way ahead.'

'There is no hope for me, for my last hope is lying in my hut...shattered and lifeless,' Rupali turned around to walk back to her hut, but then stopped after taking a few steps, 'and you want to know why....come with me!'

Simran wondered if it was indeed a wise move to take the stranger inside her house. Was Rupali alone? Babu had always taught her never to trust strangers, never to accept things from them and this daft girl...she was taking him inside the house. She gently shut her eyes and a silent prayer caressed her lips.

A strange panic filled his heart as he started following the girl. An earthen lamp lit one corner of the room that was very stuffy. His eyes scanned the room, while the girl walk towards a charpoy. His eyes were still trying to adjust to the light in the room and he could not actually figure out if there was something on the bed. The girl sat on the edge of the charpoy and he realized that someone was lying on it with the entire body covered in a black tattered quilt. Rupali gently removed one end of the quilt. From that distance, the man could see the forehead of a woman as the girl started caressing her hair. Tears filled her eyes as Rupali looked at the woman.

'This is my last hope, my mother. Last night, she died....'

Simran stood there stunned and the bunch of papers slipped out of her hands. Her eyes moved sideways, numbed by the shocking revelation. The mother was dead. The thought of Rupali's father's whereabouts dwarfed in front of the shock that was unfolding in front of her eyes. He must be away for work. He must come back soon to his daughter who was alone.

She left the last word hanging. The man stepped back in shock, letting out a gasp. Hope had suddenly acquired a different meaning in this small space, this world of hers.

'You talk about hope,' she said faintly, 'My mother died last night and that is what this word means to me.'

'What happened?

'She felt a sudden pain in her chest while cooking and I asked her to rest. I had my back to her when I heard a groan, but I ignored it. I kept cooking and did not look at her till I finished the chores in half an hour. She must have died that very moment.'

The man looked at her in stunned silence. The stuffiness of the room and the shock of what he had just seen and heard were now engulfing his senses. He inhaled the musty air and it made him even more uncomfortable. He wanted to breathe fresh air now.

'She could never recover from my father's death a year ago, when the police rained lathis on his head in a freedom rally in Red Fort. Ironically, my father was not even a part of the rally. He was just a bystander. My father believed that the freedom struggle was not his fight. His war was against hunger. We are daily wage workers from Uttar Pradesh and had come to Delhi for a better life. This city and your fight

for freedom took away my father...and now...,' she pointed at
the lifeless body of her mother as her voice broke.

Rupali's father would never come back. The chill in the air
suddenly increased. She could feel each and every strand of Rupali's
vulnerability. The girl by the hut. The girl with no parents. The
orphan. She was now worried about the man who had just entered
her life. She could not read his intentions.

The man had seen death closely so many times during
rallies, but this was not some martyr. This was certainly not
death with dignity. And certainly not death with hope at the
end of the tunnel.

'My father would come back in the evenings after a hard
day's work and sit with us and talk endlessly about his day,
the freedom struggle, the men leading the movement – Bapu,
Chacha Nehru. He was fascinated by them, but never did he
muster the courage to go and participate in these rallies.
I would admonish him and ask him if he was afraid and
that he could be construed as a coward. But he was never
apologetic. He just said that his world was his family and
that the condition of his lot would be the same, whether it
was the British or our own people. I could never understand
his pessimism. He said that our society functions according
to a strict feudal norm. He said that he was a worker, a
labourer, and that the powers to be would conspire to see
that he continues to be at the lowest echelon. He was not
resentful though. He said that all of us have come to this
earth with a distinct karma and that his karma was to serve.'

Rupali now looked at the man and said, 'Your freedom
struggle is yours, not mine. I have no share in your hope. My

world stands here...right in front of my eyes, dead and lifeless and hopeless on this wooden charpoy...'

The man realized that every stain of tears on her face, every unruly hair falling across her eyes and every pain-filled frown reminded him of just one thing – uncertainty. Dignity and self respect acquired a new meaning in her world. After all, this was what they were fighting the British for. He would have never understood her father's stand had it been some other time and situation. But here he was, staring at the girl's dead mother. Hope was certainly not meant for her. It was romanticized and overrated here. After half an hour, he asked the girl to wait in the hut, as he hurriedly got some of his friends to arrange for the last rites of her mother.

The funeral was performed in the next two hours as the man's friends bathed and clothed Rupali's mother for her last journey. From a distance, Rupali watched the funeral pyre being lit by the stranger. A stranger whom she had met a few hours ago. As the fires leapt and kissed the chill of the morning, the sun rose at a distance. When the first ray of the winter sun hit Rupali, she felt a strange sense of relief. It was indeed the end of all the trauma that her mother had been enduring for the past one year. She was alone, but her mother was not. Hopefully in a better and a just world, with her father. She looked around and saw many faces, all strangers to her. Then she saw him. The stranger in her life.

The man put his hand on Rupali's shoulder and she looked straight into his eyes. She did not know how to read them, not yet. She was not completely sure what that grip on her shoulder meant. She did not know if she could trust him. She wanted to feel reassured, though.

Trust was still an ambitious word for Rupali. But he was her final hope.

Hope....

Rupali did not know that she would find her share of hope at the funeral pyre of her mother. But it was certainly something she was ready to cling on to.

Abhimanyu Sharma
9th B
Roll number 11
Title of the story: The Girl by the Hut

Simran got restless; she wanted to know more about Rupali. The ray of hope that she was ready to cling on to! Did it lead her to the bright future that everyone in India had hoped for? Or did Rupali's story end like Simran's beginning? Thoughts crashed on her tender heart with tremendous ferocity and her hands shook. Something was not right, she thought. Something had been left unfinished. Did Babu finish the story and leave it hidden somewhere? Did he?

She looked at the rack and the books stacked in it. Her eyes started scanning each book and signs of any folds in the volume of the books. She stood up and took out the first book in her hand and started turning the pages. Nothing!

She took a second one. Nothing again!

The third, the fourth and the fifth

She was breathing heavily and checking each and every book in the shelf and then throwing it on the floor. The sound travelled to other rooms too. Mahima was the first to wake up, followed by Ujjwal. Not finding Simran next to her, she called for her, 'Simran beta!'

Ujjwal walked into their room, his ears still on the sound from his father's study.

'Where is she?'

Without uttering another word, they rushed to the far end of the house to Daddu's study.

Simran was now throwing books randomly on the floor; saliva oozed from her mouth. She had the look of a possessed girl. Knowing that she now had company did not deter her. She was still searching for the conclusion to Rupali's story.

And then suddenly she stopped and crashed on her knees. Mahima rushed to her and pressed her to her chest. She was not crying, but the silence was scarier than the cry that they had seen in the recent past. Ujjwal bent down and patted her head. This had to be some attack of lunacy, where she was now gradually losing control over reality. She probably was.

That's when Abhimanyu walked in.

The first thing he saw was the three-page short story lying on Daddu's study table. And then he saw the floor. He saw Simran and a dozen books lying around her. His parents looked confused and Mahima kept asking Simran what had happened. Confused and shocked, Abhimanyu walked closer to her and said, 'What happened Simr—'

'What happened to Rupali? What did you do to her? Why did you not complete her story?' She sprang up and held his shirt with her slender and trembling fingers.

'Who Rupali, Simran? What happened to you?'

'You bloody well know what I am talking about Abhimanyu Sharma...you bloody well know!'

This was the first time Simran had addressed him by his name. The very first time. He was after all just a year older to the twelve-year-old Simran right now. He looked at the bunch of papers again, and understood everything. He spread his arms around her and embraced her.

Simran pushed him back and asked him, 'Why did you not complete Rupali's story? What happened to her? Did she live happily ever after?'

'Simran, this was just a short story that I had written twenty years ago.'

'But you have to...you have to. You can't leave Rupali like that. She deserves a happy future, doesn't she?'

'Simran, you are unnecessarily—'

'I am not mad, I am not!' This time she yelled, her voice carrying outside the house. 'But you need to tell her story. You have to...'

'I will Simran, but you need to get some rest.' This time there was a hint of curtness in his voice. Ujjwal moved towards the desk and picked up the papers.

'You have to tell me now...what happened to Rupali? How did her story end? You have to....'

'If I tell you her story, will you promise me that you will be fine soon? Promise me that you will be the Simran I once knew.'

She kept quiet, but in her eyes raged a thousand questions and she sought an answer for each one of them.

'Will you complete her story?'

Abhimanyu lifted her in his arms and covered her in a warm shawl. As they walked the length of the house towards the exit, her gaze was fixed on his face, still expecting an answer from him.

He sat with her under the banyan tree that faced the mausoleum. Abhimanyu said, 'There was a time when I wanted to tell this story to the world, and nobody wanted to hear it. I am shocked that you ask me to complete it now...after so long.'

'Babu, you pause her story at a time when it was screaming to be told. How can I be unaffected after reading it?'

Suddenly, his Simran sounded older that her twelve years. Abhimanyu smiled for he had never imagined that "the girl by the hut" would reveal herself like that. That too, to Simran. As if she had been written precisely for this day. He felt hopeful that Simran would be fine. Soon.

'Can I ask you something, Simran? You want me to tell this story because you want to know what happened to Rupali, right?' Simran nodded feebly, her eyes still teary. 'Because for some reason, you wish to seek the answers of your life through the fate of Rupali?' She remained quiet, her gaze blank. 'You want to know if she had a happy life, if she found love...if she could trust the stranger in her life? Right, Simran?'

Simran was quiet, wondering how her Babu could read her so well. 'You seek a happy ending for Rupali, don't you?'

'Yes, I do,' she finally mumbled.

'You cannot control a story, just like you cannot always control life. And what if Rupali does not have a happy ending? What if she marries the stranger and he gets killed in the riots that were sparked off during the division of the country? What then? Does this mean I should not tell the story because this is not how you want it to end?'

'But why can't you? Why can't you at least tell her story to the world? You never answered any questions that I asked about my life, Babu.'

Shocked, Abhimanyu asked, nearly protesting, 'When have I not?'

'You think I don't know what happened to my parents? You think I don't get a hint of it from all my classmates and auntys who pity me for being born on the day my parents died? You think I can't fathom this simple truth about my life?'

Abhimanyu stared at Simran, not knowing what to say. He had waited for the right time to break the truth about her parents' death. But all along, she had known it. And she did not even give the slightest of hint that her tender heart was bearing the burden of the massacre.

'I kept asking you but you won't tell me. So I decided to find out myself. I have been reading newspaper articles about the genocide in the library archives. You deny me the truth because you think that it would harm me. But I seek the truth because that is the only thing that can liberate me.'

'I thought the truth would harm you...that you were not prepared you handle it,' he reasoned.

'Have I asked you about my parents after that incident in school, when I was six years old? Have I ever made you feel that you have been a bad parent, that I have missed my real parents for even a single day? Have I?'

He knew he could not protect her anymore. The imaginary cocoon that had sheltered her, had now finally ruptured. His fingers trembled as he caressed her head. He felt content. He felt reassured as she spoke. Those were the most comforting words that he had heard. He wondered if he had undertaken this journey to Santpur to rescue her, or to be rescued by her. There was so much strength in her eyes.

Simran held his hand and pressed it gently. 'Tell me,' she asked, 'Why did you abandon Rupali, and that too in Daddu's study room?'

'I did not abandon her!' He spoke softly. 'I told you that a story has a soul of its own. She did not wish to be told. She was waiting for you to discover her. I let her go because the cost of pursuing her was too much for me to bear. The death of my grandfather! That is the price I paid for 'The Girl by the Hut'. I still remember the pride in his eyes when he read the story. My Daddu felt my pain that day. I often wonder if I had pushed him towards his death that night. That night when I argued with papa. I wonder if I had provoked him against his own son. There was no way he could have died so soon Simran...' He looked at Simran as if seeking an apology for his sins.

And then her Babu told her how a story had changed his entire life. She looked at him intently. What she saw was a thirteen-year-old boy looking for recognition. And almost apologetically.

'You've been so strong for me. You have always sheltered me. You have to stop blaming yourself for every incident in my life. Do you realize what you are doing to yourself?'

Abhimanyu looked away and heard her reprimand, 'Don't turn your face away from me. I know it makes no difference to you if I tell you that you may be hurting yourself, bit by bit. Every day! But...' Abhimanyu now turned to look at Simran. '...but what if I start blaming myself for the mess in your life. Are you ready to live with that? Can you handle that Babu?'

He had no answer.

'You can't, na? Even I can't! I can't handle the fact that the most important person in my life that could ever be, blames himself for the unfortunate events that surrounded my birth or the incidents after that.'

After a small pause, she said, 'I am strong enough to handle the truth, Babu. You've got to have faith in me. But I want the truth from *you*,' she paused, 'and no one else.'

At that moment, he knew hiding the truth was also a lie. He knew that he would have his share of battles to fight. And Simran would have to fight along with him. His battles were hers and hers his to fight. He knew she was right. That she was strong...strong enough to handle the truth.

For the first time in his life, Abhimanyu's mind felt uncluttered. His past and his relationship with his father were still ringing inside his mind, but he was ready to give it a chance.

He wondered if Simran was ready to let go? This was just the beginning for her. Ghosts of her past would still haunt her and he would have to exorcise them for her.

As he held her hand tenderly and as they took their steps gingerly towards the fields with the gentle breeze encompassing them, Abhimanyu smiled.

He smiled. And he knew why.

He remembered the expression in her eyes, when he had held her as an infant. For the very first time.

You saved me, and in time, I shall rescue you back.

www.ingramcontent.com/pod-product-compliance
Lightning Source LLC
Chambersburg PA
CBHW052027020726
47501CB00004B/1288